THE O ZONE

KELLY JAMIESON

OWEN

She's here tonight.

A few steps in front of me, the guys are yammering about the game tonight. They stride right past her where she sits playing and singing into her microphone, not noticing my steps slow as I walk by her. I feel like I'm in a slow-motion scene from a movie, her song the score as my head turns and our eyes meet...and hold for one step...two... three. It feels like time stands still but it's seconds—a flicker of her eyes as she sings, a tiny dip of her head.

A guitar case on the floor in front of her holds bills and coins. Any time I've seen her, she attracts a crowd and always seems to have money in the case. I've never given her money. I don't know why. I often toss cash to subway buskers.

As I walk through the subway station behind my teammates, the soulful melody floats around us and all the other people in the underground tiled space. I don't know much about music or how to describe her voice—soft, high, clear, and utterly beautiful. Combined with the notes she plays on her guitar, her music never fails to give me shivers when I hear it.

One time when I was alone, I stopped to watch her for a few songs, trying to blend into the crowd. I didn't want to be creepy, but there's something about her music that's…mesmerizing.

Her hair is green. I can't say I find that attractive. I've always been into blondes. Okay, it's not *all* green—it's like, dark brown with a green tint, shoulder length, with long bangs. She wears big gold-framed glasses, and her full lips are shiny and natural. Today she's wearing loose, ripped up jeans, and a massive, chunky-knit brown sweater that hides her shape.

I make myself keep going so I don't fall too far behind my team-mates, letting her voice fill my head then gradually recede behind me as we distance from her and emerge from Penn Station onto the street.

It's game day, so the area is busy, lots of fans in New York Bears jerseys filling the streets even though it's a couple of hours before the game. I brace against the cold January wind as we walk to the Apex Center and duck into the staff entrance, showing our security badges and greeting Homer. He waves us all in with his usual beaming smile. "Good luck tonight, guys!"

We head straight to the locker room to change and go through our game day routines. Game day is all about getting ready for puck drop. Every player's routine is different. I'm not superstitious—okay, maybe I am a bit—but I do the same things in the same order, every game day, from getting up in the morning until I skate onto the ice.

Not only game day. My entire life is organized into a routine that keeps me busy. I eat, sleep, practice, and study. I have to work hard so I don't waste this gift I've been given. A gift not everyone gets.

After I change from my suit into athletic shorts and a T-shirt, the first thing I do is go to the training room, where I roll out my quads and do some stretches. Then I have my bowl of oatmeal with a banana on top.

"What's up, Cookie?"

I look up at Axe, who joins me in the lounge for a snack. He takes a bite of his protein bar.

My nickname comes from my last name—Cooke.

"Good. You?"

"Feeling fine. What'd you think about that fine for Reynolds?"

"Ugh." I take a spoonful of my oatmeal and chew while I think. Reynolds, who plays for the Condors, was fighting with a Leafs player in their last game and punched him in the head while he was face down on the ice. He got fined five thousand dollars, and the public outcry has been loud. He's a repeat offender and should have been suspended in my opinion. And in a lot of people's opinions. "How does he keep getting away with shit like that?"

Axe shakes his head. "I don't know, man."

I'm not a fighter, but I'll drop the gloves if I have to. I follow the rules, though. And believe me, I know the rules. That's why I have an "A" on my jersey. I may be a jock, but I'm also a giant nerd. I spend hours watching hockey—video of our own team but also watching other teams on TV. I read everything I can get my hands on about hockey.

When I see guys get hurt, it makes me sick. But hockey's a dangerous sport, and shit happens. We all take that risk every time we step on the ice. We can't let that distract us from doing our jobs. Over the years, I've learned how to focus on the things I need to. Which is playing the best game I can.

After my oatmeal, I join some guys in the hall for a little soccer. And some laughs. This warms up our muscles but also relaxes us.

Around five-thirty, we have our pre-game meetings with the coaches with last minute reminders about the team we're playing tonight, the Flames. Coach gives a quick review of the game plan from the morning five-on-five meeting. He also reminds us that the Flames' power play has been hot lately, so our penalty kill guys have to be on top of them.

"Remember, bump and run!" Coach says. "We don't need the big check, just harass them, put pressure on them, but don't take yourselves out of the play."

In the dressing room, I put on my equipment in the same order I always do, left to right. I tape my stick while music plays, the sound of tape ripping mixing with the tunes. It's always something fast paced to get us going. Right now, Imagine Dragons gets us grooving. Our dressing room DJ, Bergie, puts the play list together, and he's good at it. I mean, *I* think he is.

"The fuck is this?" Jake whines as he tosses a wad of tape toward a garbage can and misses. "Come on man, where's Blake Shelton? Kenny Chesney?"

Bergie laughs. "Patience, my friend."

I hear the words of the song. *Whatever it takes.*

I get myself ready to do whatever it takes to win.

The game is close. And frustrating. I feel like we're playing great, but we can't get ahead, and things are tied one-one. Then we end up with a goddamn penalty for too many men on the ice.

"Okay, we gotta kill this, boys," I say as our penalty kill team jumps over the board. "Let's do this!"

This could be the end of the game with a loss. Just what we didn't want, another penalty against a team with a hot power play. That's how they got their only goal. We can't let it happen again.

Barbie is our penalty kill god. He always has his stick in the right place and isn't afraid to block shots. He's a maniac that way. I watch him throw himself in front of the puck and wince along with him. But he gets up and keeps skating.

"Attaboy, Barbs!" I shout.

Then I'm out on the ice, watching JBo take the faceoff. He wins it, gets the puck back to me, and I have lots of room to head toward the Flames' net. I skate my ass off, knowing I'm being chased, keeping the puck on my stick, watching the goalie, my mind racing, planning. I watch him come out, and I shoot over his glove hand and fuck yeah! I light the fucking lamp!

Shorthanded!

"Fucking beauty," JBo crows.

We're still short one guy for another minute, but my goal gives us a huge boost, and we kill the rest of the penalty.

With frustration mounting, a scrum develops around the Flames' net after a whistle. I'm watching from the bench. Hellsy and Barbie hang at the blue line. The linesmen break things up, and the guys disperse to their benches. I jump on the ice.

Peters, one of the linesmen, skates to the neutral zone for the faceoff.

"Hey, hey, wait. Hold up." I skate over to him. "The faceoff has to be inside the blue line."

He shakes his head. "We're doing it here."

"No, that's wrong. Our D-men stayed on the blue line. That means the faceoff happens inside."

He frowns.

"Seriously. Following a stoppage of play, should one or both defensemen who are the point players enter into the attacking zone beyond the outer edge of the end zone face-off circle during an altercation, the ensuing face-off shall take place in the neutral zone near the blue line of the defending team." I'm practically reciting the rule book. "But they *didn't* enter the attacking zone."

The refs skate up to us to see what's going on. I explain it to them.

They agree with me.

With a sharp exhalation of relief and satisfaction, I take my place for the faceoff. With another quick faceoff win by JBo and a pass to Bergie, Bergie pops it into the net. We fucking score again!

In the dressing room, I peel off my jersey and shoulder pads and sprawl on the bench with a bottle of Gatorade. Now the music is "Winner Take All" by ABBA, which cracks me up.

"ABBA?" Jammer shouts, dancing. "This is fucking perfect!"

I swipe sweaty hair off my forehead, laughing. Then it's time to talk to the media, and I take off my pants and switch my skates for a pair of sandals to answer questions. They ask about the shorty, of course. "Hey, it was a great faceoff win by JBo," I say. "He got the puck to me just like we wanted."

Then I head back to the training room to ride the bike for a bit.

Three of my teammates and I live in the same apartment building, so we often take the subway to and from games together. But tonight they've got other plans. They're all boo'd up, as the kids say. I kind of envy them. It'd be nice to have someone to go home to. Maybe even a dog, like Millsy has.

But I don't need distractions. The occasional hookup is enough for me. I need to focus on the game.

I trudge to Penn Station through dark but still lively streets and then through the station. As I pass where the busker was playing earlier, I glance at the empty space. She's gone. Good.

Not that I don't want to hear her music; I love it. But she shouldn't be hanging out alone in the subway at night.

2

EMERIE

"Hey, Eddie, you done for today?" I walk over to Eduardo in the 14th Street/Union Square station, carrying my prized LX1 Little Martin in its case and my amplifier. He's putting away his pan flute.

"Hola. Djess, I am done," he replies in his thick accent, flashing a smile. "Juss for now. I weel be back for the lonch crowd."

I nod. As he turns away briefly, I quickly drop my wad of bills in my hand into his case. "I'm going to Penn Station."

"Be careful." He looks up and frowns at me. "Those wack jobs got in a duss up with Cherry a few days ago."

I grimace. "I know. They usually leave me alone." The wack jobs he refers to are a group of break dancers who attacked another busker for being in "their space." There are often turf wars over the best locations, like 42nd Street and Herald Square, which make the best money. There are unwritten busking rules and one of them is first come first served, but lately some groups have been using their numbers to push individual performers out. These guys actually have weapons, and they check to make sure there are no cops around before they attack other musicians.

"Lucky you usually got lots of people around watching."

I shrug. "Not as many as you."

7

Eduardo's music is remarkable. He's from Peru originally and has been doing this for years—busking in the subway and on New York streets. He does it to support his family, a wife and two young kids. Since I've been a regular here, we've become sort of friends.

He grins. "Theengs are peeking up. The money ees coming een again."

Times have been tough lately, and I feel for him and the others who do this to survive.

"Things are looking up!" I wave as I head up to street level.

My stomach is rumbling. I never eat breakfast, and I've been here since about nine. I stop at a cart and buy a falafel rice platter, which I devour sitting on a nearby wall, and then I continue on to Penn Station. Every station is unique, and I like to move around.

I find a spot where another friend is finishing. "Hi, Em," he greets me with a smile, removing the mouthpiece from his saxophone.

"Hi, Nash. How's it going?"

"Going good."

Nash plays amazing jazz music on his sax. He's really talented but struggled with performance anxiety and found a place busking with not as much pressure.

"How's the SoundCloud thing going?"

He grins. "Great. It's seriously dope. And I'm making money. You should try it."

He's told me that before, but meh, I've got enough on my plate.

"Have you seen this?" He holds out a flyer.

I take it and scan the words. It's an advertisement for a competition—American Busker. It'll be held in June in Central Park, with cash prizes and a recording deal. It's like an American Idol kind of contest for buskers. To enter, you have to go through a series of auditions. "No," I say. "I haven't." I hand it back to him. "Are you going to enter?"

"Ha. No way." He waves a hand. "Keep it. You should enter."

I look back down at it. I don't need the money, and I don't think I'm going to ever get a recording deal. "I don't think so." I tuck the flyer into my guitar case.

"You should! Your voice is amazing."

I shrug, as always uncomfortable with the compliment. "Thanks, but I doubt it's good enough to win."

He shakes his head.

"*You* should enter," I say.

He holds up his hands. "Okay, point taken."

"Maybe we can both enter."

"Ugh. Forget it."

I grin. "Done."

I set up, tune my guitar and finger a few notes, then start playing and singing.

I love singing. I love music. I've loved it all my life. My father was a Broadway musician, and there was always music in our home. When my mom started my piano lessons, I was so eager. I never had to be forced to practice. After Dad died and my mom remarried, my stepdad bought me a gorgeous grand piano, more to impress her than me, but I loved it. I wanted to learn to play more instruments. At school, I played clarinet and saxophone in the school band. I learned guitar more or less on my own.

I had dreams of making music my career, but that was years ago. I'm realistic about my talents—I don't have a Broadway show voice— but I possibly could have followed in my dad's footsteps or...who knows. I gave that up when my little sister needed me.

About a year ago, I decided to try busking. I was terrified at first. But most people walk right by and ignore me, and that's fine; it was mostly the possibility of attention I was afraid of. I spent my teenage years feeling invisible, and busking suits me for that reason. I can make music and be invisible.

I've never told anyone else about the busking. I'm not ashamed of it, but it's...personal. Something just for me that I want to keep just for me.

My stepfather? I don't think he's ever even heard me play that grand piano. After my mom died, he never came to my recitals or concerts. He's never asked me to play for him like Mom did. Whatever.

I'm singing a song I wrote, "Darkness," when my attention is diverted by...him. The guy.

There's a bit of a crowd gathered for this song and he's at the back, but he stands out because of his height. He has to be six and a half feet tall. I've seen him a few times here at Penn Station. His tawny hair often curls out from under a knit beanie he wears, and his trimmed beard and moustache are also dark gold. He's usually dressed in a suit and tie and a long black coat. The suit makes me think he's a businessman of some kind. I can tell his clothes are expensive, so he must be successful, whatever he does.

The guy moves and I realize it's not him.

Damn.

I was actually thinking of talking to him today.

"Darkness makes the stars shine," I sing, my gaze drifting about the crowd. "Never stop looking up at the sky."

I finish that song to a smattering of applause and money tossed into my guitar case. I smile thanks at people as they move away. I move on to my next song.

As I sing, people rush by while others stop to listen. I concentrate on my fingering, singing slowly,

I lose myself in the music as I often do, and when I finish, I smile at the people watching, some giving me money. Sharing my music with people is both scary and intensely gratifying.

"You should just stop," a woman calls. "You can't sing!"

My stomach knots, but I keep my face pleasant. People around me make an unhappy sound as a group.

"You're entitled to your opinion!" I call back with a smile.

"Damn right! And my opinion is you should get out of here and let someone with talent play."

Another murmur of concern ripples through the air.

"Hey," a man says to the woman. "Shut your face. She's damn good."

"You shut your face!" she yells back.

I close my eyes. Great.

I open my eyes and shake my head at the man defending me. I play some notes on my guitar leading into the next song, ignoring the woman, but others aren't inclined to let her comments go, and voices rise as several people confront her.

The uglier her comments get, the more money people toss my way. Yikes.

This happened to me before, and I got upset. Now I know I have to keep my cool. Rewarding this woman with attention is not the way to go. But how do I control my "fans" who want to stand up for me? I speak into my microphone. "Hey everybody, let her go. She has her opinion and that's fine. I just want to make music."

I start my next song, not the one I was going to play, but a more up-tempo ballad called "Sure as the Sun." "Even the moon glows in the sun's light," I sing.

I try to show my gratitude to everyone who gives me money with eye contact, smiles and nods.

When I'm done, I bundle into my old jacket and wrap a scarf around my neck. I haul my stuff down 8th Avenue, the street packed with traffic, the sidewalks bustling with pedestrians, and around the corner onto 36th. I pass little shops, restaurants, a hair salon. This is the worst part about busking—lugging all my gear around. Luckily, I have another friend who helps me out. I enter Cantor's Luggage.

"Emmie!" Mr. Cantor calls to me.

"Hi!"

He bustles down the main aisle of the small shop filled with suit-cases of every size and shape and takes my stuff from me.

"Thank you."

He beams and nods. "How was your day?"

"It was great. Other than one person who told me to leave and make room for someone with talent."

He rolls his eyes. "You have the voice of an angel," he pronounces, turning to the back of the shop. Mr. Cantor stores my precious Little Martin for me here in midtown, making my life easier.

"Aw. Thank you." My chest fills with warmth. I follow him to the back, taking off my jacket. I pull my Versace puffer coat out of the locker and push my arms into the sleeves while Mr. Cantor slides my cases in, then I shove my old jacket into the locker along with the wig I pluck from my head.

Some of the best people in my life are the ones I've met through busking. And Mr. Cantor is a sweetheart. I give him a quick hug. "See you tomorrow!"

And I rush out. I have to get to the school to pick up Cat and take her to gymnastics. Busking time is for me, but the rest of my time belongs to my little sister. I want to make sure she never feels as alone as I did.

3

OWEN

She's back.

My subway folk singer. Ha. She's not *mine*. But now I look for her every time I'm in this station. And sometimes at other stations.

Today I'm by myself. We have a day off and I decided to...ah hell. I don't need to be here in midtown today. I told myself I'd do some shopping, but my favorite clothing store is in SoHo. I'll head there later. This is on the way. Sort of.

I have all the time today to stop and listen to her, but hanging around too long would be creepy. As usual, I stay at the back of the crowd, hopefully out of her notice.

People pause, listen, then move on, some tossing money into the guitar case.

I'm fascinated with this woman. She has a beautiful voice and plays the guitar with amazing skill. At least it seems like that to me. Why is she busking? This has to be a tough way to make a living. Is she homeless?

I don't know anything about busking.

She starts another tune, a wistful melody, her fingers moving on the guitar strings as she sings about a soulmate. "And suddenly...all my love songs are about you."

I get goose bumps on my arms and a shiver runs down my back.

I've never really thought about having a soulmate. I'm not sure if I even know what that is. The person who's perfect for you, I guess. Loneliness hollows out my chest for a moment. I doubt I'll ever be someone's soulmate.

Jesus. Why am I thinking about shit like this?

It's the music. It makes me feel things. I try not to feel things. I keep myself too busy to feel things.

When she finishes her song, she stands and sets down her guitar. I guess she's done. As people disperse, I duck around a corner so she won't see me. Shit. I need to get out of here, but I have to pass her to get out.

I pull out my phone and unlock it then stare at it so I don't look weird.

"Hi."

My head snaps up. It's her. Standing in front of me, a curious half-smile perched on her pretty lips.

"Hi." I'm swamped with awkwardness, staring at her.

"I've seen you watching me," she says.

Busted. Crap. I search for a response that's cool and not weird. "I like your music," I blurt out.

Her smile deepens. "Thanks."

Oh hey...does she want money? I reach for my wallet. "I should give you..."

She holds up a hand. "No, no. That's okay."

"It's not that I don't think you're good enough," I babble. "You're really good. I give money to buskers all the time."

"That's not why I'm talking to you." Her lips tighten minutely.

Great. Now I've pissed her off.

"I'm a good guy," I say. "I'm not creeping on you."

I totally am creeping on her. Also, why did I say that? Jesus.

Her eyebrows lift behind the long bangs. "I didn't think that."

"Okay, good." I attempt a smile, also non-threatening and chill.

Hopefully I don't look like Christian Bale in American Psycho. "Are you done playing?"

"I am." She pushes back her greenish hair. "Would you like to get a cup of coffee?"

I blink. "With you?"

Jesus. Could I be any more of a fuckwit?

Her lips twitch. "Yes. I noticed you're not wearing a suit, so I thought maybe you had time…?"

I don't know what to say. If I say yes, does that prove I *am* a stalker? If I say no…I don't get to have coffee with her. My curiosity about her wins out. "Sure. Okay."

"Okay." She smiles fully, and wow, it's dazzling. "Let's go. I know a place near here."

I follow her. "Can I carry that for you?"

"That's okay."

Out on the street, she turns right and leads me around a corner to a small diner. The old-fashioned sign above the door says LANGLEY LUNCHEONETTE.

We pause inside the door, enveloped in warm air. I guess we seat ourselves, as this musician—hell, I don't even know her name—leads us to a small booth upholstered in green vinyl. Round stools line the counter where I spy a glass container of donuts. Framed prints of various sizes cover the walls, photos of people who've probably eaten here.

"Looks like this place has been here for a while." I shrug out of my jacket.

She slides in opposite me and does the same, parking her gear in the inside corner of the booth. "It sure has. I think sixty years."

"It's cool." I finish my perusal of the place and focus on her. "I'm Owen."

She extends a small hand to me across the table. "Nice to meet you, Owen. I'm Emmie."

Her hand is soft except for the tips, which are calloused. Strangely, those callouses dragging over my palm is…erotic.

"Emmie. Nice to meet you, too."

Face to face, I can indulge in studying her up close. Her full lips are pouty and smooth, her nose what I think people call "snub" with a slightly blunt and upturned tip. Behind the big gold-framed glasses, winged dark eyebrows sit above expressive blue-gray eyes heavily coated with mascara. Smooth, glowing skin, perfect white teeth and shiny eyes don't give the impression of someone who's homeless. Is that stereotyping? I don't know.

A waitress approaches the table to take our order.

"I'll have a coffee," Emmie says.

The waitress looks at me. I don't drink coffee. They probably don't have kale smoothies here. After a pause, she says, "Our milkshakes are world famous."

Jesus. I can't drink a milkshake. "How about a bottled water?"

She nods and disappears.

"So." Emmie adjusts the sugar dispenser on the table. "You pass by quite often. You must work in this area."

"I do." I don't offer up what it is that I do. For some reason, I don't want to come off as rich and famous. Which I kind of am.

"I pegged you as a successful businessman," she says with a smile. "Am I right?"

"Pretty successful."

Wait. She thinks about me? Huh. With slightly increased confidence, I smile. "I've been trying to figure you out, but I can't."

"Because I'm a busker."

"Yeah."

The waitress returns and sets and a cup and saucer in front of Emmie, then fills the cup from a pot of coffee.

I watch Emmie dump in a staggering amount of sugar, then cream.

"You're a very talented musician," I offer.

"So why am I playing in the subway?" she responds with a crooked smile.

"I have wondered."

"I like it." She stirs her coffee and shrugs. "I can do my thing.

People can ignore me. Or not." She lifts the cup to her lips and takes a sip, meeting my eyes.

Or not. "A lot of people stop to watch you."

She smiles. "Sometimes, yeah. Different locations have different audiences. I do pretty well at Penn Station. Also Times Square and Grand Central."

"I never would have thought of that, but I suppose the location makes a difference."

"It does. Also the time of day. I never play during the end of day rush hour. Everyone's too busy and focused on getting home to enjoy my kind of music."

"It's very..." I stop. "I don't know anything about music. Except that I like it."

"That's okay." She eyes me. "It's very what?"

"Emotional? It makes me feel stuff. Oh, shit. That sounds dirty. I mean, inappropriate." My eyes widen in alarm.

She laughs softly. "I know what you mean. And that's the perfect compliment. So thank you."

Relief flows through me. I make a face. "Your music is beautiful."

"Aw, thank you." She seems genuinely pleased by this compliment.

She's beautiful too, in an offbeat kind of way with her funky glasses, green hair, and the tiny diamond piercing that glints on the side of her nose. I keep this to myself, though. For now.

"I'm not super talented," she adds matter-of-factly. "But I do really love music."

"I think you're amazingly talented."

Her smile is appreciative but her tone still pragmatic. "Thank you."

My water arrives and I thank the waitress with a smile.

"Would you like a refill?" The waitress holds up the coffee pot.

"Sure. I'm going to need extra caffeine tonight."

"Ah. More busking?" I frown, thinking of her alone in the subway late at night.

"No, actually, I have to go to a party." She bites her lip and eyes me appraisingly. "That's actually, um, kind of why I asked you for coffee."

Her slight stumbling is a change from her confidence, and endearing. But I frown, uncomprehending.

"I need a date," she adds bluntly, dumping more sugar into her cup.

I give my head a small shake. "Uh…you want me to go to a party with you tonight?"

"Yes." She peers up at me tentatively through long eyelashes and green bangs. "Are you married?"

I already noticed her checking out my left hand. "No."

"Girlfriend?"

"No.

"Okay, good."

"I don't get it."

She sighs. "It's a long story. My ex-boyfriend is going to be there. I just want him to think I'm with someone else now."

"Ex-boyfriend?"

"Yeah." She sinks her teeth into her plump bottom lip. Her lips tighten. "We broke up and he didn't take it well. And my stepfather wants us to get back together." She rolls her eyes. "He talks about Roman all the time to me. Roman's family and his family have been friends forever. He thinks this would be the perfect match for me."

I can tell her opinion of it from the eye roll and tone of voice.

I nod slowly. "So you want your ex to think you're in love with someone else."

"Not 'in love with.'" She pauses. "Well. Maybe. But it doesn't have to be that involved. Just someone there. Maybe you can pretend you like me."

I huff out a laugh, shaking my head. "I'm trying hard not to be insulted."

Her perfect eyebrows pull together above that cute snub nose. "What?"

One corner of my mouth lifts. "Usually, women ask me out because they're attracted to me." It's my turn to be pragmatic.

Her eyes fly open. "Oh! I see what you mean." She smacks her forehead. "I'm sorry! I'm not trying to insult you!" She covers her mouth and regards me with remorseful eyes. "I just thought it would be easier to convince someone if it was just…you know…transactional."

"I get it."

"You *are* attractive!" She bobs her head enthusiastically. "Very attractive."

"Gee, thanks."

She closes her eyes. "Never mind. I totally botched this. It's a stupid idea anyway."

"No, no. It's fine." I pause. "You don't even know me."

"I know, but you look perfect." Her eyes widen with enthusiasm. "You dress well. I know you own a suit."

I choke on my water. "Your bar is pretty low."

She grins. "You don't know my stepdad."

I grimace. "True." I'm not getting a good impression.

"You look nice," she continues. "I mean, better than nice. You're…" She stops. "This is so awkward."

To be honest, I like seeing her falter. It makes me feel better. But it also makes me like her. More.

"I guess it's not much different from a blind date. Except we don't have a friend vouching for us."

"True. We don't know each other, but I've seen you a lot and you seem decent."

"Decent and owns a suit." I nod. "That's me."

Her laugh is a soft ripple. "You don't look like a serial killer."

"More high praise."

"I'm fucking this all up, aren't I?" She gulps her coffee. "Shit."

"Nah. I'll go to your party with you." What the hell? Am I crazy? This is definitely not part of my carefully planned routine.

For some reason, I want to do this. She's a little unconventional, but I don't get any sinister vibes from her.

"Really?"

"Yeah. What time and where?"

She swallows. "Okay. Wow. I can't believe this. The party starts at seven, which means we should show up around eight."

"Ooookay."

"We can meet somewhere…" She pauses. "Okay, let's meet at The Carlyle."

I tilt my head. That's a pretty swanky hotel. "Fine."

"Just before eight," she adds. She sinks her teeth into her bottom lip. "Wear a suit."

"Yeah, I got that." I pause. "Do we need to make up a story about how we met, how long we've been together…?"

"No." She waves a hand. "We don't need to go into that much detail. I just need someone to be there."

"Okay. I'll be there."

"Perfect! Okay. I have to get home. Thank you, thank you!"

She pulls out a small wallet to pay for our drinks. I wave it away. "I got this. Though it looked like you did make a lot busking today."

She yelps out a surprised laugh, seeing I'm teasing. "Thank you, Owen. See you later."

She gathers up her things and hustles out of the diner into the late afternoon chill.

I drain my water bottle.

Well. This turned out weird. Guess I have a date tonight.

4

EMERIE

I can't believe I did this.

I stare at my reflection in the mirror. I'm ready for the party. My first plan was to not be here at all. That would get me irritation from Vince. Bringing a date is likely to get *more* than irritation. My stomach flutters with nerves. But somehow, I have to put an end to this bullshit. I can't handle Roman hanging around all the time, and Vince pushing me to get back with him.

I lift my chin. Time to go meet Owen.

I can't believe he agreed to come. Or maybe he was just humoring the crazy lady and has no intention of showing up. Honestly, I pretty much expect him not to show. That's been my experience most of my life—people I need don't come through for me.

That's okay. I'm used to it. I know I can count on myself.

The party starts at seven. Nobody will show up that early, but I need to get out of here before someone does. So I grab a coat and purse and sneak out of the Park Avenue penthouse where I live. I walk the couple of blocks to the Carlyle, my chin tucked in the collar of my coat against the cold night air. I enter the hotel through revolving doors and stride into the lobby. Here, I'm not out of place in my cocktail dress and heels.

I walk into the gilded glow of the bar. A pianist at the grand piano plays "The Nearness of You." The dulcet music soothes my nerves as I find a seat at a small table in a corner. I take off my coat and lay it on the banquette next to me.

This guy's pretty good. As always, the urge to play comes over me, but I like to listen as well.

A waiter approaches to take my order.

I smile at him. "A dirty martini, please."

"Of course."

I pull out my phone. I didn't even exchange numbers with Owen, so he can't cancel on me. I'll just have to wait and see if he shows.

I scroll through social media to occupy myself, sitting alone in the elegant bar. My cocktail arrives and I sip it slowly, enjoying the dry vermouth and salty olive juice. I lose myself in the smooth jazz music. When I check the time on my phone, I'm surprised to see it's nearly eight.

I don't know if Owen will look for me in here, so I gather up my things and quickly take care of the check, then emerge back into the lobby, scanning it.

He's here.

Sweet prancing Christ.

And he looks amazing.

My heart knocks against my breastbone and I suck in a breath. Standing near the entrance in a long dark coat, he hasn't seen me yet. Tonight, he eschewed the knit beanie he sometimes wears, his dark gold hair gleaming from the pot lights and chandelier above. He's big —tall and broad, an imposing figure who catches the eye of more than one woman passing by.

I walk toward him and he lifts his head as I enter his peripheral vision. For a moment he gives me a blank gaze, then blinks a few times. "Emmie?"

"It's me." My smile is sheepish. I know I look different. "You showed up. I didn't think you would."

"Your hair…"

I touch my locks. "I wear a wig when I busk."

He blinks again, his gaze moving from my hair, over my face, then down to my dress. It's not super revealing—a black velvet sheath with sheer black sleeves and upper bodice—but also very different than my busking outfits.

"I'm a little confused."

"I'm sorry." I shake out my coat and start to put it on. He automatically takes it from me and steps behind me to help me into it. My heart does another thump.

Then we face each other again. He still looks...dazed.

"Are you okay?" I ask. "With this, I mean."

"Not sure what I've gotten into," he mutters. "But what the hell. Let's go."

He barely touches the small of my back to shepherd me into the revolving doors ahead of him. I push through, and then he follows my lead down the sidewalk. The night is clear and crisp, the sky matte black above, glittering skyscrapers towering around us.

He casts a glance at my heels.

"I'm fine," I say, sliding my arm into his. "And it's not far."

"Okay. The party's not at the Carlyle?"

"No. It's at my stepfather's home."

"I see."

"It'll be fine. Lots of people. We can grab a drink and hide. I just have to make an appearance, look like we're hot for each other, and then we can leave."

"Jesus." He rubs his face.

"Are you still okay with this?"

His chuckle is dry. "Like I said, I'm not sure what I've gotten into."

One-way traffic streams slowly past us. We pass closed shops and other businesses, then turn and walk another block to the building where I live. "This is it."

"Good evening, Ms. Ross," Anthony, one of the doormen says.

"Good evening," I greet him. Owen and I step into an elevator. "I guess I should know your last name to introduce you."

"Right. It's Cooke. Owen Cooke."

I nod. "Thanks. I'm Emmie Ross." We ride silently to the top floor and step out. There are two units up here, and I turn left to open the door to Vince's apartment. As soon as I open the door, we can hear the noise within—chattering voices, loud laughter, more smooth jazz piano music.

I'm used to this. I'm not sure about Owen. He seems okay with it all.

I knew he'd be perfect for this.

A maid takes our coats to hang them. "Thanks, Sophia. This is Owen Cooke."

"Nice to meet you, Mr. Cooke."

I cross the foyer beneath the coffered ceiling, my sharp heels sinking into the thick rug. We enter the living room through double doors. Yep, lots of people. I stop to survey the space, the scent of expensive perfumes reaching my nose, a burst of laughter coming from the far end of the room near the window. That's Vince.

"First things first," I mutter. "Drinks."

Vince has a bar with a bartender set up in here and we make our way over there. I greet a few people I recognize. None of these people are close friends of mine. Finally, I have another dirty martini in my hand and Owen holds a crystal glass of scotch.

We stand to the side.

"I told you everyone would just ignore us," I say. I sip my martini. "Uh oh. I've been spotted. Brace yourself."

Vince has seen me and is walking toward us.

Owen has his back to him. "Should I look?"

"Don't look. Be casual." I give him a loving smile.

"Emerie, you're finally here," Vince says. "Where the hell were you?"

"We stopped for a drink at the Carlyle," I say lightly. "Sorry we're late. Vince, this is Owen Cooke."

Owen turns to face him.

"Owen—"

Both men wear identical expressions of shock and recognition.

"Mr. D'Agostino," Owen says, his voice cracking.

Vince's eyes widen. "Owen."

Now I'm staring. "You two know each other?"

Vince gives me an incredulous look. "He plays for the Bears."

The hockey team Vince owns.

My stomach swoops. I swivel my gaze to Owen. His look confirms this. What the fuck?

For a moment, my head goes empty. Then thoughts rush in. Can I save this? No. Yes. I don't know. How? How could I not know the guy I'm supposedly dating is a hockey player? Who works for my stepdad? How the fuck did this happen?

"You didn't tell me you know Vince," I say with a light laugh, sliding my arm through Owen's.

He stares at me, as incredulous as Vince.

Shit. I can't blame him. "Sorry, since our names are different you had no way of knowing we're related," I add quickly. I pat his hard chest. It's very hard. *Focus.* I turn back to Vince. "I may have kept it a secret from him."

His eyebrows pull together.

"Way to spring it on me, sweetheart," Owen says with a tight smile.

"Emerie, for God's sake. You can't date one of my players."

I frown. "You don't *own* them, Vince."

Tension vibrates off Owen's muscled body.

"And you certainly don't own *me*," I add.

We're approached by another man, and while I welcome the diversion, it's Roman. Ugh.

"Hi, Emerie." He gives me the usual covetous look he always does, gets way too close, and kisses my cheek. His aftershave nearly suffocates me. "Great to see you. You look gorgeous, as always."

He's never seen me busking. Actually, he has. One time he walked right by me and didn't even recognize me. He also didn't pause to listen. He doesn't believe in giving money to buskers or panhandlers. He thinks they should "get a job."

"Thank you. Roman, this is my date—" I try not to choke on the word. "Owen Cooke. Owen, this is Roman Moretti, a family friend."

Roman's eyebrows snap together, and he turns a hostile gaze on Owen. "Cooke."

Owen meets Roman's eyes. He's probably six inches taller than Roman and a lot broader. His oblong-shaped face wears an intimidating notch between his brow, his jaw strong. The hand he extends to Roman is large and grips Roman's in a forceful shake.

Roman's eyes are slitty. Owen's face is grim and slightly baleful. Oh hell. That turns me on.

"Good to meet you, Roman," Owen says.

Vince's pinched expression doesn't bode well, but he won't make a scene here.

Roman looks between Owen and me. "I didn't realize you're seeing someone." Disappointment tugs the corners of his mouth down.

I smile and take Owen's arm again, hugging it like a life preserver. "Yes." I flash Owen a loving look.

Roman takes this in then chugs back a swallow of whatever he's drinking. The air around us is thick and heavy.

"We'll talk about this later," Vince says, outwardly calm, but I can practically see steam coming out his ears.

"Owen!" Another man joins us. It's Brad Julian, the general manager of the Bears hockey team. "What are you doing here?" Brad slaps Owen on the shoulder. Brad's smiling, unaware of the undercurrents. Clearly, he likes Owen, his smile friendly and genuine.

"I'm here with Emmie," Owen replies. "Er, Emerie."

"You can call me either." I lean into him with another adoring smile, fluttering my eyelashes up at him. *Don't be mad. Don't be mad.*

He has every right to be mad. Holy shit. My insides quake.

"Oh." Brad's a little taken aback, but not nearly as much as Vince and Roman. "Small world."

Clearly, he's questioning Owen's judgment. Dating the team owner's daughter might not be the smartest career move. But I'm only

Vince's stepdaughter, and Vince doesn't really care about me other than for making Roman Moretti happy.

"Right?" Owen chuckles. "I just found out Vince is Emerie's stepfather." He casts a chiding glance my way, but I can see a glint of censure in his eyes, matched by the tightness at the corners of his beautiful mouth.

"You two can't know each other that well, then," Roman says with an edge.

"I wouldn't say that," Owen replies with a smile bordering on dirty. *Thank you.*

"It's my fault," I say. "I just wanted him to know me for who I am, not my family."

I meet Roman's eyes when I say it, and even though I'm smiling, his face stiffens. "Emerie..."

"I said we'll talk about this later," Vince interjects, laying a hand on Roman's shoulder and squeezing. "So, Owen, how are you feeling about the season so far?"

As if a microphone has been shoved in his face, Owen switches into pro mode. "We're having a good season," he says. "We're playing the right way and getting better all the time."

He, Brad, and Vince launch into hockey talk, which makes my eyes glaze over. Here I'm trying to convince everyone I'm dating a hockey player when hockey is the last thing in the world I'm interested in.

I keep an interested expression in place as I down my martini. Heat from the alcohol runs through me. I'm going to need another one of these, ASAP.

What have I done?

5

OWEN

Holy fucking shit.

If I didn't know better, I'd think this is a huge practical joke. The guys have done some crazy pranks on each other, but this would definitely take the cake.

Did someone set me up here?

Nah. Not possible.

I'm doing my best not to look like a fucking idiot in front of the owner and GM of the team, but I strongly suspect I'm failing.

Who is this chick? Oh yeah—apparently the owner's daughter. How the hell did she pick *me* to drag into this nightmare? Why the fuck is she busking in the subway when her stepfather is a billionaire? Or something. I have no idea how much money he has, but it's a lot.

"Obviously, our goal is to be ready for the playoffs.," I say. I don't know what the hell I'm babbling. I take a sip of scotch. My buddy JBo once tried to get me into scotch, but I can't stand the stuff. I mostly avoid alcohol during the season, but right now, I'm glad I have this.

Eventually, Mr. D'Agostino ushers Roman away to talk to someone else, but not without a stern look at Emerie and a reminder they'll talk later. That takes a little of the stress off. Then Mr. Julian's wife joins us. I've met her a few times over the years I've been playing for the

Bears. She doesn't know what's just gone down, so the atmosphere lightens as we chat about the holiday season we just had, what we all did for New Year's Eve, and the snowstorm apparently headed our way.

Then Emerie excuses us, and her arm hooked through mine, leads us out of the living room and into the kitchen. The people bustling around in here must be hired—they're preparing appetizers and arranging them on platters, and a man carries a case of liquor through. Emerie pauses at the island.

"How's it going here, Klara?" she asks.

"Things are fine," a woman assures her with a smile. "Thanks for checking in."

"Let me know if you need anything."

Is she...in charge of this party?

In her high heels, she clips over to a huge refrigerator, opens the door, and pulls out two beers.

"Do you live here?" I ask in a low voice, following her through another door and into another living space, this one more casual. And empty.

"Unfortunately, yes." She doesn't stop. "Come on, I have to check on my little sister."

What?

I trail behind her down a hall. She knocks on a door and when a small voice calls to come in, she enters.

I'm not following her into a little girl's bedroom, so I hover in the hall as she walks in.

"Hey! What are you watching?"

To All the Boys I've Loved Before." I can't see the person belonging to the voice. "How's the party?"

"Boring."

"You're just saying that so I won't feel bad that I'm not there."

"No. I really mean it." Emerie turns and beckons to me. "Come meet Cat."

I wave a hand and shake my head. I'm already in this deep enough.

"Who's there?" the young girl's voice asks.

"My friend, Owen," Emerie says. "He's shy."

I roll my eyes. I've never been called that before. I poke my head in. "Hi."

The girl is curled up in an armchair in the corner with a remote control in her hand, the picture on the big TV near her paused. "Oh, hi," she says with a smile.

She looks nothing like Emerie. Her hair is long, wavy, and dark, more like Emerie's wig, her eyes big and brown. Okay, their face shape is the same. And their smile. She's cute.

"Just wanted to check on you," Emerie says. "Make sure you didn't sneak a bottle of booze in here or something."

Cat rolls her eyes. "As if."

Emerie grins. "Bedtime is nine," she reminds Cat, and we leave. "Let's go to my room."

"What? Jesus."

She ignores me and struts down the hall in her wicked heels, her ass twitching in the form-fitting black dress. Under those baggy clothes she wears in the subway, she's...wow. Small waist, curvy hips, and stacked.

Reluctantly, I trudge after her. She opens another door and steps inside, flicking on a light.

It's another spacious bedroom with a queen bed at one end and near us, a sitting area with a small couch and chair. I don't take in a lot of details, focused more on Emerie, but the overall impression is luxurious and serene. My gaze lands on the guitar on a stand in the corner, then takes in the papers covered with music notes strewn on the low table.

"Here." She hands me a beer. "I have a feeling this is more your taste."

She's not wrong. If I drink, it's usually beer. But I hold up a hand. "No thanks. I don't drink much."

She shrugs, quickly gathers up the papers, then kicks off her shoes and sits on the couch. "Have a seat."

I take the chair. "Okay," I say, letting out a long gusty breath. "What the hell is going on?"

"I'm sorry. I'm so sorry." She lowers her head into her hand. "I had no idea you play for the Bears."

"Really?" I'm not prepared to believe anything she says at this point.

Her head snaps up. "Really!"

"Your father owns the team."

"My stepfather." Her tone is icy as she corrects me. "And I can't stand hockey. I don't know anything about the team."

My eyebrows fly up. "Really." I'm a little offended by her dislike of my sport.

"Really." She opens the other beer and takes a guzzle.

My lips twitch with the urge to smile. Diamonds glitter at her ears. She's dressed in an elegant, knee-length black velvet dress, bare legs stretched out with her feet on the table, toenails impeccably pedicured in matching black polish, ankles crossed—one of them tattooed—and swilling a beer.

Her natural hair color—assuming this is natural, who knows?—is dark blond with pale honey highlights, parted in the middle and hanging in waves just past her shoulders. I assume she's wearing contacts now. Or the big glasses were fake.

She's stunning.

But then, I thought that when her hair was green. It's not about the hair and the clothes...it's the sweet, luminous smile and warm, shining eyes.

Never mind that. We have a huge-ass problem here.

"I can't believe it," she moans, letting her head fall back against the couch. "How did this happen?"

"You're asking *me*?"

"That was rhetorical." She rolls her head side to side. "I thought you were some random hedge fund trader Roman and Vince would never see again."

I'm kind of believing her now. She seems really perturbed.

She lifts her head and meets my eyes. "I had no idea. I'm so sorry I dragged you into this."

I nod slowly.

"Thank you for going along with it out there."

"I had no idea what to do." I pick up the beer and take a gulp, waiving my no alcohol rule because, Jesus.

"You did great." She sighs. "What do we do now?"

"Another rhetorical question?"

"No, we really need to figure that out."

"Oh. I guess we do. I could just disappear, and you could claim I dumped you." I smack my forehead. "No, that would probably piss off your stepdad and get me fired."

"He can't fire you!" she says on a gasp. "Can he?"

"He can trade me. Buy out my contract. Bench me. Make my life living hell."

"Oh, Jesus Krispy Creme Christ."

I choke on a laugh. "Yeah."

"Okay." She holds her hands up in a soothing gesture. "Realistically, he won't do that. He doesn't care enough about what I do."

"Except for skeevy Roman, there."

"Oh right. Shit. Vince is pissed because of that." She nibbles her full bottom lip in a gesture that makes my groin tighten. "It's true he might want you out of the picture."

"What does that mean?" Alarm heats the blood in my veins. "Is your family...you know..."

"What?" Her forehead crinkles.

"Is your family in the, uh, garbage business?"

She squints. "No. Vince owns a bunch of different businesses, but not garbage."

"No, that's a euphemism."

"For what?" A notch forms between her perfect eyebrows.

"You know..." I don't want to say it. "The mob."

She bursts out laughing. "Oh my God! Because he's Italian?"

My face heats. "Is that stupid?"

"Yes." She laughs more. "But you're not alone. Other people assume that, too. It's ridiculous."

"I wouldn't put it past Moretti," I mutter. "How long were you together?"

"A few months."

My gut twists. "He didn't want to end things."

"No. But I can't marry him." Her firm words ease the tension in my belly. What is that tension? Not…jealousy?

"He looks like a creepdog."

She laughs more, then takes a breath. "He's not that bad. He's rich and thinks he can have whatever he wants. But I don't think he's mobbed up. You're not going to get whacked."

"Good to know." I gulp more beer. "However, my career is fucked."

I hope I'm exaggerating, but that's how I feel. How could this happen? To me? The hardest-working, most focused and serious guy on the team. The *last* thing I'd ever do is get involved with the owner's daughter!

She groans, head falling back again. "No. It can't be. Let's think about this."

After a moment of heavy silence, I say, "Your sister is a lot younger than you."

"Um. Yeah. She's my half-sister. She's twelve. My mom married Vince when *I* was twelve. They had Cat a year later." She pauses. "Mom died when I was fifteen. Cat was only two."

My body stiffens. Talking about losing loved ones rattles me. "Oh. I'm sorry for your loss." I clear my throat and try to relax.

"Yeah." She sighs. "Cat doesn't even remember her."

"Your biological father…?"

"He died when I was nine."

Hell. Both her parents. Heat burns over my skin. "That's a lot of loss."

She meets my eyes and hers shine in recognition of my sympathy. "It is. My dad was a cello player. He played on Broadway in orchestra pits for lots of big musicals."

33

"That's where you get your talent from."

"Yep. Wish I got more of it." She pushes hair back off her face. "Anyway, he's not around either. Vince isn't exactly paternal, so Cat and I have been mostly on our own since Mom died."

"On your own." I look around. "When I saw you in the subway I wondered if you were homeless. This is a far cry from that."

"I know!" She sits up straight. "Don't think I'm a privileged brat. Well, okay, I am, in some ways. I live here, Vince has lots of money, and we have a privileged lifestyle. I know that." One corner of her mouth hooks up. "But people need more than just food and shelter."

I can't help the small snort that escapes me. "Again...this ain't just food and shelter, sweetheart."

She pins me with a long look. "I know. But love is pretty important too. Belonging somewhere." She sweeps out a hand. "I've never felt like I belong here. Especially after Mom died."

That renders me silent.

"I had to make sure Cat didn't feel like that, too," she adds quietly.

She's looking after her sister. I feel like a hand is reaching inside me and twisting my guts up. Of course, I think of my brother. But I shove those thoughts away.

I have a million more questions for her. She's intriguing and interesting and puzzling. "Why do you say you've never belonged here?"

She doesn't answer right away. Finally, she says, "Vince loved my mom, but he never loved me. This is a beautiful apartment..." She sweeps out a hand. "But it never felt like home. And when Mom died...well, then I *really* felt alone here." With a shake of her head, she lowers her feet to the floor and leans forward, elbows on her knees. "But we don't need to get into that. We just need to figure out how to handle this without you losing your job and without me ending up married to Roman."

"Your...Vince can't make you marry anyone," I point out reasonably.

She lifts an eyebrow. "You don't know him."

I rub my jaw. "I don't know him personally that well, but he does have a reputation as a...er, tough negotiator."

"What Vince wants, Vince gets. He has his ways." She holds up a hand. "Not by whacking people."

"Why does he want that so bad? You're not his daughter."

She sighs. "I suspect there's money involved. Lots of money. Roman's family is very wealthy."

I get a sick feeling in my gut. This is fucked up. She can't really think Mr. D can make her marry that asswipe.

"I thought about just leaving," she says. "But I have to stay for Cat."

I could see they love each other. If Vince is an asshole to his younger daughter too, I get why she wants to stay.

"If I can make it a few more years, I can leave," she adds. "Cat'll be old enough to look after herself." Her lips push out. "Who am I kidding. I'll never be able to leave her." She falls back again, emitting another groan and closing her eyes.

She says all this without an ounce of self pity. It's all just presented as established facts. For some reason, this makes me like her. I don't feel sorry for her. Well, I do. But in a way where I want to help her. "It's okay. We got this."

"No. I'll figure this out. You don't need to be involved."

"I already am. Look." My mind rolls. "What if we keep seeing each other?"

One eye opens. "What do you mean?"

"We keep pretending we're together. Roman will leave you alone, and Mr. D will give up on that idea."

"What if he trades you away?"

My back teeth grind a little. "I don't think he'll do that. Not to brag, but I'm a pretty good player. They just signed me last year again. The team's been through a bunch of changes lately. He has to care more about winning than about marrying you off."

She purses her lips and thinks this over. "Possibly."

"Also, he isn't the manager or the coach. I guess ultimately he could tell them what to do, but most owners are more hands off. If he told Coach to bench me, he'd probably get a fight." *I hope.*

"I can't ask you to do that."

"You've got other ideas?"

She falls silent. Finally, she says, "No."

6

EMERIE

"Vince doesn't even like hockey that much," I tell Owen. "He just likes making money."

He snorts. "Owning a hockey team is a tough way to do that."

"I wouldn't know." I nibble on my lip. "How long would we have to do that?"

"You tell me."

"I don't know."

"Maybe...a month?"

My eyes pop open. "A month is nothing. Roman will still be hanging around." Then I slump into the couch. "See? I can't ask you to do this. I don't know how long it'll take. Unless..."

"What?"

"We find someone else for Roman to marry."

He bursts out laughing, then sobers when he sees I'm serious. "You are batshit crazy."

"I know." I sigh. "But what if we did? What if Roman fell in love with someone else?" I tip my head back. "That could work."

"You could just tell Vince the truth. You don't want to marry Roman."

"I *have* told him that! Repeatedly! He just brushes me off." I grimace. "Finding a boyfriend actually might help. Other than Roman, I've never had a boyfriend before." I give him a shy look.

He blinks. "I find that hard to believe."

"Why? I'm weird. And I've been busy looking after a kid."

"And hanging out in the subway."

"That just started." She waves a hand.

"Well, that's my offer. Take it or leave it." He finishes his beer and sets down the bottle as if he's leaving.

Panic flashes through my chest. "Okay! I'll take it."

"For a month."

I already pointed out a month isn't long enough, but it's the best I have right now. "Okay."

"Let's go back to the party."

"Ugh."

"Believe me, I feel the same. But we need your stepdad to see us."

"I suppose so."

I don't know why he's willing to do this. It's bizarre, and he seems pretty normal. "I'm really grateful," I say quietly. "I know this is fucked up."

He purses those gorgeous lips. I bet he's a good kisser. "It really is. But I said I'll do it, so I'll do it."

I gaze at him for a few long seconds. "I really appreciate that."

I stick a foot out and slide my shoes closer to me, then slip them on. "Okay." I stand. "Let's go."

I'm pretty tall, and even with my four-inch Louboutins on, I'm still a good six inches shorter than him. "You're really tall," I say as I lead the way out of my room.

"So I've heard."

I flash a smile. "Just call me Captain Obvious."

"Ha."

The party is in full swing, the music now more up-tempo, the voices louder. We stop at the bar again for refills of liquid courage.

"No offense," Owen says as he picks up another glass of scotch. "But I'm probably not gonna drink this. It's disgusting."

I bite back my smile. "You don't have to drink it. I can get you another beer."

"No, that's okay. I'll just carry this around and look sophisticated."

I give him an up and down look. His expensive suit fits his athletic body perfectly, accessorized with shiny, stylish shoes. Definitely sophisticated. His big hands are clean, with neatly trimmed nails, although his knuckles are a bit red and rough. And his face...sophisticated is not the correct word to describe his face. More like...tough. A small scar creases the skin near his mouth, barely visible beneath his stubble, and his nose isn't perfectly straight at the bridge. The twin lines between his eyebrows give him a perpetual glowering look, although when he smiles, they disappear. His smile is...warm. Like an incandescent bulb in a dark room. It's bright, safe, reassuring.

Also sexy as fuck.

I've never been into athletes, but now I'm getting the attraction.

"You look great," I murmur, then sip my cocktail.

"So do you. I never would have guessed...this..." He gestures at me. "...was underneath those baggy clothes."

"This?" I lift an eyebrow.

He eases me away from the bar so others can get there. "Fishing for compliments?"

"Yes."

A surprised laugh snaps out of him.

"I'm kidding," I say. "I'm just bugging you." I look down at myself. "I try to look different when I'm busking."

His smile sends a bolt of heat straight to my girl parts. "You succeeded. But even with the wig and baggy clothes, I thought you were beautiful."

Heat unfurls in my chest. "Thank you." I duck my head and take another sip.

"Hello, Emerie."

I turn to see one of Vince's business partners. "Hi, Zev," I say, and we exchange air kisses on the cheek. "How are you?"

"Very well, thanks." His gaze moves to Owen.

I make the introduction.

"You play for the Bears," Zev says.

"Yes, sir, I do."

"That was an amazing goal in the shoot out last week."

Owen smiles. "Thanks. I hate shoot outs."

"You looked pretty comfortable."

I listen to their hockey talk. I guess this is what it's like to date a hockey player. Hockey bores the socks off me, but I got myself into this, so I hang on Owen's every word, smiling and nodding.

We mingle a bit more. I make sure Roman sees us. And Vince. I stand close to Owen, fasten my gaze to his face, and lean in to whisper in his ear.

It's not that hard. He smells amazing. I'd like to press my nose to his neck and inhale him for about an hour. It's also quite enjoyable when he smiles down at me, his cobalt blue eyes warm and the skin around his eyes crinkling up attractively. He's good at this.

I don't think he can talk about anything but hockey, though. In fairness, everyone we meet wants to talk about that with him. I'd like to talk about Broadway plays or concerts or the police trying to arrest street performers who had a right to be there. Nobody wants to talk about that. Just me.

So I listen to a lot of hockey talk. Most of it goes over my head. I have to admit Owen sounds knowledgeable, and he's very well-spoken.

"I think we've been here long enough," I finally say to him when we're alone. "You can head out if you like."

"What are you going to do?"

"Make sure Cat's in bed. Have a snack and maybe watch a movie."

He nods slowly.

I press my fingertips to my chin. "You don't want to…join me, do you?" I'm sure he doesn't.

"Sure."

I blink. "Okay."

"Will your stepdad freak out about me being in your room?"

"He'll never know." I roll my eyes. "His suite is on the other side of the apartment. He rarely comes to our rooms."

"That's…sad." We start walking toward the kitchen. "Not so much for you, I guess, but your sister…she's still little."

"Yeah. It sucks. He's a dick."

"No love lost between you two."

"Sadly, no. I mean, well, we can talk more in a minute."

I stop again in the kitchen and fill up a plate with some of the party goodies—beef wellington wontons, antipasto skewers, crostini with almonds, bacon, and cheese. I grab a few paper napkins and throw Owen a look over my shoulder. "Sure you don't want a beer?"

"No, thanks."

I shrug and grab one for myself. Together, we carry everything to my room. I leave him to pop back to Cat's room. She's still watching TV.

"Hey, Kitty Cat, what are you doing? It's way past bedtime."

She heaves a sigh and turns off the TV. "Fine."

She's in her pajamas, so she knows. She's just pushing as long as she can until I come in. I smile. This is a far cry from her behavior years ago. "G'night," I say, kissing the top of her head when she's in bed. "I love you. See you in the morning."

"Night, Em. I love you, too."

A wave of affection floods me as I leave.

I hesitate before entering my room again. There's a man in my room. A big, sexy, delicious-smelling man. This is…unusual. My belly flutters, and I press a hand there. It's fine. Everything is fine.

Other than I now have a fake boyfriend I don't even really know and a pissed-off stepfather.

I open the door and step in. And freeze.

Sweet baby deity. Owen has removed his suit jacket and tie and undone the top buttons of his shirt. He has the remote in one hand, aimed at my TV, and he looks right at home. Glancing up, he says, "Hey."

"Hey."

I start toward him. "It occurs to me that you know my secret."

He's watching me with attentive, hot eyes. He likes what he sees. And I like that. This feeling is unfamiliar to me. "What do you mean?"

"My busking."

His chin lifts. "Ah. Your stepdad doesn't know about that."

"Nope. He'd die if he found out."

"Doubtful." He watches me sit on the other end of the couch from him.

I tuck some hair behind my ear, my belly fluttering even more now, my skin heating. "Well, he'd be pissed."

"So what?" Then he narrows his eyes, and his shoulders stiffen. "Does he hurt you?"

"No!" I shake my head vehemently. "No, he's never touched us. Mostly he ignores us. But he doesn't like things that make him look bad."

"Okay," he says quietly, visibly relieved.

"He'd be embarrassed. It's just easier if he doesn't know. You wouldn't say anything to him, would you?"

His eyebrows jerk down. "Of course not, if you don't want me to."

"Whew. Okay, thanks."

"Why do you do that?" He gazes at me, curiosity lighting his blue eyes. "You obviously don't need the money."

"It's not about the money for me. It's a way for me to make music."

"Hmm." He contemplates me wordlessly for a moment. "You're really talented."

I try to accept the compliment. "Thanks."

He looks like wants to say more, but doesn't, still contemplating me with focused intensity.

"Have some food," I squeak, waving at the plate on the table.

He eyes the food. "No, thanks."

I frown. "Why not?"

"I follow a pretty strict diet during the season."

I run my gaze over his muscular body. "I'd think you could eat whatever you want."

One corner of his mouth hooks up. "It's not about putting on weight. It's about being healthy."

"Oh. Of course."

"So, what's next?"

"Next?"

"Our next date."

"Oh." My heart quavers. "Right."

"You can come to my game Saturday night."

My jaw loosens. "Uh…I don't really like hockey."

His lips twitch. "Maybe you should learn, if we're dating?"

I wrinkle my nose. "Damn."

"That would impress Vince."

"Impress? Not sure about that."

"I mean, it would convince him that we're a thing."

"I guess it would, yeah." I sigh.

He hoists a thick eyebrow. "It's not that torturous. Hockey's fun. And we're doing this for you."

I straighten. "You are absolutely right. You're putting your job on the line. The least I can do is go to a hockey game."

"Do you need tickets? Probably not."

"I can sit with Vince in his box." I grin at the thought. "Maybe I'll bring Cat. She actually likes the sport."

"Smart girl."

"Oh, come on. It's a brutal sport."

"It's a game of great skill," he says calmly. "Speed. Agility. It's fast-paced and requires incredible endurance. Stick skills aren't something just anyone can do, especially while skating twenty miles an hour on thin blades."

"Twenty miles an hour."

"Yep."

I remain unconvinced. "All I know is you like to hit each other. A lot."

His eyes glint with amusement although his expression stays neutral. "True. Watch the game, then see what you think."

"I've been to a game." I toss my hair back. "Once. I was seventeen. I wore the opposing team's jersey, and the press took pictures of me and put it all over social media. Vince was furious."

Owen observes me closely. "Is that what this is about? Pissing off Vince?"

"No." I shake my head without hesitation. "I went through that phase years ago. Trying to get attention any way I could. I got over it when I realized my priority had to be looking after Cat. Making sure she gets attention…even if it's just from me."

His eyes warm.

"This is about me controlling my life," I add quietly. "Really."

He nods. "Okay. Well. Let's exchange numbers and I'll see you Saturday."

7

OWEN

I have no idea how I got myself into this.

I'm lying on my bed in my darkened bedroom, trying to have a game day nap. But every time I close my eyes, I think about Emerie.

I should have walked away from that whole bizarre proposition.

But how could I? There's something about her that pulls at me. At first it was her music. Then meeting her in person...well, I couldn't say no to the date, and then I couldn't just leave her hanging with her ex trying to get back together and her stepfather pushing for it. That tossbag Moretti may be rich and good-looking but I wanted to punch his face for no real reason. Even though I'm a hockey player, I'm not one to go around punching people.

I flop over onto my stomach, eyes crammed shut.

This is going to mess things up for me. This'll take time away from hockey. Playing. Watching. Studying.

During the season, I'm intense about hockey. I eat, breathe, and sleep hockey. I don't have time for anything else other than a hook up once in a while, because hey, there are health benefits to sex.

That sounds clinical. Look, when I'm in bed with a woman, I make sure we both have a good time. But it's never about intimacy. Or love. It's just physical. It's endorphins and hormones. Stress relief.

But I won't be hooking up with Emerie. That's not what this is about.

I roll onto my back again and stare at the ceiling.

So what if she's hot? That was a shock, seeing her in her little black dress, the sheer parts revealing slender shoulders and arms. Without the wig and glasses, she's exactly the kind of woman I'm usually attracted to. The weird thing is, I was kind of attracted to her even *with* the wig and glasses.

But that's not going anywhere now I know she's the team owner's daughter. Jesus! I'm still not entirely sure I haven't fucked up my career doing this. That would be the worst thing that could happen to me!

Goddammit! I need my game day nap. I have to be at my best by game time and my routine is important to me. I punch my pillow, once, twice, then smash my head back into it. I need to think of something else.

What if I run into Mr. D at the arena tonight? What am I supposed to say to him? What are my teammates going to think? They know I don't have a girlfriend.

Sleep, goddammit. I need to sleep.

The wheel. Think about the wheel. A hockey play where a defenseman has the puck. If he has space from the forechecking opponent, he skates behind and as close to our net as possible. The other defenseman stays near the crease in front of the net and tries to pick out opposing players trying to close in on the puck. Once the net has been cleared, the D man with the puck passes it to our center or a winger (me) to attack.

I picture another one. I'm leading the rush into the zone on the left side, staying close to the boards. Our opponent will protect the center of the ice so I don't get behind them and go to the net. Once I cross the blue line into the O zone, I stop fast, close to the boards, and pass to Burr, the right winger on my line, or Murph, our center, as one of them crosses the blue line. The goalie will be off angle because he's concentrating on me and not them coming in the zone, setting my line mates up for a chance to score.

I'm still not asleep, but I feel calmer. I can do this. I just have to make sure that nothing interferes with hockey—not Emerie, not Mr. D and sure as shit not Roman fucking Moretti.

My alarm wakes me, and I take a moment to blink myself back to consciousness. Fuck. I dreamed about Emerie. I was listening to her sing in the subway, but the guys were trying to drag me away from her and I was getting pissed.

I'm still pissed. Maybe that's a good frame of mind to be in for a game.

I dress in a suit. I don't usually pay much attention to which suit I wear, but knowing I'll see Emerie after the game, I mull over a couple of choices, settling on a gray Tom Ford suit with a windowpane check. I pull a light purple shirt off a hanger and grab a darker purple tie.

I meet up with the guys in the lobby of our building to take the subway to the arena. We walk up to Broadway then descend into the station. I guess I won't be hearing Emerie tonight. That kind of bums me out, which is ridiculous.

At the arena, I change and do my usual stretches and massage with the foam roller, eat my oatmeal and banana, and play some soccer.

Here it's easier to focus, to close my mind off to everything except hockey. Except when I catch a glimpse of Vince D'Agostino talking to Coach and one of our scouts.

I'm going to have to face him at some point. How the hell did we think we could pull this off?

We have our pre-game meetings with a review of the game plan, then I put my equipment on, following my pattern, blocking out the team owner. I think about our opponent and how I'm going to play against them.

I've watched video of this team, especially their second line, which is who I'll be matched up against. They have some good goal-scorers, and we need to be sharp on our defense tonight.

As I stand at the bench listening to the national anthem, I lift my eyes up to the press box. I can see people up there, lit up from behind, and I search out the owner's box. It's up so high it's hard to recognize individual faces unless you know the person and where they are. I see tiny faces that aren't usually in that space. Not that I usually pay much attention to who's up there, but I know which box is his.

She's up there.

It doesn't matter. I play my same game no matter what. Even knowing she's watching, and because she's there, Mr. D'Agostino likely has his eyes on me, too.

No pressure. Ha.

I like pressure. I've never been a choker. I thrive under pressure. I will tonight.

EMERIE

"Well, this is different," Vince says as Cat and I settle ourselves in the box. "Having you here."

"I know." I adjust my sweater and take a seat at the counter that runs along the balcony we're in.

"We're so high," Cat says. "I love this!"

Cat actually likes hockey, and I momentarily feel bad that I don't bring her to more games. Vince wouldn't even think of it. For me, it'll be about two and a half hours of excruciating boredom.

"Too bad you don't have Owen's jersey," Cat chatters. "You could have worn it! And maybe painted his number on your cheek!"

I blink at her. Good lord. "Maybe next time."

I had to carefully tiptoe around when she asked if he's my boyfriend. I hate lying to her. But I need Vince to believe he is. So I made up some shit about we've been seeing each other and I'm not sure if it's serious, but I really like him.

Ugh.

It's not that I *dislike* him. He wouldn't eat the snacks I got us because they weren't healthy enough for him, and he doesn't drink, and all he talked about was hockey, so my impression is that he's a jock who's interested in hockey and not much else. But I also don't *like* him. Like *that*. You know what I mean.

Vince and I had a weird conversation last night, the day after the party, where he asked a bunch of questions about Owen and I gave him vague answers, trying to sound as if I really like Owen.

"It's just odd," Vince said, eyeing me. "You hate hockey."

"I know! I didn't know he was a hockey player when we first met. I thought he was a hedge fund trader."

Vince's eyebrows shot up.

I pressed a hand to my chest. "The heart has its reasons which reason knows nothing of."

"What?"

"It's a quote. Blaise Pascal. A French philosopher."

He couldn't get away fast enough after that.

Now we're here at the game, I fully expect more questions. We stand for the national anthem, then sit again as the game is about to start.

Then Roman walks in.

Oh, for fuck's sake.

He's not giving up, apparently.

My body stiffens and I resist the urge to lower my forehead to the counter. I take a couple of deep breaths as Roman greets Vince, then me. He ignores Cat.

Asshole.

I shoot Vince a slitty-eyed glare. He ignores it.

Roman takes a chair next to me and leans forward to see what's happening on the ice.

"I didn't know you were a hockey fan," I say to him.

"Oh yeah. Sure."

Huh. He never talked about hockey while we were dating.

I want to see what's happening, so I lean forward too. I did a little research so I wouldn't look too out to lunch. I know Owen is number twenty-seven. I now know he is six feet, five inches tall and weighs two hundred and twenty-five pounds. He plays left wing, although I'm not sure what that is.

The players move so fast, it's hard to tell who's who. I squint, but I don't think Owen's on the ice. I scan the guys on the bench, but I can't tell which one is him. Oh wait...they stand, and one guy is taller than the rest. That has to be him.

Sure enough, he hops over the fence or whatever and onto the ice, and as he skates toward the end, I see his number. A small shiver works through me, and I bite my lip, watching him. He's fast!

He slams another player into the wall and the glass rattles alarmingly. The crowd cheers, but I flinch. Yikes!

This is why I don't like hockey. They're clobbering each other out there! That can't be good.

Owen could be hurt.

But he doesn't seem to be, streaking down the ice again. Another player gives the puck to him and he skates toward the goal. I watch intently as he aims the puck and...the goalie catches it.

The crowd groans.

"Damn," Vince says. "Beautiful play."

Okay, then! "It really was!" I agree.

Roman scowls.

"Which one is Owen?" Cat asks.

I find him on the bench and point him out. Even though he's not on the ice, he still seems intently focused on the game, his head following the puck.

But watching him and not the game, I completely miss the other team scoring a goal. The arena goes nearly silent.

"That sucked," Roman says. "Crappy defense."

I grimace.

Then the other team gets a penalty.

"Okay." Roman rubs his hands. "It's a five-four. Good chance to score."

"Okay." I nod, not really knowing what he's talking about.

"It's not a five-four," Vince says. "It's a power play."

"It's called a five-four," Roman says.

"Jesus," Vince mutters.

My lips twitch. Vince seems genuinely irritated by Roman's disagreement with him.

The announcer blasts out, "And it's a Bears pooooowerrrr plaaaay!"

I slide a smirky smile toward Roman.

"It's also called a five-four," he insists.

"Owen's out there." Cat points.

"They only use the worst players for a five-four," Roman says.

"Why would that be?" I ask doubtfully.

"Because it's so easy to score," he replies. "They save the good players for when the other team is back to five players."

"Oh." After a pause, I say, "So you're saying Owen is one of the worst players on the team?"

On the other side of Cat, I hear Vince snort.

"Well, maybe not the *worst*," Roman says.

"What was the penalty for?" I ask.

"Holding," Roman replies.

"So they can hit each other but they can't hold each other?"

"Right."

I point at the ice. "Is that holding?"

"No."

"Then what is holding? That looked like holding to me."

"It's…holding. You know. Stopping another player."

I wrinkle my nose. I try to find Owen, but he's gone off the ice. The five guys down there are passing the puck back and forth and around, over and over again.

"Shoot the puck!" Roman yells.

It makes sense to me. Why do they keep passing it instead of trying to score?

And then they do! The horn blares, the crowd cheers and jumps to their feet. Vince nods and smiles.

"Yay!" Cat cries. "That was Owen!"

"No, hon, I don't think he was on the ice," I say, clapping.

"Yes, he was. That's him." She points.

We watch the replay on the big screen on the scoreboard. It's still hard to tell who scores, but Vince says, "Yep, that was Cooke."

They announce the goal and the crowd cheers wildly. For Owen. That's...cool.

"Well, damn," I mutter. "I missed it."

"It's a fast-paced game," Roman says. "You have to pay attention."

I want to tell him to fuck off. But I don't.

I'm skeptical of his hockey knowledge, but he's right. It is fast, and I don't know enough about it to understand everything.

Okay, the score is tied now, so it's important that we score another goal. I'm going to watch carefully.

When one of our players shoots the puck down the ice, the ref blows the whistle and stops the game. "Why did he do that?" I ask with frustration.

"Icing," Vince answers.

"What does that mean?"

"Icing is when a player tries to delay the game," Roman says. "They can give a penalty for it."

"Oh." I frown. "So we're getting a penalty?"

"Yes."

"No, we're not," Vince says.

I sigh.

"It's a delay of game penalty," Roman maintains. His complete confidence convinces me. But there's no penalty. Both teams keep playing with five players after another faceoff.

I'm so confused. "Stupid sport," I mutter.

"And yet you're dating a hockey player." Roman's lip curls. "What does that say about him?"

My jaw tightens and my eyes narrow as I keep my eyes on the game. "Owen is not stupid."

"Sure, sure."

My stomach tightens. Ugh.

During the first intermission I make a trip down to the three hundred level concourse to get a drink. I need a good stiff one.

That sounds dirty.

Of course that makes me think of Owen. Ever since the party the other night, I've been thinking about his muscles and flat abs and the way his pants fit over his thick thighs and butt. It was magnificent. He probably has a good stiff one.

I gulp back the vodka and cranberry and order another one to take back up. Cat wants popcorn, so I indulge her in that.

This time, I sit next to Vince and make Cat sit on the other side of me so Roman can't. But Vince disappears for most of the second period. Probably down in the suites, "networking." Of course Roman slides over into Vince's seat. And shifts the chair even closer so our arms are touching. Ugh. He literally makes my skin crawl. I make short work of my second drink and feel a little more relaxed.

Trying to understand the game helps divert my mind from Roman, who keeps explaining things to me even though I stop asking him questions. It's not that I really care about hockey, I just don't want to have to pay any attention to him.

Owen's on the ice now, so I'm watching especially closely. They're near their own goal, and one of the Bears breaks his stick trying to stop the other team from scoring. Owen hands his stick to the guy! What?

"What is he doing?" I cry, shifting to the edge of my seat. "He needs a stick!"

The guy with Owen's stick now shoots the puck to another player as they skate up toward the other team's goal. I watch as Owen races to the bench, grabs another stick from someone who holds it out, chases after the player with the puck, who then passes it to him and... he scores!

I jump out of my seat with a scream. "Yes!" I clap and cheer loudly, joined by Cat. Roman claps politely. I love the way the entire building full of people is cheering for Owen.

They show him on the big screen as he skates by the bench to bump gloves with the other guys. This seems to be a tradition, as it happens every time there's a goal. The other players are all laughing, and so is Owen. I guess it's funny that he grabbed someone's stick and immediately scored.

The camera's on his face as he sits on the bench, grinning. A guy behind him hands him a towel, and he wipes off the inside of the glass visor on his helmet. Someone must say something to him, because he laughs.

I'm mesmerized by that smile—the utter joy of it. He is absolutely in his element.

This is his passion. He loves this sport.

That's kind of hot.

8

OWEN

Emerie wanted me to come up to the press box level after the game so her stepdad would see us together, but I nixed that idea. I don't want to go up where the media is. I have to talk to them enough. So she comes down to our level, where the dressing rooms are, and waits in the family lounge until I'm done.

When I've talked to the media, cooled down, stretched, showered, and changed back into my suit, I walk in and see her and Cat standing by themselves in a corner. I guess she doesn't know any of the wives and girlfriends, AKA WAGs. I say hi to Lilly, Kate, Sara, Nadia, Layla. They're all happy and laughing after the win.

"Congratulations, Owen!" Lilly calls to me.

"Thanks."

The girls give me a curious look, no doubt wondering why I'm down here. I stride over to Emerie. "Hi."

"Hey." She beams at me. "Good game."

My chest puffs up a bit. I did play great. "Thanks."

"You scored two goals!" Cat says.

"I did. And got an assist."

"How do they decide who gets an assist?" Emerie asks. "I asked

Roman. He said the last players to touch the puck before a goal get an assist. And what does it mean?"

I open my mouth, then snap it shut and frown. "Wait. Roman was watching the game with you?"

"Oh yeah." She rolls her eyes.

My jaw tightens. I pull in a breath through my nose. "An assist is given to the players who take part in the play immediately preceding the goal," I say stiffly.

"Is it always two?"

"At the most. Sometimes only one. Sometimes none."

"I see."

"Do you have a lot of points, Owen?" Cat asks.

I catch the amused glances of the WAGs who overhear. "I have forty-two points," I mutter.

Emerie and Cat nod but look blank. Emerie leans closer. "Is that good?" she whispers.

"Yeah, it's pretty good." My best season yet.

Millsy walks in, looking for Lilly. He shoots me a surprised glance, his gaze tracking over Emerie and Cat. Here we go.

"Hey, Owen," Lilly says, walking toward us with Millsy. "We're going to the Amber Horse. You coming?" She smiles at Emerie.

I make the introductions. Luckily, I now know Emerie's last name is Ross. "And this is her sister, Cat," I say.

"Nice to meet you." Lilly shakes Emerie's hand. "You're welcome to join us."

"I need to get this lady home," Emerie says with a smile and a hand on Cat's shoulder. "But thanks."

"Next time." Lilly rejoins the others just as some other guys walk in.

"Okay, let's head out," I say.

Out in the corridor, a few people are still milling about—communications staff, media, trainers, a couple of players. I wave and lead Emerie and Cat down the hall to an exit.

"How did you get here?" I ask. "With your, uh, Mr. D'Agostino?"

Emerie shakes her head. "No. Taxi."

"Okay, let's go find you one to get you home."

We step out into the cold night air to the sound of cars honking, and walk around the corner to Eighth Avenue, dodging pedestrians on the sidewalk. Most of the fans have cleared out by now, but it's Saturday night in Manhattan and busy.

I scan the traffic on the street and lift my hand to hail a yellow cab approaching. He swerves over to the curb.

"Wow, that was fast," Emerie says. We move toward the car. "Um... are you coming with us?"

I hesitate. "Why?"

"You didn't come up to Vince's box. He didn't see us together."

"Oh. Right."

"He'll be home in a while and...you could be there."

After I brief pause, I say, "Okay."

I join them in the back seat of the taxi and Emerie gives him the address.

"We had a lot of hockey questions," Emerie says as the driver takes us straight over to Park Avenue, then zips up and around Grand Central Terminal. "Right, Cat?"

"Yeah. It was fun going to a game. Hockey's cool."

Emerie bites her lip. I almost laugh.

"I can probably explain stuff to you," I say. "I know a little."

Cat laughs. "Maybe sometime we could watch a game on TV," she says. "And you could watch with us and explain it to us."

"We could definitely do that," I agree.

Man. How do these two women suck me into these things so easily?

"I love watching hockey," I add. It's true. I'm always studying the game to learn more and be better.

"Okay," Emerie says. "We'll figure out a time." She's about as enthusiastic as if we were planning a tonsillectomy for her.

"Hockey's fun." I bump her shoulder with mine.

"Sure. Right."

I pay for the taxi and follow the ladies up to the penthouse apartment again. This time the place is dark and quiet. Emerie flicks on lights, opens a closet, and takes off her coat. "I'll take yours," she says to me. I hand it over. Then she walks into the living room. "Have a seat. Can I get you something to drink?"

"I'm okay, thanks."

"Bedtime," she says to Cat. "Go get ready and I'll come tuck you in, in a bit."

Cat grumbles something about it being Saturday and not that late but trudges off down the hall. I sit in a big armchair near the fireplace and look around. This place is super formal, not my style at all, with some uncomfortable looking chairs against the wall, a small sofa, and a big crystal chandelier above us. Oil paintings hang on the walls as well as a huge, gilt-framed mirror above the fireplace.

Emerie sits on the other chair flanking the fireplace. She's wearing loose jeans, black Chelsea boots, and a black and white striped sweater, looking more like her busker persona than the sophisticated socialite she appeared to be the night of the party.

I gesture toward the grand piano at the far end of the room. "Do you play that, too?"

She glances at the piano. "Yes."

"I'm impressed."

She smiles.

"Why was Roman there?"

Shit. Why did I blurt that out?

"I don't know. I assume he invited himself. Vince probably told him I'd be there."

This annoys me. Dammit, the man's basically my boss. I can't be annoyed at him.

"Your teammates will think we're together," she says. "But I don't think they know who I am."

"I don't know if they do." I pause. "This is bigger than I thought when I suggested this crazy idea."

"I know." She sighs. "I hated not being totally honest with Cat." Her bottom lip pouts out.

Damn, that's cute. And hot.

"Do you still want to do this?"

She meets my eyes. "Do you?"

"Answer me first."

"I haven't come up with a better plan, so...yes."

I nod. "Okay. Me too." I always stick to my commitments.

"Thank you."

The door of the apartment opens and closes. We both straighten. Then Emerie jumps up and scoots over to the sofa, beckoning wildly at me. I get it, so I throw myself across the room to sit next to her. We're just settling in when Mr. D'Agostino walks in. He stops when he sees me but recovers and strolls toward us.

"Great game tonight, Owen." He extends his hand.

I stand and shake it, my stomach clenching. "Thank you, sir. Things were clicking for all of us." Then I add, "Maybe Emerie being there had something to do with it."

Mr. D'Agostino's lips thin, but then he smiles. "Maybe so." He looks around me at Emerie. "Now you'll have to come to every game. Hockey players need their good luck charms."

She laughs. "I don't think I'm a good luck charm."

"A win over Pittsburgh is excellent," Mr. D'Agostino says. "They're right behind us in the standings."

"Yeah." I sit again as Mr. D'Agostino moves away. "They've got a good team. Some really good goal scorers."

"We need to stay ahead of them in the standings."

"Yep."

"Why?" Emerie asks.

"Well, for one thing we want to make the playoffs," I say. "The top three teams in each division earn berths in the playoffs. The next two teams in terms of total points in the conference, regardless of division, earn the wild-card spots."

Her eyes glaze over.

"The top seed in each division plays one of the wild-card teams in its conference. The division leader with the most points plays the wild-card team with the fewest points. The second and third seeds in each division face each other in the first round. So where you finish in the standings effects who you play in the first round."

Mr. D'Agostino nods, eyeing me attentively. He's not all that involved with the day-to-day stuff, but he has to know how this works.

"And if there happens to be a tie, the number of wins can break the tie. Wins, among other things."

"Fascinating," she says, trying to stifle a yawn.

"You asked," I remind her gently with what I hope looks like an affectionate smile.

"You've got your work cut out trying to make Emerie into a fan." Mr. D stands. "I'm going to bed. Good night."

"Vince?" Emerie speaks up.

"Yes?"

"Could you say goodnight to Cat? I'm sure she's still awake."

"Oh. Right. Of course."

We both watch him walk out, then turn to each other. Emerie makes a "yikes" face, then mouths, "Thank you."

I nod, my stomach unknotting somewhat. "This is fucked up," I say in a low voice.

She laughs softly. "No shit."

Our faces are close together. Her scent teases my nose—both earthy and sweet, flowers mixed with spice. Her skin is smooth, her tip-tilted nose adorable, her big blue eyes a different, lighter blue than my own, with flecks of silver sparkling in them like tiny diamonds. Like the diamond that glints on the side of her nose. Her pink lips are bow-shaped, the lower lip plumply curved.

My cock thickens.

She's studying me as well, her gaze moving over my face, and when it lingers on my mouth a powerful urge to kiss her rockets through me. A desire to feel how soft her lips are, to know how she tastes, to have her tits pressed against my chest.

She swallows, her eyes darkening. "I don't like jocks," she whispers.

I don't even react, I'm so stupefied by her loveliness. "Okay."

She jumps up, clasps her hands together and takes a few steps. "Well. I guess our mission for tonight is accomplished."

I stand, too, more slowly. "Are you kicking me out?"

She grimaces. "Maybe?"

"Do you want to go to the Amber Horse?"

She blinks extravagant eyelashes. "Oh. Um. I don't think so."

"Okay."

"Are *you* going?"

"Not if you're not."

"Why not?" She stares at me curiously.

"Because that looks douchey, when a guy takes his girlfriend home and then goes out without her."

"But we're…"

I lift an eyebrow.

Her voice trails off. "Right. Well. That's very, um, noble of you. But you can totally go hang out with your friends if you want."

"I know." I start toward the French doors to the foyer.

"Okay then." She follows me and retrieves my coat from the closet for me.

"When do you want to watch a game?" I ask, pushing my arms into the sleeves.

"Oh. I don't know. What's your schedule like?"

"Games Monday and Tuesday." I think. "Thursday and Saturday again. They're all here, except Monday we play the Islanders."

She nods. "You're a busy guy."

I shrug. "Yeah."

"How about Friday?"

There goes one of my off days. Being a Friday, the guys will probably try to convince me to go out, but I usually resist and stay home with a couple of good books and a hockey game on TV. Ah well. I'll still be watching the game. "Sure. Here?"

"Okay."

I nod. "Sounds good. See you then."

Out on the street, I stop and tip my head back. Fuck! I wanted to kiss her! I damn near did. That's not cool.

I start walking. Where I live is almost exactly on the other side of Central Park from here. Central Park is a lot safer than it used to be but still, I'd probably get lost in there in the dark if I tried to walk home through it.

I hail a cab and sink into the back seat as we travel through city streets. And again, I ask myself what the fuck I'm doing.

The fact that Roman Fuckface showed up at the game tonight affirms that we need to keep up this ridiculous charade. The fact that I'm going up against the man who signs my paycheck confirms that I have lost my goddamn mind. And on top of that, my entire organized life is being fucked up.

9

EMERIE

I'm not here at Penn Station a couple of hours before game time because I think I'll see Owen. Not at all. This isn't unusual for me, especially on a Tuesday when Cat stays late at school for pottery club.

I have to stop myself from constantly scanning the people walking through the station. That's not like me. Usually, it's easy for me to lose myself in my music. So I do that.

Somehow, I look up just as he's walking by. I recognize his size and shape immediately. He's wearing a smile before our eyes even meet. This time I notice he's with a couple of other big, well-dressed men, but he's the only one who slows down as he passes by.

My lips pull up into a smile as I sing. He gives me a tiny nod and a bubble of happiness swells in my chest. He keeps walking, though, quickening his steps to catch up to his friends.

I can't stop smiling for the rest of my time there.

We share this secret.

The only other person who knows my secret is my best friend, Janiya. We've been friends since high school. She was my best friend when my mom died, and she knew the shitty years after that when I was grieving and rebelling against the hurt, not getting the love I needed because Vince didn't give two shits. I told her when I started busking and she swore to keep it secret, and she always has.

Now she's living in India, it's not that hard to keep it secret.

Tonight, we're doing a video chat. I miss her so much. I've let other friendships slide over the years, my attention focused on Cat, but I try to stay in touch with Janiya even though she's far away now.

Now I have another secret. But I have to tell her this one, too. I can't keep it from her.

When it's time to go, I pack up and chat with Elijah, another musician ready to take over my spot. "You coming to open mic night at the Mystic Nomad on Monday?" he asks.

"No." I grin. He doesn't know me that well. Everyone else knows I don't do open mic nights.

"You should come! Acoustic solos or duets. You can play two songs. You'd do great there."

I shake my head. "I'm not interested. Plus, they start early, don't they?"

"Four-thirty."

"Yeah, I have to pick up my little sister from school."

He shrugs.

As we talk, I manage to slip some of my haul of cash into his bucket. I'll drop the rest in another busker's case later. I leave my gear at Mr. Cantor's luggage store, then take the subway to Cat's school.

She's chatty about her day, and I'm grateful for that so I don't have to pry things from her. I want to know what's going on in her life, what her problems and fears are, what her successes are and who her friends are. We walk home from there. Klara has dinner ready for us to heat up a bit later.

"Thank you, Klara, you rock."

She smiles. Her steel-gray hair is in a low bun, her eyeglasses low on her nose. She's worked for Vince for a few years. At first, she was distinctly reserved and professional with all of us, but I can't handle having "servants," so I treat her like a friend who helps us, and gradually that's what she's become. She sees what happens with Vince, and I think she feels sorry for us, although she never says a word against Vince. She just steps in and does what needs to be done, and I kind of love her for it.

"I rock," she repeats. "This is a good thing, yes?"

"Yes."

"I am off tomorrow," she reminds us. "But dinner is in the fridge for you to heat up. There is enough for Mr. D'Agostino if he's home. I made the potatoes you love," she adds for Cat. "Good night, my lovelies."

"Good night, Klara."

After dinner, I settle into my couch in my bedroom with my computer to talk to Janiya. She's living in India now, working in her family's business.

"Hi! I miss you!"

I smile at her face on my screen. "I miss you, too!" I hold up a small, wrapped parcel. "I got your gift."

"Ohhh! Open it!"

I peel off the tissue and reveal a small stone sculpture. My eyes widen as I take in the couple portrayed in a…sexual position.

Janiya laughs. "The look on your face!"

I bite my lip and raise my eyes to my computer. "It's lovely."

She chortles. "It's an erotic sculpture from Khajuraho temple. We went there. It was amazing!"

"Okay."

"No, seriously, it is beautiful. There's all kinds of symbolism. Not all the sculptures are erotic, and it's believed that the temples are a celebration of womanhood."

"Oh." I study the small carving.

"Another story is that the carvings of Mithunas are symbols of "good luck." Also, they could be a form of sex education by rekindling passions in people who were probably influenced by Buddhism." She shrugs. "Anyway, I thought it might bring good sexual luck to you."

I choke on a laugh. "Good sexual luck?"

"Yes." She nods firmly. "You need some of that. Since you have no man in your life."

"That's not entirely true."

Her dark eyes widen. "What? What happened while I was gone?"

I make a face. "Well, nothing really. Except I sort of have a boyfriend now."

Her hands fly up. "That is not nothing! Who is this? How did it happen?"

I pat my hands in a calm down gesture. "I'll explain."

"Yes! Spill the Darjeeling."

I laugh. "You're going to think I'm crazy. Wait. You already do."

She rolls her eyes.

"Roman is not giving up on us getting back together. He keeps showing up at the apartment. He's got Vince on his side, and Vince is really pushing for us to get back together, too."

"Ugh."

"So I got this idea that I'd bring a date to a party Vince was having last week. Act like we're in love. That would end that."

"Hmm. Not a bad idea, actually. So, who did you ask?"

I grimace. "A stranger."

She frowns.

"I see this guy in Penn Station when I'm playing. He looks nice and well dressed. I thought he was in finance or something. He stops and watches me. He likes my music."

"Of course he does. Because you're amazing."

"Well, one day he was there, and I asked him for coffee, and he seemed nice and normal, so I told him I needed a date for the party. And why. And he agreed."

"Okay. So…he went to the party with you?"

"Yes."

"And did that convince Roman to leave you alone?"

"No." I sigh. "I took Cat to a hockey game the other night, and he showed up in Vince's box."

"You went to a hockey game?" She stares at the camera open-mouthed.

"Yes." I bite my lip. "It turns out that Owen—that's his name—plays for the Bears."

Once again, her eyes nearly pop out of their sockets. "Vince's hockey team?"

"Yeah."

"Holy crap."

"Right? They know each other. It was all sort of...chaotic. Neither of us knew what to do. So we kept up the pretense."

"Yikes."

I nod. "Owen doesn't think Vince would trade him away...but he could."

She narrows her eyes. "I wouldn't put anything past Vince when it comes to money."

"I know." I sigh. "So we agreed we'd keep going with this sham relationship."

She stares at me. "That's your boyfriend? It's fake?"

"Yeah."

"Damn." Her bottom lip pouts. "I thought you'd for real found someone."

"You know I don't have time for that with taking care of Cat. And my music."

"Cat is doing great. And she's twelve now, hon. She can stay alone. She'll be driving soon."

Laughter bubble up my throat. "Not for a while. And you're right, but I still want to spend time with her. She still needs attention and love."

"Of course." Her eyes soften. "You've been a great sister to her."

"Thanks."

"I think you could take more time for yourself now, though. You could be dating. Having fun!"

"I do have fun!" Well, not that much, actually.

"Tell me about Owen."

67

"Owen Cooke. He plays left wing for the Bears."

She grins. "Do you even know what left wing is?"

"I do not." I shake my head. "Cat and I went to the game on Saturday to watch him. Because that would be a girlfriend thing to do. I had no clue what was going on. And Vince must have told Roman and invited him."

"Wow." She tilts her head. "You hate hockey."

"I know. Ugh. I mean, it turned out to be kind of fun. Owen got two goals!"

Janiya rolls her lips inward on a smile. "Good for him."

"And the Bears won."

"Uh huh." She nods. "Are you seeing him again?"

"Yes. He's coming over on Friday to watch a game with Cat and me. She was at the game too, and she really likes hockey, so he offered to explain it to us."

"This must be torture for you, watching sportsball."

I open my mouth and catch her observant gaze. "What?"

"What's Owen like?"

"A jock." I roll my eyes. "All hockey, all the time. Doesn't drink, doesn't eat junk food. Probably obsessed with working out and admiring his muscles in the mirror. I'm sure he can't have a conversation about anything but hockey."

"Is he good looking? Wait. Let me check." Her attention refocuses as she taps on her keyboard. "Whoa." She clicks a couple of times to share the screen. "Is this him?"

"Yes." It's a team headshot. He looks angry.

"Hot. Intense."

"I guess he's attractive. He's very big."

"Ohhhh. Big feet?"

I choke. "Janiya!"

"You know what they say."

"It's a myth." I cough. "And yeah, his feet are big. He's six-five!"

She nods. "That's tall. I like big men."

"Well, it doesn't matter if his penis size matches his shoe size, because I'm never going to know."

She sighs and ends the screen share. "Disappointing."

"I'm just trying to get Roman and Vince off my back."

She nods thoughtfully. "Lucky Owen doesn't have a wife or a girlfriend."

"I wouldn't have asked him to do this if he did."

"Right." She pauses. "He knows about your busking, obviously."

"Yes. He was a little surprised when he saw me again at the party without my wig and glasses."

"Do you trust him to keep your secret?"

I consider that. "I...do." I wrinkle my nose. "For some reason, I trust him. He clearly hasn't told his teammates, or they would have stopped and gawked at me when they walked by earlier."

"You saw him today?"

"Just in passing. They were on their way to the game."

She nods.

"He hasn't told Vince. So far. He could have."

"He still could." Her face sobers.

"I guess. Trusting someone with your secrets is risky. Maybe I should be worried, but instead I feel like it makes us..." I stop, searching for the word.

"Conspirators?"

"Eh."

"Accomplices?"

"More like...friends."

"Friends. Hmmm."

I ignore the speculative look on her face and change the subject.

10

OWEN

I feel like I can't show up empty-handed, so I pick up a big bag of popcorn and some root beer on my way over to Emerie's place. I grab a bottle of water for myself, since root beer has so much sugar.

I prepare myself to see Mr. D'Agostino. I've been lucky I haven't run into him at the arena. He doesn't come to the practice facility very often, which is where we usually are other than game days.

The doorman sends me up and Emerie lets me into the apartment.

"Hi!" Her gaze falls to the popcorn. "Oh, yum! I love popcorn."

"Good. I brought it for you and Cat." I hold it out.

"Thank you!" She sounds surprised. "We're going to watch in the den, this way." Instead of the French doors to the living room, she turns the other way and leads me to another set of doors.

This room is a lot more casual and comfortable, thankfully, with a soft-looking patterned carpet, built-in bookshelves overflowing with books, and cozy lighting.

Cat's already curled up on a big gray sectional in front of large windows. "Hi, Owen!"

"Hey, Cat. How's it going?"

"Good! Come on, the game's starting soon."

"Owen brought popcorn." Emerie holds it up. "I'll go get bowls."

"I brought drinks too." I set the root beer down on a square table.

"There are glasses in the bar there." Emerie points to a small nook.

I find what we need and take a seat on the sectional too. The TV on the wall opposite us is massive. Perfect for watching hockey.

Emerie hesitates before sitting, then lowers her butt to the cushion right next to me. We exchange a glance and she does a tiny shrug, her arm pressed against mine.

Once again, I breathe in her scent. It's distinctive and recognizable and dammit, erotic. She's dressed in ripped-up jeans and a well-worn sweatshirt, which is *not* erotic but even so, something stirs in my southern region.

Great. Her little sister is sitting right here with us.

"Is your stepdad home?" I ask her.

"No. I think he's out for dinner. But he'll probably be home in a while."

I nod.

"You're not having root beer?" She eyes my bottle of water.

"Nope."

"Are you going to eat popcorn?"

"Yeah. I like popcorn."

"I thought maybe it's not healthy enough for you."

"Popcorn's a healthy snack."

"What kinds of things do you eat?"

"Smoothies with protein powder. Lots of lean protein and fresh veggies and fruit. I've been trying new grains—quinoa, millet."

"That's weird." She wrinkles her nose.

"It's not that weird. Just healthy."

"I guess."

"What do *you* eat?" I ask with amusement.

"We eat healthy," Cat says. "Emerie makes us."

I smirk. "Oh yeah?"

"Well mostly," she says. "But sometimes we have ice cream or cookies."

"Not very often," Cat protests.

"Not often enough for you," Emerie retorts. "You'd eat ice cream every day if I let you."

Cat makes a face.

"I don't make you eat millet," Emerie says. "I don't even know what that is."

She bugs me about how I eat, but makes her sister eat healthy, too. Ha.

"Okay, a penalty!" Emerie says. "It's a four-five."

"A what now?" I frown.

"A four-five. No, wait. A five-four. That's what it's called, right?"

"No. That is not what it's called. It's called a power play."

She wrinkles her cute nose. "Roman was sure it's called a five-four."

"Roman is a pinhead."

She bursts out laughing.

"Seriously. What the f—" I stop myself with side eye toward Cat. "It's called a power play for the team with the man advantage. And a penalty kill for the team who's short a man."

"Because they're killing off a penalty," Cat says.

"Exactly."

"Roman also said that you get a penalty for delay of game when you...what's it called...icing."

"When you ice the puck. A penalty?"

"That's what he said."

"Jesus." I shake my head. "Don't listen to him anymore. Icing isn't a penalty, like two minutes in the box, but the team does get penalized in that the puck is brought back for a faceoff in their own end."

"Why?"

"If teams could shoot the puck all the way to the other end, that's all the game would be. It would be boring."

"Ohhhhh. Right. Okay." She nods.

Holy shit. I don't know if I've ever met someone who knows so little about hockey. I mean, it doesn't make me think less of her. It's just…surprising. My whole life is hockey, and it pretty much always has been.

Maybe that's not a good thing?

I push that thought aside and explain offside. Then a delay of game penalty when the puck goes over the glass.

"It was an accident," Emerie protests. "Maybe there should be a rule that if they shoot the puck over the glass, they have to go get it."

"Uh…" I have to laugh at that.

A while later, she screeches. "Oh no! What is he doing?"

The Blue Jackets' goalie is leaving the ice. "It's okay. The other team's getting a penalty."

"But they'll score on the Blue Jackets!"

"Nah. As soon as they touch the puck, the whistle blows. The only way they could get a goal is if the Blue Jackets shoot the puck into their own net."

"I don't understand that," she says. "Is there anything you can't explain?"

"Yeah. Goaltender interference." My tone is dry. "*Nobody* can explain that."

She gives me a look.

"Really. Basically, the rule is simple—don't interfere with the goalie. But there are so many other rules around it and they're applied so inconsistently, nobody really knows what that is. The goalies don't know. The players don't know. The coaches don't know. And the referees don't know."

She laughs. "Okay then."

I have to say, she learns quickly. By the third period, she's calling offside and even a tripping penalty. And Cat is really into it, too. I feel kind of proud. Seeing the game through their virgin eyes, hockey virgin that is, opens my eyes to things too. And I've actually had fun teaching them about hockey.

Then Emeries tries to make Cat go to bed.

"What?" Cat whines. "The game's not over. And it's Friday night."

"This isn't even our team. We don't care who wins."

"Actually, we do," I put in. "Those teams are in our division. Washington has fewer points, so we want them to win."

She blinks. "Oh. Okay. Well. Cat, you can watch the rest of the game in your room. Brush your teeth."

Grumbling, Cat trudges out.

"You're like her mom," I comment.

"I know."

"That's a lot for someone your age to take on."

"Lots of women my age are mothers."

"Not of twelve-year-olds."

"Okay, true. The thing is...I had to." She pauses. "I love her. When she was born, I was so excited to have a baby sister. I wanted to take care of her all the time. Even change her diapers." She laughs softly. "She was so tiny and precious. And so little when Mom died. I had a hard time myself, dealing with that. But then when Cat got into school, she started having problems. Behavior issues. She'd refuse to go to school. I thought she was faking being sick, but when Vince or I tried to make her go, she'd have a total melt down."

"Oh man. And you were...what? Seventeen? Eighteen?"

"Yeah. She wasn't sleeping at night. She still doesn't like going to bed, but it was more than that. She'd be up at night and of course without enough sleep, her mood wasn't great. She wasn't eating. She started getting in arguments at school with other kids. Even her teachers. I was at my wit's end, but thank God for a good school counselor who realized what was happening. We got referred to a wonderful child psychologist. *I* even got some therapy." She makes a face as if she doesn't like to admit it. "But it was a good thing. And I realized I had to do better. I had to be there for her. Vince hired a bunch of different nannies, but she needed a more normal, structured life." She wrinkles her nose. "With one consistent person. I was about to go to college, but instead I stayed home with her."

Wow. She really loves her sister. I loved Eric, too, but I couldn't be there for him like she was for Cat.

"I feel guilty that I let her down at such a tough time," she adds quietly.

Yeah. I lower my chin, my jaw tightening. I know how that feels. Shit. I don't like remembering how that feels. I swallow and say, "And now you're trying to make up for it."

She glances sharply at me. "Uh..." Then she purses her lips. "Maybe I am."

"Why are you looking at me like that?"

"You're very...perceptive." She sounds surprised.

I shrug and focus on the TV.

"Do you have any siblings?" she asks.

Shit. "I had a brother," I say, trying to keep my voice even. "Eric. He died a few years ago."

"Oh no!" She gazes at me, her sharp eyes softening into sympathy. "I'm so sorry."

I feel her curiosity, but I don't want to talk about Eric. So I don't answer her unspoken questions, and we sit in silence and watch the game.

When the Blue Jackets score, I say, "Nice. You gotta like that back door play."

Her head swivels and she gapes at me. "Back door play?"

I realize how it sounded and grin. "Yep." Her face is so expressive. It's adorable.

"Well then."

The filthy innuendo lightens the leaden atmosphere. Good.

I explain a high-sticking penalty to her and why the guy who got hit keeps checking to see if he's bleeding.

"So he *wants* to bleed?" she asks incredulously.

"Well...it's a longer power play if he's cut."

"Weird."

We continue watching. Then I say, "Blue Jackets are trying hard to get into the O zone."

"The O zone," she repeats.

"Yeah." I glance at her.

She's smirking again. "I like a guy who can get into the O zone."

My head jerks around. "It's the offensive zone."

She tosses her head. "In hockey, sure."

Aw, fuck. Why'd she get me thinking about orgasms? Jeez.

"Offense is trying to score. Defense is trying to stop the other team from scoring."

She tips her head. "So Roman is on the offense. And I'm on the defense."

I stare at her. "Yes. Exactly." He better not fucking score.

I turn back to the game, my focus shot. I didn't anticipate this hockey lesson going into sex territory. The Blue Jackets score. "Yesss!"

"You said that before the puck even went in the net."

"No, I didn't." I laugh.

"It seemed like it. How did you see that?"

"I'm watching."

"Huh. That was the wrong team, though. I thought you wanted Washington to win."

"I do, but it *was* a nice goal. Löfgren has silky mitts."

She stares at me.

"He has good hands."

She blinks. "That's what she said."

I burst out laughing. "Come on. You're making everything dirty."

"*I* am?" Her mouth falls opens. "Ha!"

Maybe it's just that I'm sitting beside a hot woman, but everything does seem sexual.

She sighs. "I'll never get this game."

I bump her shoulder with mine. "It doesn't matter, Em. You just need to pretend to be interested. Right?"

Her lips part and her eyes hold mine for a moment. "Right."

"You learned a lot tonight."

"I'll be able to school Roman next time."

"There better not be a next time," I growl.

She gives me another look. "You sound like you care."

I go still. "Well, I do," I say slowly. "That's the whole point of this, isn't it? Making sure he leaves you alone."

"You're right."

"What do we do about that? I could have a word with him…"

"Eeek. I don't think that's a good idea."

"Why not? Wouldn't a real boyfriend do that?"

Her eyes narrow and she bites her lip. "Maybe?"

With our gazes connected and her right next to me, the air around us crackles. We watch each other.

We completely miss Washington tying the game up. Whatever. We both blink away from each other to stare at the screen. Heat prickles over my skin.

Then Mr. D'Agostino walks in.

"Thought I heard noise coming from in here," he says. His gaze lands on me. "Owen."

"Hello, sir."

"Hi, Vince," Emerie says. "We're watching hockey."

I can see his effort to keep his face neutral. "I see that. Which game?" He steps farther into the room. "Ah. Tie game."

"Yep. Hoping for another goal from Washington."

He nods as he strolls over to an armchair.

Crap. He's joining us. So much for avoiding him.

"I'm learning so much," Emerie says. "Owen knows everything about hockey."

I smile and nod at the TV. "I've been watching Washington's point shots, where they're coming from, and where they all line up around the net."

"Hmmm."

We watch as Löfgren nearly scores again, robbed by the Washington goalie. "Wow, what a save!"

Emerie lays her hand on my thigh. I immediately tense, heat flowing south as I'm hyperaware of her touching me only inches from my groin. I'm also hyperaware of my boss sitting near us, his expression grim. Of course, that's his usual expression, which explains why most of us feel our assholes pucker when we're called to his office. I'm not convinced he doesn't have mob connections.

Okay, that was a dumb thing to say to Emerie that night.

The game ends in a tie.

"What happens now?" Emerie asks.

"Overtime," I say. "Sudden death. First we play three on three."

"Just three players?"

"Yep. For five minutes. If nobody scores, it goes to a shoot out."

"Owen won the game for us the last time we had a shoot out," Mr. D'Agostino tells her.

"Really?" She beams a smile on me.

A cold knot in my chest softens. "Nah. Our goalie won the game for us by making the next save."

Mr. D'Agostino's eyes flicker.

"I don't understand that," Emerie says. "But you sound modest."

My face warms and I shake my head.

"They're starting right away," Emerie observes.

"Yep."

"Do you get tired?" she asks. "Overtime must be hard."

"Yeah, we get tired. But that's what we train for."

She squeezes my thigh. "That's why you only eat healthy food."

"Sure."

I'm kind of hoping Mr. D'Agostino leaves, but nope, he remains seated, watching the game with us. Great.

"I'll go check on Cat," Emerie says. "Be right back."

She disappears, leaving me and Mr. D alone. Hoo boy.

I'm tempted to make a comment about how much time Emerie spends looking after her sister, but keep my lips zipped. Then I'm tempted to say something about Moretti being at the game in Dr. D's box. Big nope to that too. "Whoa," I say, eyes on the game. "Close one."

If it weren't for the game, the silence in the room would be excruciating.

Emerie returns only a few seconds before Washington scores.

"Yes!" Mr. D lifts his arms.

"Wait, was that Washington?" she asks. "Did they change ends?"

"Yeah, for the overtime."

The game over, Mr. D and I talk about standings for a few minutes while Emerie tries to look interested. I take pity on her. "Hey, want to go out and get a drink?"

She gives me a blank look, then says, "Oh, sure!"

My fingers are crossed (figuratively) that Mr. D doesn't tag along with us. That would be pretty ballsy.

We're in luck. He says goodnight and leaves.

"We don't have to go anywhere," Emerie whispers when he's gone. "I gather you were trying to get rid of him."

"I was. Your call. We can stay here a while longer."

She picks up a bowl of popcorn. "I'm fine with that."

They cut away from the game to Sports Wrap, and the two on-air personalities immediately start analyzing the game we just watched.

"So, you have a game tomorrow night," she says.

"Ha, yeah, against Washington."

"They'll be tired. You can beat them."

I nod. "It can be hard playing back-to-backs. We'll see."

"I guess I'll come to the game again."

"We could go out after the game."

Our eyes meet. And hold. Finally, she says, "I don't think that's a good idea."

11

EMERIE

Am I imagining it, or does Owen look disappointed?

"I just mean, we don't need to get more people involved in this crazy plot than necessary. Your friends will all think we're really dating."

"They already do. They saw us at the game, remember? I got shit about it for days. And they don't even know you're Mr. D's step-daughter."

"Really?" I stare at him. "I'm sorry."

He shrugs. "It's okay. I just ignore them. But you should at least come down to the lounge before you leave after the game so Mr. D *thinks* we're going out."

"Oh. Yeah."

The truth is, I'd love to go out with Owen after the game. I'm having so much fun tonight. Believe me, I'm as surprised as anyone that I'm having fun watching a hockey game. Being with Owen is... well, fun. It's kind of exciting. We're flirting and touching—holy hotness, when I put my hand on his thigh, I thought my clothes were going to incinerate right off me. His thighs are huge. And hard. I couldn't resist a glance at his feet. Yes, they're big. I bet he's big all over. Oh God.

It's not just his muscles, though. He's funny. And smarter than I think I gave him credit for. Maybe the only thing he knows is hockey, but he knows a *lot* about it. That's...hot.

I resist the urge to fan my face as heat slides up into it.

"Okay, I guess we could go out after the game," I say.

He nods.

"Has anyone said anything about...you dating me? I mean your coach, or the manager?"

"No."

I nod slowly. "That's good."

"Yep."

I nibble my lip. "I hope Vince doesn't get involved."

"I hope so too." He grimaces and shoves a hand into his hair. I watch his fingers slide through the thick mass. I'd like to do that...

I shake my head.

"Well, I should get going."

"Okay." I nod and stand. "I'll walk out with you."

We stroll to the door and I hand him his jacket from the closet. Vince is apparently in the living room. I hear him moving around there. As Owen and I pause at the door, he walks past the French doors opening.

Owen bends his head and kisses me.

Startled, I flinch back.

He slides an arm around me and pulls me closer. "He sees us," he murmurs against my lips. "Kiss me goodnight."

My eyes are wide, staring into his, a deep, mesmerizing cobalt blue like the sky just after sunset. Then I let my eyes fall closed and I kiss him back, softening against him.

Daaaaaamn....

His mouth is as perfect on my lips as it is to look at—soft, sensual, but firm and warm. He tastes amazing as his tongue slides over my bottom lip, and he draws back.

My eyes flutter open and meet his again. A hot haze shimmers around us.

"I'd apologize," he whispers. "But…"

"I know." I give a slow blink, my insides hopping and skipping erotically.

"See you tomorrow night," he says, louder, giving me a last brush of his mouth on mine, then opens the door.

When it closes, I lean against it. Whoa. That was the hottest kiss I've ever had. Holy hell.

Vince appears in the door opening. I straighten quickly and face him.

"Dating him is not a good idea, Emerie."

I lift my chin. "Why not?"

"He's a hockey player."

"What's wrong with that?"

"That's not the kind of man for you."

"Why do you even care?" I take a couple of steps closer. "You've never cared about who I date before."

"Roman Moretti is perfect for you. He doesn't mind that you have no ambition."

No ambition.

Well, I guess that's how it looked when I decided not to go to college to look after Cat. Still, my stomach tightens, and I bite down on my bottom lip.

"I am not getting back with Roman," I say.

"You haven't given him a chance."

"And I'm not going to. Goodnight, Vince."

I flee, heading to my room.

I hate arguing with Vince. I'm used to him being indifferent to my presence, not pestering me to go out with someone. I appreciate that he continues to provide for me even though I'm not his biological child, but he's not my father, and he has no say in who I date or marry. Jeez, even my real dad wouldn't do that.

I undress and put on my nightshirt.

Most of the time Vince doesn't care what I do. But for some

reason, this has become a mission for him. I don't totally get it. And I hate it.

I sit on the edge of my bed, fingers clenched together, and stare at the rug.

Vince thinks I'm dating Owen, which is good. We're pulling it off. But it *is* annoying Vince. My insides roll unhappily. I don't know to what extent he'll go to get what he wants. It worries me. Maybe I should end things with Owen.

I'll sleep on it.

We're at a place called the Amber Horse, near the Apex Center. It's long and narrow with concrete floors, a high, dark ceiling, and big frosted windows. The bar runs all the way down one long side of the room, which is packed this Saturday night.

Some of Owen's teammates are already here, and they wave from the back. Owen clears a path through the crowd with his impressive stature, me following in his wake. I take in the looks he gets from men and women, some of them looks of recognition, others admiration. He does look amazing in a suit.

Somehow, we find a few stools and pull them up to a couple of small tables grouped together. The guys are standing, the girls sitting. Owen holds the back of the stool for me as I climb on.

"Everybody, this is Emerie," Owen calls.

I lift my hand in greeting, taking in the crowd. I don't know anyone, but they all give me friendly smiles.

"Do you want me to name everyone?" Owen asks in my ear.

"Yes, please." I'm good with names.

He goes through a list pointing. "That's Barbie. And his wife Nadia."

"Wait. Barbie?" He's pointing to a big guy with shaggy hair and a crooked nose.

"That's his nickname. Igor Barbashev."

"Igor." I nod. "And Nadia. Hi!"

"Guess I'll use real names," Owen mutters. "Hunter and Kate. Josh and Sara. Colton and Layla."

Yikes. I recognize Layla. She's a model.

"Evan and Hannah. And Easton and Lilly."

"Hi!" I repeat everyone's names, noting something about them so I'll remember.

"And single dudes Jammer, I mean Jamal, and Brandon."

"Hi guys."

We order drinks, Owen requesting just water. I decide to have a beer.

"So was Moretti in your box?" Owen asks me. He moves in close, his body pressing lightly against mine.

Heat curls low inside me. Trying to ignore it, I give him shocked eyes. "What?"

He winces. "In, uh, the box. You know."

"Oh, right!" I grin and he does too, shaking his head.

"You knew what I meant all along."

"Yeah."

"You have a dirty little mind." He pauses. "I like that."

My heart bumps. "I don't know if he was up there. I didn't sit there."

"Oh. I thought you would."

I shrug. "I bought myself a ticket." I didn't want to take a chance on Roman being there again. "It was a great seat, only three rows off the glass."

"Shit. I didn't even see you."

"Do you pay any attention to the people in the crowd?"

"Sometimes. If they're hot."

I lower my chin and give him a look.

He bursts out laughing. "I'm kidding."

"Not me," Brandon puts in. "I always notice the beautiful women. You were in section one twelve, right?"

"Uh...yeah." I blink at him.

Owen frowns. "Hey."

Brandon laughs. He's very good looking, with a charming, boyish smile. "Don't get your jock strap in a twist. I can't help but notice pretty girls." He winks at me.

I can't help but smile at his flirty comments.

"When's your next game?" I ask.

Owen picks up my hand and twines his fingers through mine. I gaze down at it, taken aback, but also...enjoying it. I melt a little inside. "Monday. A quick trip to Raleigh. Then Wednesday against New Jersey."

I nod.

"After that we're off for three weeks. For the All Star game and the Olympics."

"Oh wow. You get a holiday."

"Yep."

"Aruba, baby!" Igor shouts, lifting his drink.

"Ve vill drink rum!" Nadia calls. "Lots of rum!"

I grin. I love their accents. "You're going to Aruba?" I ask them.

"Ve all are," Nadia says, waving a hand. "Eet will be a party."

"You too?" I ask Owen."

He makes a face. "Maybe. Depends on what happens next week."

"What's next week?"

"They pick the all stars for the All Star Game. If I get picked, I won't be able to go."

"Oh. That sounds like a tough choice. All star or a week in Aruba."

"I'm not much of a partier."

I give him a look. "Oh, come on. You could let loose for a bit."

"Yes!" Nadia agrees. "You tell him, Emerie."

"Aruba's beautiful," I say. "I went there once. You'll have a great time."

"You are not coming?" Nadia asks.

I quickly shake my head. "Oh, no."

"You should come!"

"Da!" Igor says. "Yes, come!"

I glance at Owen with a tiny headshake.

"You *could* come." His hand moves to my upper back and rubs. More melting occurs. Touching is part of the deal, I guess. I just wasn't prepared for how it would make me feel. "If I go."

I turn and whisper in his ear, "We don't have to go that far."

He shrugs. "It'd be fun."

It does sound like fun. A trip with a bunch of friends. I've never done that. A wistful feeling unfurls inside me. "I can't leave Cat that long." I meet his eyes. I told him about her, about her problems when she was younger. She's so much better now, but still...

He nods in understanding.

"It's not even a week," Layla says to me. "Six days."

She doesn't understand my situation with Cat. Also, Owen and I barely know each other. I sigh inwardly. "I just can't do that."

"Weren't you just telling me to loosen up?" he murmurs in my ear. "How about you?"

I'm silent, mulling that over. I haven't had much of a social life lately. Going on a fun trip is so tempting.

I look around at the group. I don't know any of them. It could be awful. Or it could be super fun. "I don't know. I'll think about it."

"Snorkeling," Easton says. "Sailing."

"Sunset Catamaran cruise," Lilly adds with a dreamy expression.

That does sound nice.

"Snorkeling with dolphins!" Sara says.

Oh my God. I love dolphins.

"Cliff jumping!" Nadia says.

"Speak for yourself," Kate says to her with a grin. "I'm not jumping off any cliffs."

"How about the quadding?" Hunter asks her.

"I'll do that!"

They're killing me.

"What do you do for a living?" Kate asks me. "Can't you take vacation?"

"Um, yes, I could. I…I'm a musician. But not professional. Mostly I look after my younger sister."

"Oh." Kate's eyes are bright with curiosity. She seems very professional. Very "polished career woman." Which I am not.

Awkward.

Owen squeezes my upper arm. I lean into him a little, relishing the wordless encouragement.

"What kind of music?" she asks.

"Folk. I play guitar and sing a little."

Owen makes a strangled noise.

"Cool."

"How about you?" I ask, deflecting attention from me.

"I'm a sports agent," she says. "I don't rep any of these guys, but I have other hockey player clients."

"Oh, wow." That's amazing.

I learn that Sara is Sara Carrington. "Oh my gosh! My sister loves your podcasts!" I tell her.

Sara beams. "Oh, nice, thank you!"

"She'll die when I tell her I met you!"

"Maybe I can meet her too, sometime."

"So who are the all stars gonna be?" Josh asks.

"Gunner, for sure," Easton replies. He squints. "Cookie has a great shot, this year."

They all look at Owen.

"Cookie?" I ask.

"Yeah, that's my nickname."

I grin. "Can I call you Cookie?"

"No."

Laughter bubbles up inside me. "I'll call you O. For short."

He shakes his head, lips twitching. "JBo has a good shot, too."

"Maybe Bergie," Igor says.

"How do they decide who's an all star?" I ask.

"Fans vote for one player from each division, and that guy becomes a team captain," Owen explains. "Then the league picks another forty players. There has to be at least one player from each team.

I nod. "Huh."

They debate the all star picks with some good natured trash talk that makes me laugh.

These people are welcoming me into their group like I'm going to be around for a while. I love it. I've never really had that before.

But guilt pokes at me with a sharp stick. I knew this was a bad idea.

I've been thinking about ending this crazy charade, in fairness to Owen, and now I wish I had. Sort of. Being drawn into this squad is so tempting. They're all close to my age, fun and energetic. But that's not what this is about.

Now I'm even more conflicted about what to do.

OWEN

Emerie and I are out for dinner. I picked her up at home, getting dirty looks from Mr. D, which I have to admit made my nuts shrivel. So far I still have a job, but after what happened on Monday, I'm even more uneasy about that.

That night at the Horse, she fit right in with everyone. I know it's pretend, but damn, it was kind of nice having her there with me, flirting a little, laughing with my friends. They really seemed to like her, and why not? She's kind, funny, smart.

I haven't told them who she is.

I was blindsided when I found out the owner of the team is her stepfather. So I should tell them. At first, it didn't seem that big a deal, since we were only doing this for a while and it wasn't real. But now she's met them, and they like her, and she fits right in, and they even invited her on the trip. I'd hate for them to go all stiff and weird on her. So I haven't said anything.

"How did the busking go this week?"

"Good." She gives me a surprised but happy smile. "Nobody told me to leave because I suck, so that's always a good thing."

I frown. "Does that happen often?"

"No. It's not exactly predictable, though. Buskers get robbed, attacked, yelled at."

"Jesus Christ." I'm gripped with unexpected panic.

She pats my arm across the table. "I've only been robbed once."

"*What?*"

"And once I got punched in the head. But I wasn't hurt."

I think I'm about to hyperventilate. I take a slow, deep breath.

"I'm sorry about the All Star Game," she says, clearly changing the subject to distract me. "Who did they pick?"

It works. My gut cramps and I drop my gaze. "From our team, they picked Gunner of course. And JBo and Bergie."

"Are you disappointed?"

"Nah." I lift one shoulder, still avoiding her eyes. "It's not that big a deal."

"I'm sorry. The others seemed to think you had a good chance."

"JBo and Bergie are both great players. They totally deserve it."

She tilts her head, her eyes soft. "I think you're better than both of them."

She knows next to nothing about hockey, but even so, her saying that eases the cold knot in my chest. "Thanks. But on the bright side, it means I can go on the trip. Are you going to come?"

She sits up straight and her mouth tightens. "Dammit, I want to. Vince invited Roman for dinner last night."

I scowl. "What?"

"Yeah." She rolls her eyes. "I had no idea. When he walked in, I thought of making a run for it, but Cat was there. Which was totally not fair of them. She didn't know what was going on. I was so pissed."

My jaw tightens. "Shit."

"Right? Now I really want to go on this trip. That'll show them."

I nod slowly. "Then do it."

She bites her lip. "I'm still worried about leaving Cat."

"She's a big girl. And you have people to help."

"I do." She still looks conflicted.

"How would the trip work with your busking?"

"What do you mean? It's not like I have a boss I report to."

I chuckle. "I know. But do you need the money?"

She blinks. "No. Vince gives me an allowance, for Cat and me. It's very generous."

"Oh. I thought...I don't know what I thought."

"I don't do it for the money." She meets my eyes. "I do it because I love to play and sing. Actually...I give most of the money away."

My eyes widen. "To who?"

"Other buskers. There are people who have families. They need it more than me."

Something hot swells in my chest. I think it's admiration. "Wow. I had no idea."

"Nobody does, so keep it on the down low, okay?"

"Right. Your whole secret life." I meet her eyes. "Why do you keep it secret?"

"Vince would hate it. It would embarrass him." She sighs. "At one time I enjoyed pissing him off, but that's not what this is about. I just wanted a way to make music, to play and sing for people that's no pressure, no commitment. I'd tell Cat, but it's not fair to ask her to keep a secret, so I haven't. Yet."

"Don't worry, your secret is safe with me."

She searches my eyes, then says, "I know."

I tilt my head. "How do you know?"

"I have no idea." She pushes her lips out briefly. "But I feel I can trust you."

That heat in my chest intensifies. "That means a lot to me."

She nods slowly, our gazes locked.

"So what about the trip?" I ask.

"I'll talk to Cat. See how that goes. The last thing I'd want to do is trigger her anxiety again."

I nod. "I get that."

She loves her sister. I admire that, too. I'm starting to admire a lot of things about her.

EMERIE

"I need to talk to you, Vince."

Vince stops at the door of his home office. "What is it?"

"I'm thinking of going on vacation for a week."

Vince's brows knight. "A vacation?"

"Yes. With some friends."

"With Cooke?"

I lift my chin. "Yes."

His eyes narrow. "Jesus Christ."

"What is wrong with that?" I demand impatiently.

"What about Roman?"

I fight back my frustration, rising in me like it's being pumped in with a tire pump. "I've told you, Roman and I are over."

His jaw clenches. "I think that's a mistake."

"I don't love him, Vince. I can't make myself."

"Marriages aren't always about love."

"What?" I stare. "Then what are they about?"

He averts his gaze. "If you go on this vacation with Cooke, there could be consequences."

My jaw loosens. "Like what?"

His mouth firms, his gaze flinty. "Use your imagination."

"What does that mean?" I curl my fingers into my palms, heat rising from my chest into my face. "Are you threatening me? If you are, just come right out and say it."

"It's not a threat. It's a promise." He walks into his office and closes the door with a sharp click.

For a moment, I can't move. My mind races, thoughts tumbling over each other. What does he mean? What would he do? Good lord.

Then I rush to his door and knock smartly. I open the door without waiting for an invitation, step inside, and close it.

"I don't care what you do to me," I say in a terse tone. "But promise me you won't take out your anger at me on Cat."

He frowns. "I would never do anything to hurt her."

"Or Owen," I add, holding his gaze fiercely. "Promise me."

He stares at me. And says nothing. For a moment, his face takes on an expression that looks...hopeless. He rubs his forehead. "I wish you wouldn't do this, Emerie."

I stare at him. Then I whirl out of his office and stalk into my bedroom, shutting the door. Goddamn him.

Later, I talk to Klara. I talk to the mom of one of Cat's classmates who agrees to take Cat to her swimming lesson since they're both in the same class. And I talk to Cat.

She's in bed, reading. I love that she enjoys reading. I cross to her bed and sit on the edge. "What's the book?"

She shows me the cover—some fantasy story, I guess, the dragon on the front covered in glittery scales.

"Is it good?"

"So good!"

I smile. "Listen, Kit Cat. I'm thinking about going on a holiday for a week, with some friends."

"With Owen?" She asks the same question as Vince.

"Yes, and some others. They're going to Aruba because they have a break in the hockey schedule."

"Right."

I tell her my tentative plans for her while I'm gone. "And Dad would be here too, of course, if you needed anything."

"I'll be fine."

I study her face, then let out a breath. Okay, good. She's not upset.

On the other hand…I admit I'm a tiny bit let down that it doesn't seem she'll even miss me.

"I wish I could go with you!"

My heart softens. "Ah, me too! But we could go on a trip, just us, sometime. Maybe spring break."

"Yes!"

I reach out and stroke her hair. "I'll miss you."

"When are you going?"

"I haven't decided for sure if I'm going. I wanted to talk to you first."

"You should go! It'll be fun. You never have any fun."

Oh, she's noticed that, too, huh? Damn. "The trip is next week. We'd leave Thursday."

She nods. "Okay."

"You have to behave while I'm gone."

She laughs. "I always behave."

"You do." *Now. Thankfully.* "I love you."

"Love you, too."

I hug her and stand. "Lights out in ten minutes."

She rolls her eyes. She still doesn't like bedtime.

Okay. I have a plan. Cat seems okay with it all. I'm still fuming about Roman showing for dinner the other night. I wanted to go on this trip because I'm enticed by the idea of a holiday with a bunch of friends. I'm also enticed by the idea of a holiday with Owen. I'm starting to really like him. But now…I'm going to do this because I'm going to damn well show Roman and Vince that they can't manipulate me.

12

OWEN

I can't believe we're doing this.

We're at JFK about to board an Airbus to Queen Beatrix International Airport.

I'm actually taking a holiday. I won't be able to skate for a week. I might be able to work out in the gym at the resort, but I won't be able to eat my usual healthy diet or study hockey for hours. I'm a little stressed about that, to be honest. It's hard enough getting back to playing after a *short* break. There's a debate between "rested" and "rusty," and I've always found time off makes me rusty. This year our break is extra long, and I don't like it. It's going to interfere with my focus.

It's making me tense when everyone else is all relaxed and carefree.

On the plane, I catch Emerie gazing out the small window, her lips drooping. Shit...is that a tear shining on her eyelashes?

"Hey." I lean into her, speaking softly. "What's wrong?"

She shoots me a self-conscious glance. "Sorry. Nothing."

"Em."

"I'm leaving Cat." She swipes her fingertips under one eye. "I worry about her. And I'll miss her."

Of course she will.

And just like that, my own stress dissolves and I'm filled with concern for Emerie. I want her to have a good time on this trip. I don't want her to spend it worrying about what's at home. So I need to do better.

"Hey. I get it." I squeeze her arm. "She'll be fine, though. You said she didn't seem upset about it at all."

"She wasn't." She nods and takes a deep breath. "She seemed excited for me."

"And you totally deserve some fun."

She squeezes out a smile. "Right."

"We need champagne." It's part of the package, and when we have glasses of bubbly, I toast her with my glass. "To relaxing. Having fun. No worries. Both of us."

"Yes."

"Soon we'll be on the beach."

She smiles. "I can't wait."

"Did you bring a bikini?"

Oh hell. I said that out loud.

She leans closer, as if imparting highly confidential intel. "I brought three."

Heat pulses between us.

Goddamn. I am so fucked.

I didn't in a million years think she would actually come on this trip.

But she is.

And we're sharing a room.

Real talk: I've thought about sleeping with her. Okay, not really sleeping. I've thought about fucking her. Pretty much every day since I met her, but now I know we're sharing a room and a bed—yes there's only one bed—I can't think of anything else.

I have no idea if she feels the same. Which could make this extremely awkward instead of shagadelic.

Now I just have to make it through this trip without embarrassing myself by accidentally jumping her.

We pass part of the four-and-a-half-hour flight watching *Being John Malkovich,* which neither of us has seen. Probably should have chosen something a little lighter for the start of a vacation, but whatever, we get into it.

"This movie is weird," Emerie comments part way through.

"Did you ever study Maslow's Hierarchy of Needs?"

"Not really."

"I took a few university courses when I was playing in Kitchener, and after I got drafted and was playing in the AHL I took a couple more. We learned about the hierarchy. Basically, it's a theory about what motivates people. People have to have their basic needs met—food, clothing, shelter—before they can be motivated to work toward things like self-actualization. Being the best they can be."

"Okay." She nods.

"Everyone in this movie is working their way through the hierarchy. They're all on a search for self-actualization. Reaching their full potential."

She gives me a weird look, but we continue watching.

At the end of the move, she turns to me, a small pucker between her eyebrows. "That's the end? He's stuck there forever?"

"Yeah, I guess." I pause. "I have questions."

"Me too."

"Okay, if you think about the self-actualization thing...and that's what they all were seeking...they all had different ways of getting there. And in the end...he didn't."

"Right."

"He thinks the only reason he's not successful is because people don't understand his work." I peer at her. "You're an artist. What do you think of that?"

"I'm not an artist."

"A musician."

"No." She shakes her head. "I'm not really a musician."

"Yes, you are." I frown.

She waves a hand dismissively and it bugs me. "Being a successful artist means reaching people with your art. Maybe..." She hesitates. "Maybe changing the world with your art."

I nod slowly.

"But that's not what Craig wanted," she continues, her brow furrowed as she thinks it through. "He's too narcissistic. He doesn't want to change the world with his art. He just wants praise and recognition. That's what he thinks success is."

I nod, examining that. Damn. "I think you're right."

"This was pretty heavy for a vacation."

I smile. "Yeah. We need more champagne."

"You wild man, you!"

A face appears over the seat back in front of us as Nadia goes onto her knees and peers over. "You have finished your movie?"

"Yep."

"Good. We need you to vote on an important topic."

I grin. "What's that?"

"Would you have surgery to get bigger balls?"

My mouth drops open. Emerie makes a choking noise beside me.

"I don't need bigger balls," I finally reply.

"That is not the question. Would you do it if you wanted bigger balls?"

Barbie also turns around. "The vote is tied right now."

"Who says they would do that?" I demand.

"Brando. And me."

I shake my head. "What is happening?"

"I'd do it so my balls would match the size of my dick," Brando says from behind us.

Emerie collapses into giggles.

"Because my dick is huge," he adds, grinning.

"Jesus. What is wrong with you people?"

"Yes or no?" Nadia prods.

"What's involved with the surgery?" I ask. "I can't say yes or no unless I know the risks."

She sighs. "I give up."

Emerie is still shaking with laughter, her face pressed against my upper arm.

"Nobody is getting near my junk with a scalpel," Morrie says.

"Me either," Russ adds.

Everyone's now crowded in the aisle around us.

Russ's girlfriend Hannah elbows him in the ribs. "Someone already did, honey," she reminds him gently.

Everyone laughs.

"I was a baby! That's different."

"Now we've gone from testicular implants to circumcision," I note. "I did not expect this conversation on my vacation."

The seatbelt sign comes on, and the chime bing-bongs.

"Sit down, you goofs," I tell everyone. As they move back to their seats, I meet Emerie's dancing eyes. "You'll get used to their bullshit."

She grins. "I like it."

We get checked in at the resort, which is fucking phenomenal, from the expansive marble-floored lobby to the restaurants, bar, and casino, to our room with more marble floors, a big ceiling fan with palm-shaped blades, dark wood furniture, and *one* king-size bed.

Emerie goes straight to the balcony, plants her hands on the railing, and tips her face up to the sun. "Oh my God, this is gorgeous!"

"It really is." I leave our suitcases and follow her out there, absorbing the view of clear turquoise waters, white sand, and palm trees. The soft, warm breeze ruffles her hair and I smile at the blissful expression on her face. "Hard to imagine it was snowing in New York when we left."

"Right?" She laughs, and her delight makes me feel as light as the ocean breeze.

We all agreed to meet down by the pool as soon as we unpack and settle in. I find the big closet and set our suitcases inside, and we take a few minutes to pull things out and hang them up or arrange them in drawers. Well, I arrange them. Emerie stuffs her things in.

She catches me side-eying her. "What?"

"Nothing."

"You're very...neat."

"Yes. I am."

She shoves the drawer closed. "Does this give you hives?"

I grin. "Just about."

"Sorry, O."

"No, you're not."

"You're right."

She's holding a bathing suit in her hands, and she disappears into the bathroom.

Yes, I'm disappointed I won't see her naked. But soon I'll see her in a bikini.

While she's in there, I change into a pair of board shorts and pull a T-shirt on. I check out some of the resort info and find we can get towels down by the pool.

Emerie emerges wearing a loose tank-style dress that's some kind of crocheted fabric. Through it, I can see hints of bright red. A red bikini. I lower my gaze to her bare legs and my tongue instantly becomes as big as a ham. Christ. Her legs are long and smooth and shiny, and all I can think is that I want them wrapped around me.

She picks up a straw hat and plops it on her head, then starts tossing things into a big straw bag.

"Okay, I'm ready," she announces.

"Can you put this in your bag?" I hold up my sunscreen.

"Sure."

"We'll be the first ones there," I say. "Everyone else is having sex."

She blinks. "Uh...how do you know that?"

"I know them. They're all still 'newlyweds.'" I make air quotes. "Still fucking like bonobos."

She spreads her hands and gives me a what-the-fuck look.

"Bonobos?"

"Yes…?"

"A kind of chimpanzee. They're sex-crazed." I hand her a key card and she drops it into her bag. Moving toward the door, I continue. "Males with females, females with females, males with males, apparently pretty much any combination you can imagine."

"Wow."

We start down a long hallway. "They also perform every position and variation you can think of."

"I'm…dumbfounded. Also a little impressed."

"Right? Apparently, sex isn't just for pleasure, for them. It also strengthens bonds, relieves tension, and keeps the peace."

"Again…wow."

We leave the resort on a path that winds through elegantly manicured grounds. I slide sunglasses onto my face. "Humans could learn a lot from bonobos. Apart from the incest."

Emerie chokes. "Incest?"

"Yeah. Like I said, they'll have sex with anyone."

"Oh my God." After a few seconds she says, "How do you know that?"

"I read a lot."

"I thought you only read about hockey."

I slant her a smile. "You underestimate me, hot stuff."

Her flip flops slap against the paved path as she strides with me. "I think you're right," she murmurs.

"There's Brando." I point to the far side of the pool. "And Jammer."

"So we're not the first ones here."

"Well, they're not fucking each other." I pause. "Not that there'd be anything wrong if they were."

We head their way. They've already got drinks in their hands, sitting on the side of the pool.

"Hi guys," Emerie calls.

"Bon bini," they both reply. Hello in the Aruban language Papiamento.

We find a couple of lounge chairs nearby and drop our things. And yeah, I'm watching when Emerie pulls her crocheted dress over her head.

Oh yeah. She's fucking gorgeous. Her skin is pale compared to others here, but it's smooth and her curves are perfect. The red bikini top is a halter-style and the bottom is modest, but it's sexy as fuck.

She kicks off her flip flops and bends one leg to dip her toes into the water. "Ohhh, nice."

"Sunscreen, my fair-skinned friend," Jammer says.

"Right." Then Emerie tortures me by pulling out a bottle of sunscreen and rubbing it all over her nearly naked body. I watch her hands glide up and down her legs, over her abs, then her arms and shoulders. God, I want to do that.

She catches me watching her. "Can you do my back?"

"Sure," I croak. I hope the water in that pool is cold, because I'm going to need it. I spread lotion on her back while she holds her hair out of the way, exposing the soft downy hairs at the nape of her neck.

"I'll do you," she says when I'm finished.

I gawk at her, my mouth dry.

"Your back." She motions with her finger to turn around.

"Oh. Right." I peel off my T-shirt and give her my back, and she spreads sunscreen on me. The feel of her hands rubbing over my skin is not helping the wood situation below. Jesus.

Once we're all greased up, I say, "Come on. Let's swim over to the bar."

"Okay."

I'm only too happy to jump into the water where my semi will be hidden. I hope.

I am not going to make it through this trip without losing my mind.

EMERIE

I can't believe I'm having so much fun!

It's been a long time since I could just lie around and do nothing. I'm drinking fruity rum drinks and soaking up the sun, cooling off in the pool, and listening to Owen and his buddies chirp at each other. That's a new word I've learned.

"I still can't believe they call you Cookie," I say at one point.

"Yep. We all have nicknames. Jammer, Brando. Hellsy. Barbie."

"Right. I remember being curious about Barbie. He doesn't look like a Barbie." I peer at Owen over my sunglasses, raking him up and down with my gaze. "Nor do you look like a Cookie."

He definitely looks edible, though. Holy hotness, seeing him shirtless has a warm slide of lust pooling in my belly. He's not bodybuilder huge, but his shoulders and chest are muscled and his abs defined. And his legs...those muscular thighs and bubble butt are literally mouth-watering. No wonder I'm so thirsty. It's not the heat...it's him.

"Thanks?"

I laugh. "I like cookies, though."

"Good to hear." He lifts an eyebrow suggestively.

I'm melting, and not from the sun. He's softening me up, somehow, just by being him. Analyzing that movie. Talking about chimpanzees having sex. The affection he shows his teammates even when they're arguing about what sun protection factor means, and he says to Brandon, "You ever look at someone and think, holy shit, you have the IQ of a crayon?"

I choke on a laugh, as does everyone else. Owen's friends like him, too, I can tell, including Brandon, that charmer with the sexy smile, twinkling green eyes, flirty manner. When he flirts with me I know he doesn't mean it, and so does Owen. This group is tight-knit and clearly loyal to each other. I guess that's what it's like being part of a team. I haven't experienced that much in my life. It gives me a wistful, hungry feeling.

The wives and girlfriends are all nice, too. At first, I fear feeling out of the loop, but I can see that Kate is also fairly new to this group, while Layla and Nadia seem close, as do Lilly and Sara.

Nadia is the self-declared "director of fun." She's the one who gets us involved in the volleyball game in the pool, and after that, floating beer pong. She's got us booked for a trip to the nearby water park the day after tomorrow and a sunset catamaran excursion the day after that.

As the sun gets lower, we all head over to the hot tub and lounge there with our cocktails until Nadia and Igor get out to return to their room. "We get ready for dinner," Nadia says, and arranges a time and place for us all to meet.

"Do you like swimming in the pool or the beach better?" Owen asks as we walk back to our room.

"I like both. Can we go to the beach tomorrow?"

"Ask Nadia," he says dryly.

"Eeep."

"I'm kidding. We can do our own thing. We all agreed we don't have to stick together every minute of every day. So if you want to go to the beach, we can do that."

"You don't have to join me," I say, sliding him a glance. "If you want to do something else."

He shrugs. "We'll figure it out."

"I do want to go to the water park. That sounds fun."

"Yeah, me too."

Owen lets me jump in the shower first, but I can't help but think of showering with him. Sharing a room is personal and I'm conscious of his big presence near me as we move around the bed. One. Big. Bed.

We're going to have to sleep together tonight. Those flutters I keep getting low inside me are making me worry that I'll molest him in his sleep. Like, I either need sex or to masturbate. Soon. And having sex with Owen would not be a hardship.

Would he...want that?

In the luxurious shower, I shampoo chlorine and sunscreen out of my hair and let the water run all over me to rinse, my eyes closed. My inner muscles squeeze again, thinking about Owen's body down by the pool—hard-packed abs, firm pecs, chiseled calves. I think about his hands on me with the sunscreen and how my insides had twisted with excitement. Which they are again now.

I cup my breasts, wet and soapy, my nipples hard. Maybe I should take care of things right here... I lean against the wall and spread my legs, sliding my hand down between them. The shower's not perfect for this, because it washes everything away, but I move out of the spray and stroke myself until everything is tightening, pulling up in a hard spiral that fractures, pleasure sliding down my legs. I pant. I think I made some noise...I hope the sound of the shower drowned that out. Jeez.

I swallow and step out, reaching for a couple of towels, one for my hair and one for my body. In the steamy mirror, my cheeks are pink. Sunburn? Or an orgasmic flush? Yikes.

I have a robe, so I pull it on and tie the belt at my waist before leaving the bathroom. Owen is out on the balcony reading a book. "I'm done!" I call.

He rises and walks in, taking in my robe and turban. As he passes me, he touches my nose. "Looks like you got some sun today."

My cheeks heat even more. "Uh, yeah."

While he's in the bathroom I quickly pull on a black sundress and rub moisturizer into my skin. I'm picturing him in the shower, water running over that amazing body. I had my hands on him earlier—well, on his back—and it was glorious. My palms itched to cup his ass cheeks and squeeze to see if they're as firm as they look. And I'm dying thinking about what's beneath his board shorts. Oh my God. I could paddle the pink canoe again already.

I take a few deep breaths. *Settle down, girl.*

Owen comes out of the shower in a cloud of spicy-scented steam, a towel wrapped low around his hips. I almost whimper.

He moves to the dresser and, his back to me, pulls out underwear. Then my dreams come true when he drops the towel, giving me a front-row seat to that top-notch ass. Admiring the divots at the base of his spine and the bulge of his thighs, I bite my knuckle.

He walks to the closet and pulls out a pair of gray pants that he steps into, thighs and glutes flexing beneath the snug black boxer briefs. He turns to me as he zips and unselfconsciously adjusts himself. And sees me watching him.

I guess I look a little lust-struck, because he stops. Heat blasts through the room like an inferno as we eye each other. I swallow. "I should dry my hair." I jump up and scamper into the bathroom again. With the door closed, I brace myself on the marble counter. Hoo boy. Okay. Wow.

It's okay. I can do this. I have to stop staring at him, though.

He was staring at me, today, too. At the pool. At the swim up bar. In my robe. Gah.

I quickly blow dry my hair. I usually use a curling wand to get the beachy waves I like, but today that seems like too much trouble, so I just scrunch a little product in with my hands. I pat some bronze shimmer onto my cheekbones and eyelids, add mascara and a swipe of lip gloss, and I'm ready for dinner.

Owen has covered his amazing physique with a short-sleeved shirt, blue with dark blue palm trees on it.

"Nice shirt, O," I say, staying casual.

He glances down. "Thanks. I bought it for this trip." He looks up. "I like your dress."

"Thank you." I grab a wristlet that will hold my room key, phone, and lip gloss. The resort is all-inclusive, so I don't need to carry much around with me. "And just in time to meet up with the others."

"Yeah. Let's make like an atom and split."

I splutter out a laugh. "Oh my God."

He grins and holds the door for me.

This time Nadia and Igor are there before us, along with Brandon. They've found a couple of big tables together in the buffet-style restaurant and are sitting there with glasses of wine, waiting for everyone. We pull out chairs and sit opposite them. The smell of food makes my stomach growl. All those rum drinks and no food...maybe I'm drunk. That's why I'm thinking about sex so much.

"Would you like some wine?" Owen asks me.

"Um, no, I'm good right now. I'll have some with dinner."

"Okay. Think I'll have a beer."

All afternoon he'd been drinking bottled water. I lift my eyebrows. "Wow. Really breaking bad tonight, huh?"

He laughs and strides away to fill a glass with draft from self-serve taps.

"He's dedicated," Brandon says. "He doesn't drink much when we're playing."

"I know. But I understand why. You play at a really high level. He needs to take care of that—" I clear my throat. "His body."

Brandon gives me a knowing wink. "True that."

He probably thinks we're already banging. I sigh.

"But it is nearly three weeks until we play again," Igor says. "So this won't affect his play."

I nod as Owen sits again. We're joined right away by Lilly and Easton, and Kate and Hunter. Everyone's a little tanned and relaxed and happy.

"I'm starving," Easton announces. "I'm not waiting for the rest of them."

We all shrug.

"Sure, let's eat," Owen says.

"I will wait here for the others," Nadia says. "Go! Eat!" She waves her hands in a "shoo" motion.

There's so much food to choose from it's hard to not overdo it. I fill a plate with mahi-mahi with a mango salsa, coconut shrimp, and triangles of what look like polenta with melted cheese on them called funchi. I take a sample of fried plantains and add some salad.

Owen's in his seat before me. "Holy shit," I say, eyeing his plate as I sit. "Are you going to eat all that?"

"I sure am." He digs into a beef stew, scooping up sauce with the bread called pan bati. "I've got lots of time to lose weight if I need to."

"I doubt you need to lose weight ever."

"He does not," Igor confirms. "Me, I put on weight when I look at food."

"He loves sweets." Nadia pinches Igor's waist. "Did you look at desserts?"

"Yes." He grins.

Sara and Josh appear with Jamal, and soon we're all eating. Owen gets wine for me and even a glass for himself!

"You will be drunk tonight," Nadia teases him.

"Could be." He grins.

"Try this," Jamal says to Brandon.

"What is it?"

"Siboyo tempera. Try it on your fish."

"But what is it?" Brandon looks suspiciously at Jamal's plate.

"It's made from onions and peppers."

"Haha, is hot!" Nadia says. "Be careful."

"It's not that spicy," Jamal says, eyes gleaming.

"I'll try it," Owen says casually.

My eyes widen. I have a feeling it is five alarm hot. "Are you sure?'"

"I like things spicy."

"Ha. Good to know."

He laughs.

Brandon forks some up and pops it in his mouth. Two seconds later his eyes bug out and sweat appears on his forehead. "Jesus!" he wheezes.

Owen tastes it, too. He swallows and nods. "Yeah, that has a bit of heat."

"A bit of heat!" Brandon croaks.

"It's made with Madame Janette peppers," Jamal says. "They're like a habañero."

"Christ," Brandon gasps, grabbing a glass of water.

"No, no, drink beer!" Nadia shoves his glass at him. "Is better."

He downs his beer, then shakes his head, his face red. "Asshole." He glares at Jamal. "You know I can't handle spicy foods."

Jamal chortles. "But it's delicious!"

"It *is* good," Owen says, grinning.

"Now I want to try it," I say.

"Are you used to hot things?" Owen asks me.

I smile. "Not until I met you, O."

"Ha. Good one."

"I like things spicy, too." I toss my hair back and pick up a fork.

"You two are so cute," Nadia says.

Cute? Uh... I glance at Owen, my eyebrows lifted.

He shrugs.

I taste a tiny bit of the siboyo tempera. I do like hot spices, but I'm also a little nervous, given Brandon's reaction. The burn takes a few seconds to develop, but Owen's right—it is delicious. "I like it!"

"I'll probably have heartburn," Brandon complains, rubbing his chest.

"You're such a drama queen." Jamal rolls his eyes. "Just remember —if you hook up with some chick tonight, don't go down on her."

I burst out laughing.

"If I hook up with some chick tonight, you're sleeping on the beach," Brandon replies, wiping sweat off his forehead.

Jamal shrugs. "I figured that would happen at some point."

I don't really have room for dessert, but I manage to try some pan bollo, a bread pudding made with Ponche Crema liqueur and served with ice cream. "I can taste the booze in this," I comment. "But yum!"

After dinner we meander down the path to the stage area where there will be entertainment starting shortly. We laugh at a comedian, dance to the live band, attempting badly to salsa. Then there's a karaoke contest. The entertainment team goes table to table trying to get people to sign up.

"Do it," Owen says to me.

I shake my head. "No."

"Oh, come on," he cajoles.

I'd love to sing. Should I? I bite my lip and look around.

"You'll be great," Owen says softly. "You want to sing. I can tell."

He's right.

"Do it for me. I love hearing you sing."

Oh my God. As if I can resist that. "Gah. Okay."

And I sign up.

Looking over the song selections, I purse my lips. Hmmm. I know my voice and I'm not going to sing a Beyoncé song. Finally, I make my choice.

"You are brave," Nadia says. "Igor, pupsick, sing with me."

He snorts. "No."

I turn big eyes to Owen and mouth "pupsick?"

"It means baby," he whispers.

"Come on. Pozhaluysta?" She bats her eyelashes.

He sighs. "Okay."

We watch a few people sing—one man sings "Sweet Caroline" and gets the audience singing with him, laughing. A couple sings "Up Where We Belong" really badly, but they're laughing as much as anyone. Igor and Nadia get up and sing "Empire State of Mind" and damn, they're good. Not necessarily the best singers, but they dance and give it their all and put on a good show.

We all clap and cheer them on, a couple of guys whistling for them, and they return to the table laughing and flushed, taking bows.

One more singer, then it's my turn. I make my way onto the stage and take the mic. This is familiar to me, but in a weird setting. I'll just pretend I'm in Penn Station.

My song starts, slow and sensual, and I move to the seductive beat. This is *not* what I would sing in the subway. I launch into the lyrics, soft and low, then hit it hard. "Damn! I wish I was your lover."

I hear the burst of applause from our table. Or maybe more than just that table, as people perk up and pay attention. I love Sophie B. Hawkins. I have to dance to the song as I sing, and I hold the long note on the word "ever..." drawing it out...and out...and out. That earns me more applause. I catch my breath before starting the third verse. I seek out Owen in the crowd and find him, his gaze riveted on me, and I sing to him, the words raw and vulnerable. I feel them in my chest.

I drop my head when I finish, the applause gratifying. With a smile I hand the mic back to the emcee and return to the table.

Owen's still clapping, watching me with blazing eyes and a proud smile.

"Holy shit!" I'm greeted with. Also, "You can sing!" and "That was amazing!"

I smile, my face hot, and take my seat. Owen's gaze burns into me, but I can't look at him. There's a tension vibrating off him that I can feel on my arm closest to him. He leans closer and says in my ear, "I can't take any more of this. We're going to be hot and naked and all over each other in about two minutes."

14

OWEN

Emerie shivers even though I feel like there's a bonfire burning right next to us. She turns her head and meets my eyes, so close I can see every one of her eyelashes, all the pale gold freckles that appeared on her snub nose today, the smooth texture of her skin.

Did I say too much? Did I read too much into that song? Is she going to shoot me down? I'm vibrating out of my skin.

"Let's go."

I leap out of my seat and hold out my hand to her.

Ignoring the others, she takes my hand and we bolt. I don't care what they think.

The path back to our room is different at night, shadowy with waving palms. Glittering stars fleck the black sky above us, the breeze a tropical caress against our skin and through our hair. My dick is throbbing, my heartbeat a primitive drumbeat.

We don't talk as we walk. I want to sprint but restrain myself.

We take the elevator to the third floor, a hot haze shimmering around us in the small space, the presence of other guests keeping us from jumping each other. Watching me, Emerie purses her lips around the straw in her drink she brought with her, and her cheeks hollow as she sucks. Fuuuuck, that's hot.

Our room is dark when we walk in, only pale, silvery light filtering in through the sheer curtains over the sliding doors. I flick on a lamp next to the bed then turn back to her. I remove the drink from her hands and set it down then reach for her.

"Fuck, I wanna kiss you," I groan, pulling her against me.

She melts into me like candle wax, forming to my shape, her arms twining around my neck. Her soft tits press against my chest and our mouths crush together. I groan again, one hand on her ass, pressing her closer still. She has to feel my hard on.

I lick over her bottom lip, tilt my head, and go deeper, gently sliding my tongue inside her mouth. She makes a small noise in her throat and her tongue meets mine, plays, sucks, the kiss turning hotter. My brain is short circuiting.

"You are so fucking beautiful."

She intrigues me. Enchants me. Fucking seduces me.

Opening my mouth wider, I kiss her deeper, exploring her mouth...she tastes tart like lime, sweet like sugar, her scent filing my head and sliding into my veins like a drug.

Lush and lovely, she smells like an angel, all warm spice and sweet flowers. I kiss her again, and again, sliding a hand into her hair and twisting my fingers into the long wavy strands, her scent and taste infusing my senses, and she moves with me, her mouth, her hands, her body, all hot need, curves, and longing. Heat runs like wildfire from my heart to my groin.

"Owen," she murmurs.

"Yeah, baby."

She slides her hands into my hair and holds my head as she presses sweet soft kisses to my cheekbones, along my jaw, and my lips again.

She's a star here on earth, incomprehensibly alluring, her voice magical, her kisses lush, the erotic softness of her body against mine freeing something inside that wants out.

She's the first person in a long time who has made me feel things. First, with just her voice. Listening to her in the subway gave me goosebumps. Tonight, I felt like she was singing to me. *Only* me, the purity and clarity reaching inside me, smooth and light, like whipped cream, making me happy and calm. But her voice is also substantial, and deep down, it tugs up an aching feeling, like a yearning for something. Watching her sing—her utter joy and energy—intensified all the feelings. I feel appreciation for her gifts, admiration at her for sharing them, affection because she's sweet and caring and talented and funny. And yeah…I feel lust.

I slide my hand up her leg, under the skirt of her dress, over her hip. She moves her hips against mine and that's it, I'm going down, all the way down. I cup my hand over her bare ass, my fingertips brushing her thong underwear. Her fingers are at the button of my pants, then my shirt, and she's undressing me button by button.

"I love your chest." She presses warm lips to the center of it, parting my shirt.

"How does this come off?" My fingers explore the back of the dress and find nothing. There's a knot between her breasts so I draw back.

"It's elastic." She hooks her thumbs under the edge of the fabric and tugs it down, baring her sweet tits.

Heat slams into me like a slapshot.

The dress falls to a pool at her feet, and I'm deaf and dumb, blood roaring in my ears, unable to speak. I can only drink in the sight of her, so lush and smooth and silky, and I'm getting impossibly harder. I clasp her waist with my hands, admiring the tiny black silk stretched across her hips.

She pushes my shirt back over my shoulders and I shrug and let it fall. Then she lowers my pants and boxer briefs.

"Oh, God." She gazes down at me as my cock springs up. "Owen…"

Just her looking at me is nearly enough to make me come, pleasure surging through me. I toe off my shoes and kick my pants aside.

"These are sweet." I snap the side of her panties. "They're coming off."

I ease them down, then slide my hand between her legs, finding soft heat, beautiful and mysterious, silky, warm and wet.

Her fingers trace over my shoulders, the bump on my clavicle from a fracture years ago, my pecs. It's getting hotter and hotter, every touch, every breath, every soft kiss. She curves her hands around my biceps, then curls them over my shoulders, hanging on, both of us naked now, rubbing against each other,

"Bed." I nudge her toward it. "Be right back."

I make a speedy trip to the closet to retrieve the box of condoms from my suitcase. I turn back to see her tossing aside the blue cushions on the bed then roll onto her back against the white pillows.

"Christ, you're gorgeous." I'm amazed the words come out coherently. Or maybe they don't. I advance on the bed pulling out one condom. I toss the box onto the dresser and climb onto the bed. From my knees, I gaze down at her.

She smiles and plucks the condom from my fingers. "You brought these...why?"

My blood runs hot through my veins. "Desperate, painful hope."

She laughs softly as she opens it then reach for me. My dick is like a divining rod seeking her touch, bobbing toward her in anticipation. The sight of her slender fingers on me, the feel of her touching me as she rolls the rubber down, has sensation burning through my body, right to the soles of me feet and the top of my skull.

"We're doing this," I whisper, lowering myself over her and pressing my cheek to hers. "Yes?"

"Yes." She bends her knees, cradling me in her thighs, and I push inside her, slowly, carefully. "Oh yesssss."

I ease into her tight heat, every nerve ending in my body electric. She gasps. I kiss her mouth. "Okay, baby?"

"Yes. It's good. So good."

"I don't want to hurt you."

"I haven't done this...much," she confesses.

My heart squeezes. "Then we'll take it slow."

Her thighs tighten on my hips, and I rock into her, savoring the sensation of being inside her, clasped by her, so intimately and snugly. Her hands move over my back, fingers pressing into skin and muscle, sliding up and down. She moves with me, perfectly,

I need to fuck her, but fuck her sweetly. She's a star, bright and fragile.

We're wrapped around each other, immersed in lust and longing. I need to move faster, to take her harder, to make her mine...but also for her to take all of me and make me hers. Her slick wet heat flutters around my dick, her arms holding on tight, and she cries out. Fuck, I'm electrified, so turned on I hurt.

I slide deep over and over again, pleasure rising, and I want it, so bad, then it hits me, swamps me, and I bury myself deep inside her as ecstasy pulses through me. She tightens around me, I groan at the euphoria, nearly blacking out. Slowly, I slide out and just as slowly push back into her. I love how she feels around my cock, hot and slick. Her breath is damp on the side of my neck as she pants.

Something inside me comes wildly, shockingly alive.

So many feelings. This is more than sex. This is life.

Our arms around each other, her head in the crook of my shoulder, one of her legs over my thigh, we curl together. Her body softens against mine and she brings a hand between us to lay over my heart. I feel it thud against her palm. She sighs, a sweet, satisfied exhale that brings a smile to my face. Precious woman. Sweet woman.

"We should talk."

"Do we have to?"

I smile, my eyes closed, idly playing with a strand of her hair. "No. Not right now."

"'Kay. 'Cause I wanna sleep." Her drowsy voice infects me.

"Go to sleep, hot stuff."

She makes a small snuffling noise and nestles in closer to me.

It's impossible to feel regret or worry about what just happened. My system is flooded with endorphins right now. The building could be burning down around us, and I wouldn't care.

And yet, I know we just complicated things even more.

Ah well. We'll figure it out. I let myself drift off to sleep as well, waking to the feel of Emerie's hand on my hip, sliding around to my ass to squeeze. I'm already half hard and blood rushes south, engorging me.

We turned out the lamp, and it's still dark. I don't know what time it is, and I don't care. We're on vacation. I don't have a practice to go to. I don't have a game tonight. We could stay in this bed for the rest of the goddamn trip and nobody would care.

In fact, that sounds like a great idea.

Emerie's fingers curl around my dick, now shamelessly pushing against her and begging for attention. "You're beautiful," she whispers.

I groan.

She drags the covers down. The languid breeze billows the sheer curtain and drifts across my hot skin. Desire rushes between us again like a rising tide.

She pushes me flat on my back, shifting next to me, her hands stroking me.

"Christ," I choke out. "Emerie…" I'm not used to just letting go, letting someone else take control. I usually don't like being the focus of someone's attention. I mean, I like blow jobs as much any guy, but when it's intense…like this…I feel like I don't deserve that kind of care. But it's Emerie, and she wants this, and I'll give her anything she wants.

"Mmm." She's studying me as she touches me, and in the faint light, I can see the look on her face—fascinated, hungry, covetous. That makes me even harder.

I want to give this to *her*. This time, it's not about me, about protecting myself. It's about *her*, about giving her what she wants, letting her drive things, letting her do what she wants. I feel cared for, and that scares the hell out of me, but also I love it.

The softness of her hands dragging over me has pleasure pouring through me. Then she bends her head and kisses the tip. My hips buck and my cock jerks. "Mmm," she murmurs again.

She licks her lips then kisses me again, licks me, all over, until I'm slick and wet and out of my goddamn mind. When she swirls her tongue around the head, exquisite pain rips through me. I slide a hand into her hair, cupping the back of her head, so carefully, not pressuring her. She opens her mouth on me and sucks me in, and sweet smiling Jesus, I can't stop the moan that rumbles up from my chest.

"Oh yeah, baby, that's so fucking good. Suck me…deeper…"

And she does take me deeper, right to the back of her throat. I swear I'm nearly weeping with ecstasy as her hands and mouth work me over, bringing me up to a fast climax. She pulls off and watches me come on my belly, hands still moving, bringing every feeling in me skyrocketing.

"Jesus," I gasp. "Sweet lord Jesus."

She bends and licks the crown, then falls back down beside me. "Wow."

"Fuck yeah. Wow." I'm gasping for air, my chest rising and falling. Then she blows my mind all over again, trailing her fingertips through the mess on my belly before rolling away. She trips into the bathroom and returns with a warm, wet cloth that she uses to wipe me off.

"I hope you realize that we're never leaving this bed again." I roll her into me and wrap my arms around her.

"Ever?"

"Well, for the rest of this trip."

She laughs softly. "Oh, come on. You'd be bored in one day."

I kiss her temple. "Try me."

We doze again and this time I wake up first. I've recovered and I need to make her come again, so I move over her and kiss her mouth. Her eyelashes flutter and her hands come up. She focuses on me, and her mouth curves into a smile. "Is it morning?"

"Hell if I know." I kiss my way down her throat and over the top curves of her breasts. "Don't care. I haven't paid enough attention to these beauties."

"We have lots of time," she says breathily. "All week."

"Mmm." I want to be inside her again, so bad, but first…I want to taste her. Everywhere.

I cup the mounds of soft flesh. Her tits full and round, with tight, pointy nipples, filling my hands. I plump them up and capture one nipple in my mouth, drawing on it, making her moan.

"I love that." She threads her fingers through my hair, shifting beneath me. "So much."

"Good." I take my time playing there, sucking and grazing my teeth over puckered flesh, making her squirm and gasp. She feels amazing on my tongue, my lips, and I love making her feel good. I slide my tongue over her nipple, all around it, along the under curve of one tit, then I so gently sink my teeth into her softness, marking her with soft bites all around each breast.

She's writhing, clutching my head, and I fucking love it. I shift lower, laying a string of kisses down her abdomen. She's completely bare, smooth and warm. I slip my fingers through soft lips, finding her slick and wet. So wet.

"Love making you wet," I murmur.

"Oh God. I love it too. I'm aching, Owen. I need you."

"Good." I open my mouth between her legs and slide my tongue over her. She gasps and twists my hair in her fingers. Sensation sparkles down my spine, gathering heavy in my balls.

I lick her, once, gently. My hands look huge on her inner thighs as I press them open. She curls up to watch me eat her, and our eyes meet in a collision that feels like an electric shock. I dive in deeper, my hands sliding up to her tits again, and her head falls back on a long sob.

This is it. I'm surrounded by her—her scent, her taste, the feel of her legs on my shoulders. She's beautiful everywhere, even this sweet, soft pussy. I can't get enough.

I play and tease, time drifting away, lost in the sensation of her, lost in giving this to her, barely aware of the hard ache between my legs. I twist and pinch her nipples and suck and lick the softest flesh until her breathing quickens, her noises become louder, sweet-sounding, lust-inflaming, and then she's holding my hair, her thighs tightening, her abs rippling, wailing as she pushes up to my mouth in a complete succumbing. I suck her clit through the contractions and the soft sighs.

"Need to fuck you again, baby," I mutter, rising on my knees. I reach over for another condom and roll it on in a flash.

"Yes." She reaches for me as I move over her.

As I slide inside her, her orgasm still pulses around me, and fuck, I'm lost. I lay my mouth on hers, my lips still slick from her, my tongue pushing into her mouth. Hands in her hair, I'm wild for the feel of her, the movement of our bodies together in a perfect rhythm as I thrust into her, over and over, a long, pure slide of delicious silk and friction. I pour myself into her, groaning into her mouth, breathing her in, completely engrossed and entranced. Obliterated.

Long, heaving, throbbing moments later, she says, "Now *this* is what I call the O zone."

I choke on a laugh and roll to my side, bringing her with me, still joined to her. "Oh yeah."

15

EMERIE

Everything is sexy.

I mean, everything. I've never been so obsessed.

We do eventually get out of bed, still without talking about what's happening with us. That's fine with me!

We spend the afternoon with the others at the nearby water park, which turns out to not be that great. Oh well, it's fun anyway, and we're all good sports about it. Back at the resort, we converge on one of the bars for drinks and snacks and decide to go into town for dinner tonight. Nadia has piles of pamphlets, planning our various activities for tomorrow.

Owen is very touchy feely, setting his hand on my arm, my leg, rubbing my back. This isn't just faking it—he seems to really like touching me. We're in swimsuits with lots of bare skin and it's easy to brush up against him. In the pool at the park, he carried me around, my legs wrapped around his waist, and I could feel his erection. I love it.

Every time I think about last night, my belly flip flops, and I want him again. I've never had sex all night before, and now I'm so horny I could do him right here in the bar.

Not really.

We keep glancing at each other and smirking and touching. We're kind of sickening, but I don't care.

I check the time on my phone. "I need to go video chat with Cat," I say quietly to Owen. "This is a good time."

"Sure. Let's go."

"You don't have to come."

He smiles. "I'll come with you."

Up in our room, he makes sure I'm all set up and when Cat's face appears on the screen, he leans in. "Hi, Cat!"

"Hi, Owen!"

"I'll let you talk," he murmurs to me, then takes a book out onto the balcony.

I follow him with my eyes, gratitude expanding warmly inside me, then turn back to my phone. "Hey, Kit Cat! How are things?"

"Good! I got an A on my social studies project. The one about comparing the deforestation of Easter Island with the deforestation of the Amazon Rainforest."

"Fantastic! You worked hard on that."

"Yeah." She smiles. "I'm happy about my grade, but I'm not happy about what's happening in the rainforest."

I nod solemnly.

"Did you know that the cattle business is responsible for nearly eighty percent of the deforestation?"

"Um, maybe?" Yikes. I haven't paid a lot of attention to the rainforest lately.

"I might want to become a vegetarian."

I blink. "Oh. Well, that's...cool. Can we talk about it when I get home?"

"Sure. How's your trip?"

We chat more about Aruba and her schoolwork and the surprising news that Vince picked her up from pottery class. She seems happy and at ease, and I know her well enough that I can tell it's not just an act.

When we're done talking, I set down my phone and sigh.

"Everything okay?" Owen asks from the doorway.

"Oh yeah. She's great!"

"I'm sure she misses you."

"Yes, she said she did, but she's doing fine."

Owen sits next to me. "That's a good thing. Why do you seem down? Do you miss her?"

"I do, of course. I just…well, I guess she can survive without me."

"Well, she probably *can*. But why would she want to?"

"Aw. You are so sweet." I turn into his arms and plant a big kiss on him.

"She needs you. But it's good that she can manage without you for a little while. That's what the goal is when you bring up kids…right?"

I tip my head back. "Yes. You're absolutely right." He just made me feel so much better.

He drags me into the shower with him to get ready for dinner. With soap suds and steamy hot water, we take care of each other.

"Gimme an O…" I murmur to him. "O."

He chokes on a laugh

"Another O Zone," I add.

"Oh yeah."

After, I stretch out naked on the bed, relaxed and content. The ceiling fan twirls above me, sending currents of air wafting over my bare skin. I stretch my arms above my head and point my toes.

"Jesus, you're hot," Owen says. "Stop doing that or we won't make it for dinner."

I smile. "Stop being hot?"

"Yeah."

"No, *you* stop."

He shakes his head as he finds clothes to wear. Reluctantly, I roll off the bed to make myself presentable.

I find another sundress, this one blue floral with spaghetti straps that tie in bows on my shoulders. As I apply makeup, Owen comes into the bathroom, stands behind me, hands on my upper arms, and kisses my shoulder.

"Careful," I say. "If you kiss my neck, we're not leaving this room tonight."

He laughs and grabs his toiletry bag. "Filing that away under things for later."

I can't wait.

Nadia picked the restaurant and made a reservation, and it's like a dream—located on a pier right over the water. They've set a long table for us at one railing. White lights and glowing candles surround us, the ocean breeze softly teasing skin and hair.

We eat seafood bisque, grilled garlic shrimp, and lobster tails, while drinking a delicious sauvignon blanc.

"Do you ever choose which will be the last bite you eat, so your mouth will remember it?" I ask Owen.

He lowers his chin to look at me. "What?"

"No, huh? Just me, I guess."

"You do that?"

"Yeah. I'm going to make my last bite this lobster, so I remember it."

"You're a nut." But his eyes are warm and affectionate as he says that.

I'm in heaven, leaning my head on Owen's shoulder to peer up at the stars, laughing at Nadia and Igor's antics, so at ease it's easy to forget Roman and Vince's attempt to intimidate me and how much I miss Cat.

After dinner, we move a little down the beach to a bar. It's noisier and crowded, super casual, with picnic tables on the sand and music playing. We start talking to some other people there who turn out to be Americans and further turn out to be hockey fans, so the guys have some time in the spotlight talking about the All Star Game and the upcoming playoffs. They're very gracious about it, which I like.

"He's bummed about the All Star Game," Easton says to me, looking at Owen talking to the others.

I turn to him. "He said they picked the best players."

"Sure, he would say that. But I know he's disappointed. He works his ass off." Easton shakes his head. "It's good that he's here, though, and good that you're here. I don't think I've ever seen him so chill."

Pleasure curls in my belly. "Well, that's good."

"Yeah." Easton takes a gulp of beer. "He's pretty intense about his sport."

"I've noticed that."

"Well, there goes Brando." Easton nods toward the deck.

I follow his gaze to where Brandon is standing near the wooden deck railing, talking to a woman with pale blond hair wearing sexy denim cutoffs and a loose white shirt. Their posture is one of unmistakable flirting.

"There he goes?" I question.

"We knew he'd hook up with someone sometime during this trip." He smiles ruefully. "He's a…what's a polite term? Ladies' man?"

I laugh. "Yeah, I get it."

Later, as Owen and I stroll through the lobby, both of us mellow and a little drunk, I ask him, "Are you disappointed you're not at the All Star Game?"

His fingers tighten on mine briefly, reflexively. "Nah. Then I wouldn't be here."

"And neither would I. And I'm pretty happy I'm here right now."

"I'm pretty happy about that, too. Also…" He kisses my nose. "Last night *you* were a star."

"I was, wasn't I?" I smile, remembering the rush of singing in front of an audience.

As we ride the elevator up, I check my phone to see if there's anything from Cat. She's sent me a photo of a bowl she made in pottery club. I message her back. *Wow, that's beautiful!*

Inside the room, Owen closes the door and reaches for me. "Finally."

I smile. "Finally."

With a low laugh, he moves his mouth to my jaw, then to the side of my neck, sucking gently. My head lolls back as shivers run down my spine and my lower belly heats.

"Mmmm. Now you've done it."

"I hope so." He picks me up and carries me to the bed. His strength is a turn on. He lays me down on the bed as if I'm fragile, his eyes warm with admiration as he studies me.

Emotion swells in my chest.

He follows me down and our legs twine together as we kiss again, rolling over the bed with our mouths fused, my hands in his hair, his on my ass and my back. He plucks at the ties on my shoulders and the V-shaped bodice of my dress gapes. I brush his shirt off his shoulders, eager to see and feel him again. I love the texture of his skin, the way he smells—I could bury my nose in the side of his neck and just breathe him in for hours. He smells warm and familiar. I love the heat of his body and the size of his hands, and the way he touches me.

He works my dress down over my hips. Again, I'm not wearing a bra, just panties, which he leaves on me. "Pretty." He fingers the pink lace.

I smile.

He gets rid of his jeans and briefs, and we're both nearly naked again, kissing like we're starved for each other. Like we can't get enough. I don't think I can. I'm as close to him physically as I can be, and it's not close enough. I press my hips into his, rub my breasts on his bare chest, and he groans.

"Goddammit, you're sweet." He gathers my hair in his hands and stares into my eyes. "I'm losing my mind."

"Me too." I touch his face, running my fingers over his beard stubble, down his neck, along his strong shoulder. "Oh, me too."

I glide my hand over his arm, lower to find his hip and squeeze the angular bone, then lower to the dark hair spreading at his groin. His cock is hard between us, and I'm wet and desperate for him. His size definitely matches the rest of him, and I want to admire the perfect shape of him all over again—the smooth crown, the defined ridge, the pattern of veins in the delicate skin over hard steel. I stroke him, then rub my thumb over the wet tip. "So beautiful," I whisper, loving the feel of him in my palm—virile, hot, pulsing.

"Emerie." He moves into my hand and lets out a low groan.

He slaps a hand out to fumble around for condoms, which we tucked into the drawer before leaving, knocks the phone off the hook, and gropes around to hang it back up. When it starts beeping, I start laughing.

"Fuck!" Finally, he hangs up, yanks open the drawer, and finds a condom. When he faces me, he's laughing too. "Sorry. Did I kill the mood?"

"No." I try to stop my giggles. When he kisses me, our mouths are smiling. Affection swells in my chest.

He rolls the condom on and moves back over me, his eyes glimmering in the faint light. When our eyes meet, and hold, I feel it—a connection of spirit, the shared humor a bond between us.

Oh hell. Our smiles fade as we both realize this is something… more. Something big. Something special.

He lowers his mouth to mine again, this time tenderly, exploring me, savoring me. This is how people fall in love, I think…with a shared understanding of someone's essence, a joining of hearts and minds, and maybe souls? And bodies.

Rising onto his knees, he slides my panties down my legs. I bend my knees, primly pressed together, lifting them to help him, and he tosses the panties over his shoulder and flattens his big palms on my inner thighs to spread me. He studies me with hot eyes, and heat slides from my chest into my face.

"So beautiful." One blunt fingertip grazes me between my legs. My clit pulses. "Want to make you come. Want to taste you again."

"I have no objection," I breathe out.

The corners of his lips quirk up and he leans down to put his mouth on me. It's paradise…his tongue sliding over me, his thumbs parting me, his breath teasing me. He lays soft, sucking kisses on me, licks me so slowly, gently. I lift my hips to his mouth with greedy supplication and feel his smile.

One thick finger slides inside, then two. Air escapes my lungs as he curves his fingers and strokes a sensitive spot deep inside me. I cry out and clutch the duvet on either side of me, holding on tight in case I fly up into the air. His tongue laps at my clit, right where I need it. "Yes," I gasp. "There. Right there…"

He keeps it up and tension coils sweetly, heat building. I squeeze and he groans. I tilt my hips, and he murmurs.

"I'm coming." Like a tsunami, it rolls through me, shaking me. I shudder and convulse, feeling how slick I am around his fingers. "Oh God!" My head rolls on the pillows and then I reach for him, grab his head and lift it off me. "I can't…"

He smiles, his lips shiny, then kisses my quivering belly. "Fuck, that was gorgeous."

He climbs up over me and glides inside me. Gripping my calves, he pushes my legs up and back and fucks me, urgent, focused, watching me as he pumps in and out. The sensation is nearly too much, exquisitely beautiful almost to the point of pain. I watch his face too, so beautiful, the bed bouncing with his actions, soft gasps spilling from my lips. I squeeze around him and his face contracts, his mouth opening, and he gives one last hard thrust, holding himself deep inside me, so deep I almost can't breathe. He shouts as he comes, hands tight on my legs. This man—big, strong, tough—is naked, exposed, unguarded. With me. Emotion floods me, and I reach for him as he releases my legs and falls over me, finding my mouth in long, lush tongue kisses.

My taste is faint and unusual on his lips and tongue, but so erotic. "God," I whisper, hugging his shoulders as he slides out and back in a couple more times, slow and silky and languid.

"Yeah." He eases to the side and I roll with him, staying face to face. "Fuck, yeah. That was so good, the people in the next room are having a cigarette."

After a surprised beat, I burst out laughing, pressing my face into his neck. He too shakes with laughter, and our arms tighten around each other.

OWEN

"Do you ever want to do more than busk?"

We're still in bed. We've missed breakfast, but neither of us cares. I run a hand from her shoulder to her elbow, my fingers lingering in the crook of her arm. So soft. So smooth.

"Maybe?" She focuses on my shoulder, her fingers rubbing over it. "I don't have a Broadway type voice. I could maybe have played in an orchestra, like my dad did, but I love guitar and folk music."

"You could write songs for other singers."

She laughs. "Sure."

"No, really."

One shoulder lifts. "Maybe. But right now, this is my life. It's getting easier, but I have to get Cat through school."

She's basically given up her own life, her own dreams, to look after her sister. I'm filled with admiration for her, but also…sadness. I don't know much about music, but I think it's a waste of her talent to just sing in subway stations.

"You're an amazing person," I say, kissing her forehead.

"Aw. Thank you. I'm just doing what needs to be done. Now, tell me about you."

I huff a laugh. "Like what?"

"Well, I know some stuff from Google."

"You googled me?"

"Of course." She grins. "I know you're Canadian. You're two years older than me. You're single."

I choke. "Uh, yeah."

"I knew that anyway. But…like…why are you so, um, strict with yourself? Your diet, your sleep, your routine…"

"I always have been."

"So…that's just you?"

I'm silent. "I told you about my brother Eric."

I feel her go very still. "Yes."

"He was three years older than me," I say slowly, watching my fingers move over her arm. "We both played hockey. We were both good at it. Eric was *really* good. When he was seventeen, he hurt his shoulder. He had to have surgery, and they prescribed painkillers for him. Narcotics." I swallow. "He got addicted to them. He played hockey the next season. He was ranked to be drafted in the NHL. But part way through the season, he started missing games, and when he did show up, he played like shit. Because he was high. The coach talked to Mom and Dad about it. They talked to Eric about it. He said he'd stop using drugs. And for a while he did. Then he started again."

"Oh." She presses her lips to my chest.

"He didn't get drafted. My parents tried everything. He could have still played in the NHL if he'd cleaned himself up. They sent him for expensive rehab. He'd come home and it would seem like he was getting back on track." I swallow. "He got a job at a gas station. Then he relapsed again. This went on for years. It was a nightmare."

"God. Oh, Owen. That's awful."

"Yeah. He'd steal my parents' car and disappear for weeks. He'd call in the middle of the night and ask someone to come get him—except he didn't know where he was."

She makes a soft, sad sound.

"Mom and Dad were at their wits' end, trying to help him. Their life was chaos. Everyone tried to baby Eric, treat him with kid gloves.

We never knew when he'd disappear or come home totally wasted. Or when the cops would show up at our door. I tried to talk to him. I begged him to get help." My voice hitches. "It was so fucking hard seeing him like that—all the possibility wasted. All his talent squandered. It was hard seeing Mom and Dad so helpless and heartbroken." I pause, my throat thick. "I tried to do the best I could. To try to make up for what was happening with him. I wanted to play in the NHL, and I was determined I wasn't going to waste my chances like he did."

"Oh." She strokes my shoulder again. I can feel her sympathy. Her sorrow. Her understanding.

"I felt helpless, too. And…" I stop. I've already shared more than I ever have. I don't want to tell her the rest of my feelings about Eric. She'd hate me. "Unfortunately, it's not an unusual story. It happens too often. Anyway, you've probably figured out he didn't make it. He died. We don't know if it was accidental or if he wanted to die." I stop, fighting the emotion that threatens to break my voice.

She presses her face against me. "I'm sorry I asked."

"Nah, it's okay." I slide a hand down the curve of her back. "So that's why."

"That must have been so hard. I can't even imagine."

I nod. "It was so fucking hard watching someone you love, love their drugs more than they love you." My voice is sandpaper-on-asphalt rough.

She snuggles in closer, kissing my jaw, squeezing me. "I'm so sorry."

"Thanks." I cup the back of her head.

"How are your parents?"

My gut tightens. "They're okay. I don't see them much."

"They still live…where?"

"Sarnia. That's where I grew up. Yeah, they're still there."

"They must be so proud of you."

"I guess."

"You don't talk to them either?" She peers at me with puzzled eyes.

I hitch one shoulder. "Not much." That's a whole other issue for dissection. And I don't want to do that now.

"That's too bad." Her voice is velvet soft. "Thank you for telling me about Eric."

We're sharing stuff. Not just our bodies. We're talking about things that have made us who we are.

"This fucking scares the shit out of me," I say in a low voice to her hair.

She draws back, eyes wide. "What does?"

One corner of my mouth hitches. "You know."

"This. Us."

This isn't pretending anymore. The sex definitely changed that. But more importantly...I really like her. A lot.

"Yeah."

Her head barely moves in a tiny nod. "I know. Me too."

Maybe we don't have to talk about why we're scared. Maybe it's enough to just admit it. To each other. To ourselves.

"What happens when we get home?" she whispers.

"What do you want to happen?"

She sucks on her bottom lip and peers up at me, looking adorably, heart-breakingly vulnerable.

"I want to keep seeing you," I say, saving her from having to say it first.

"I do too."

Our eyes meet and hold.

"Okay," I finally say. "Let's do that, then."

Her smile breaks free. "It does make things more complicated than they already were."

"We got this." I dip my head to kiss her. Her lips cling to mine in the sweetest, warmest kiss. I'll make sure things are okay. I'll take care of her. She knows that Cat needs someone to look after her. But who's looking after Emerie?

I want to look after her.

What is *that* about? I want to make sure she's always okay. I'm not sure if I can even do that. I'm not sure I have room in my life for someone else. This might be a huge mistake. But I want to try.

Today we're going on a snorkeling excursion.

We meet the crew on the beach in front of the resort. Carmen and Maria are friendly and helpful, welcoming us aboard the catamaran. The bar has free cocktails and lunch will be included. There's even a slide and a rope swing.

We settle in, and soon we're skimming over the turquoise waters, a delicious breeze keeping us cool. Nonetheless, I make sure Emerie is well-coated in sunscreen, assisting where needed. Completely unselfishly, of course. Today's teeny bikini is a bright yellow that contrasts the aquamarine water and blue sky. I take a bunch of pictures of her with my camera, including a few fun selfies of the two of us.

Brando is stretched out, nearly comatose.

"What's with him?" I ask Jammer.

"He stayed out all night. Seems a little tired."

"Was she good?" Barbie asks Brando with a grin.

Brando lowers his sunglasses. "Jesus. It was porn star sex."

The guys all make low noises.

"Tell us more," Jammer says.

"No." He slides his sunglasses back in front of his eyes. "Let's just say some of the best moments in life are the ones you can't tell anyone about."

"So where is she?" Nadia asks.

"Gone." Brando pouts. "It was her last day here."

"Damn. That's too bad," Jammer says.

"I don't think I could survive another night with her," Brando says with a happy sigh.

I meet Emerie's eyes, lit up with laughter.

We sail in silence for a while. Then Emerie nudges me. "I've never snorkeled before."

"I have a couple of times. It'll be fine." I pause. "You know how to swim, right?"

"Oh yeah. I mean, I'm not an athlete like you…" She pokes my abs. "But I can swim." She leans in closer. "What about sharks?"

Jesus. "I'm sure there are no sharks."

The guides set us up with snorkel equipment and a brief lesson. We get our masks and fins on, clip in the snorkels, and hop into the water.

"Slowly put your face under," Carmen advises us. "Look around and start breathing. Keep looking down, to keep your snorkel nice and straight up. Kick with your feet."

I keep an eye on Emerie right next to me since she was nervous.

After we try this for a few minutes and get a few more pointers, Carmen gives us tips on how to unfog our masks and clear water out of the snorkel. We practice that, too.

Emerie's doing fine, although I do see her eyes darting around.

"What about sharks?" I ask the guide, prepared for laughter.

"Not here." He shakes his head. "Farther out in the ocean there are sharks."

I catch Emerie's eye, and she smiles gratefully.

We buddy up and are told to keep an eye on our buddies, but nobody has to tell me that. I'll be watching Emerie like a hawk watching a mouse.

We venture away from the boat, kicking our way along, watching colorful fish and sea life. Then Emerie frantically pushes her way to the surface, bubbles flowing from her snorkel. My heart jumps and I swim after her.

With her head out of the water she screams, "Snake!"

"Where? Where?" I'm splashing around, my head turning.

"I saw it! It was black and swimming around me! Aaaaaah!" She splashes frantically.

"This?" I grab the floating strap of her life jacket and hold it up.

She stares, panting, water running down her face.

The others all surface, too. "What's going on?" Millsy asks.

"What's wrong?" Sara says.

"It's all good." I bite my lip.

"Oh my God." Emerie starts giggling. "I'm such an idiot."

My lips twitch.

"What?" Lilly asks.

"I thought I saw a s...sn...." Emerie is now laughing so hard she can't talk. "A snake. In the w-water."

"What?" The girls all bolt up higher.

"No, it's fine." Emerie giggles again. "It was this." She holds up the belt.

I'm laughing now too, and the others start. Emerie's laughing so hard I'm afraid she's going to drown, so I wrap my arms around her.

"I'm sorry," she chuckles.

"It's okay. Ready to go back?"

"Yes. It's amazing!"

We spend a while enjoying the scenery in the clear blue water, then climb back aboard the catamaran. We sail to a different spot and stop for lunch—sandwiches and cold beers.

It's a blast sliding into the sea and swinging from the rope to drop into the water. Emerie's hesitant about the rope, but she does it, bobbing to the surface laughing with delight. Her joyful smiles and bright eyes make me feel something. Again. Maybe...happiness? And despite my disappointment about the All Star Game, I also feel a deep gratitude that I'm here, with her, giving her these new experiences and sharing this with her.

17

EMERIE

What. The. Fuck.

I stand on Park Avenue shivering, looking around. What am I supposed to do? Where am I supposed to go?

I just got home from Aruba and discovered my key wouldn't work in the door of the apartment. I rode the elevator back down to the lobby and approached Anthony. With an uncomfortable look on his face, he handed me a letter from Vince.

He's kicked me out.

I crumple the paper in my hand.

I'm not really sure what I'm feeling. Actually, I can't believe this is happening. And yet...I can't get into the apartment. And nobody's coming to help me.

What the fuck?

The February air feels especially frigid after just getting off a plane from Aruba, where the air was soft and balmy. My suntan isn't keeping me warm.

"You look cold."

My head snaps around to see Roman standing on the sidewalk. He's wearing a leather jacket and a scarf, his hands in his pockets. He smiles at me.

"What are you doing here?" I ask.

"I thought you might need some help."

My jaw falls slack. He knows? What the hell? Is that what this is about? Vince's note says I can't move home until I break up with Owen. Is this still about me and Roman? For fuck's sake.

"I don't need any help." I set off down the street, my suitcase rolling along beside me. I don't know where I'm going, but I need to get away from Roman.

"Where are you going, Emerie?" He catches up and strides along beside me.

My teeth grind together. "I'll find somewhere."

"You could stay with me. I have lots of room."

Yes, he does, in his expensive apartment on East 87th. "I'm not staying with you." I keep walking, looking straight ahead.

"It's cold, honey. Come on. Let me take you home."

"I've just been locked out of my home," I reply bitterly. "Thanks to you." Then I stop and turn to glare at him. "This *is* thanks to you."

His eyes narrow fractionally but his shrug is casual. "Vince thinks we should be together, too."

I slowly move my head from side to side. "I don't know what is going on here, but this seems extreme, even for Vince. He's never been exactly fatherly to me, but he's always provided for me. Kicking me out...?" I study Roman's face. His expression is neutral, but I think his eyes flicker. "Why are you doing this?"

"I love you, Emerie."

"Oh my God." I start walking again. "No, you don't."

"Jesus. Yes, I do!" The passion in his voice startles me. Roman's part of a successful family business empire. He knows how to negotiate. He knows how to get what he wants. And this isn't it. He knows to keep his cards close to his chest.

I stop again and search his face. He meets my eyes, his fiery, his mouth tight.

"I'm sorry," I say quietly. "I've been honest with you, Roman." I hold his gaze steadily. "We're over. I'm with someone else now." And then it hits me, almost like a punch. I asked Owen to come to the party as my date to show Roman I'm with someone else. But now... "The truth is, I'm..." I stop. I'm what? In love? With a guy I barely know? Yes. I think I kind of am. "I'm falling for Owen," I say. "I care about him a lot."

Roman's face returns to unreadable, but a vein throbs in his temple, and his jaw tightens. For a moment he says nothing, and I can see his thoughts turning. I liked Roman well enough when we started dating. I'd known him for years, and since his family and Vince were friends, I thought he was a decent guy. But right now, I'm a little afraid of him. Finally, he says, "You're making a mistake." He turns and walks away.

Holy shit.

This is ridiculous. Why is he being like this? I haven't led him on. I don't think. At first, after we broke up and he kept pushing me, maybe I wasn't assertive enough. But come on! I'm with someone else now!

I resume walking, turn the corner, and see the Carlyle. Okay, I can go in there.

"Checking in?" a doorman asks me, seeing my suitcase.

"Um, no, actually." I glance around. "I'm here for afternoon tea."

"Ah." He stretches his arm out with a smile, and I cross the lobby.

I'm seated on the brocade banquette, my suitcase parked to the side. I pull out my phone and set it on the red tablecloth while I drag off my scarf and coat. I feel spacey. In a daze.

This can't be happening.

What do I have to do to get Vince to let me come home?

Do I *want* him to let me come home?

Well, I have nowhere else to live, so duh. Also, there's Cat. My heart clutches, thinking about her. She needs me. Never mind me, Vince can't do this to *her*! What is he thinking?

I remember Vince's vague threat when I told him I was going away with Owen. Jesus. He was serious. But...is this coming from him? Or from Roman?

A waitress brings me a pot of Assam tea. I need this warmth. I pick up my cup and wrap both hands around it. Probably poor tea drinking etiquette.

What am I going to do? My best friend is in India. I've let friendships slide the last few years, and there isn't anyone else I'm close enough to, to ask to stay with them. I guess I could get a hotel room. The note from Vince said my credit card has been cancelled, but I have money of my own. I'm not that stupid. I've put aside money not only from Vince, but also some of my busking money. In the past, I've used it to donate to a charity that helps street musicians, but it looks like I'm now my favorite charity. Ha.

I could call Owen.

Things are new with us, but surely he'd be okay with me staying with him for a few days. Until…I don't know until when, but I'll figure something out.

The waitress brings me a selection of small sandwiches, scones, and pastries. Surprisingly, I'm starving. I wolf down a few delicious sandwiches, then spread a scone with thick cream and strawberry jam, washing it all down with full-bodied tea.

Okay. I feel better now.

My phone rings.

I grab it and see Owen's name. Oh good. I answer. "Hi!"

"Hi, beautiful."

"I'm so glad you called! You're not going to believe what happened."

"What?"

"Vince has kicked me out." I keep my voice low. It's not busy in here, but I don't want to broadcast my soap opera life to everyone in the restaurant.

"*What?*" His tone sharpens.

"I'm not kidding." I tell him what just happened. "He sort of threatened to do this before we left for Aruba, but I didn't think he really would."

"You didn't tell me that."

"I didn't think he'd do something like this!"

"Okay, okay. Where are you?"

"I'm at the Carlyle, having afternoon tea." Suddenly this strikes me as hilarious, and I start laughing.

"Are you drinking?" he asks.

"No." I swipe a tear from my eye. It's from laughing. I think. "I'm having Assam tea. And scones." I sigh. "Can I ask you a huge favor?"

"Of course."

I swallow. "Can I stay with you for a few days?"

After only the briefest hesitation, he says, "Of course you can."

I blow out a relieved breath. "Okay. Thanks. Um…I don't even know where you live. Exactly." I know it's on the West Side.

"I'll come get you."

"I can take a taxi."

"No. I'll come get you. I'll be there in about fifteen minutes."

"Okay. Thank you." My heart settles down.

I eat another cucumber sandwich and a small tart, finish my tea, and pay the bill. Then I head back outside to wait on the sidewalk for Owen.

I don't even know what kind of car he drives. This is crazy. We barely know each other. And yet…he's the one I trust to help me.

A brief wave of self-pity washes over me, and I blink back tears. *No tears.*

I hope Klara is picking up Cat from school. What is she going to think about this? God. My breathing quickens, thinking about Cat being upset.

A silver Range Rover pulls up at the curb and the door opens. Owen jumps out.

I rush at him and throw my arms around him. "Thank you for coming." More tears threaten. God, what is wrong with me?

His hands land on my back and rub. "I got you."

I sniffle and lift my chin to meet his eyes. "Thank you. Really."

"I'll get your suitcase."

He tosses it into the back of his vehicle, and we both climb in. He makes a right turn, then another onto Park Avenue. Traffic is nuts at this time of day, but then, when isn't it?

As we drive, I share more details of my arrival home and discovery that I'm locked out. "He says I can pick up all my stuff tomorrow at noon," I tell him. "Is he going to be there, though? Cat will be at school." I choke on a tiny sob. "When am I going to see her?"

Owen curses under his breath.

"Vince says I can move home when I break up with you."

"What?" His head whips around, then jerks back to focus on the road.

"Yeah. And then..." Should I tell him about Roman? I have a feeling this won't be good, but...I have to be honest. "Roman was waiting for me outside the building."

"Are you fucking kidding me?" Owen bellows.

Eeek. I knew this would be bad.

"I know. This is too much. I can't believe Vince is doing this."

Owen zigzags over to Fifth Avenue and enters Central Park. I'm talking non-stop, twisting my fingers together. We pass the carousel, then Tavern on the Green, and then leave the park. Owen keeps going straight toward the river.

"I'm sorry to dump all this on you."

He takes a deep breath. "It's okay, Em. I got you."

Warmth balloons in my chest.

He parks in underground parking at his building, and we take the elevator to the seventeenth floor.

"How long have you lived here?" I ask.

"A few years. It's a good location. Easy to get to the arena on game days, and to the practice facility in Yonkers. There are a few guys who live in this building."

On his floor, he unlocks the door and motions for me to go in ahead of him. I walk into a bright foyer with light wood floors and white walls. He hangs my outwear in a spacious closet and leads me into the living room, leaving my suitcase near the door.

I check the space out. Big windows look out over the river. A chunky sectional upholstered in stone-colored twill sits against one wall, facing a couple of squarish chairs with black metal frames and taupe leather seats and back. Between them sit two low tables, similar in style and shape to the chairs with black metal frames topped with cream tiles.

I step onto the thick black and cream rug to survey the art on the walls—a big framed watercolor in shades of taupe, mocha, gray, and black; a few handwoven baskets; and a collection of mixed-sized prints in white frames that look like neutral color seascapes.

"This is lovely." I turn to face him. "Did you decorate this?"

"Ha, no. I went to Pottery Barn and told them to put together rooms that looked good."

I grin. "At least you're honest."

"I like it to look nice, but I have no clue how to do it. Mostly I just want it comfortable."

"It feels comfortable." I sit on the sectional, shifting a couple of toss cushions aside, and run my hand over a chenille throw draped over the arm. I sink back into the couch and let out a huge sigh. "I'm okay," I say, seeing his look. "I'm just releasing tension." I do another inhale and exhale.

His lips twitch. "Gotcha."

"I still can't believe this is real. Vince is nuts."

"I have no comment on that matter."

I sit up straight, stiffening. "Oh my God, Owen. You still have to deal with him." I cover my mouth with my hand. "If he did this to me, what could he do to you?"

"He won't do anything to me. Want something to drink?"

"I'm okay, thanks." I jump up and follow him into the small but nicely appointed kitchen, all white cabinets, stainless steel appliances, and gleaming black counters. "Are you sure?"

His shoulders are tense as he grabs a bottle of water from his fridge. "I think I need to have a word with Roman Moretti."

"No!" I clasp my hands. "Don't do that."

He gives me a fierce look that should be as scary as Roman's was, but with Owen I don't feel scared. I feel safe. "He can't do this."

My insides twist painfully. "I'll leave."

"No." His tone is sharp.

"I'll tell them we broke up. Then they'll leave you alone."

He stares at me. "You want to break up?"

"No!" Tears sting my eyes. "No, I don't, but I don't know what else to do."

"Stay here, Emerie. I want to know you're safe."

I blink rapidly, his concern for me so sweet, so unfamiliar to me. "What about Cat?"

His head drops forward.

I'm putting him through this. This is all my fault. "I'm sorry."

He shakes his head and turns to face me. "Don't apologize. Tell Cat the truth."

I swallow. "Okay."

I find my phone, my stomach in knots. How am I going to tell her about this? I've always been so careful to avoid phrases like "your father is an asshole."

I dig my phone out of my purse and call Cat. She answers quickly. "Hi! Where are you?"

I swallow. "Hi, Kit Cat! I'm at Owen's."

"Oh, okay. When will you be home? Did you bring me a present?"

Her deliberately cheeky tone makes me smile. "Maybe I did. Um, listen. I'm not coming home tonight."

She's silent. "Why not?"

I can't lie to her. I suck in a big breath. "Vince doesn't want me to live there anymore."

"What? Why?"

"You need to ask him that. I'm sorry, honey. I'm going to talk to him tomorrow. I hope he'll change his mind, but I don't know."

"That's crazy, Em!"

"I don't like it." I keep my voice calm. "But I'm okay. And you'll be okay. I'll come take you to school in the morning like usual, I'll just wait in the lobby for you. And I'll pick you up."

"Um. Okay. So I'll see you tomorrow?"

"Right. For sure."

After a few seconds of heavy silence, she says, "I don't understand this."

"I know. I'm sorry. And listen…I doubt your dad will ask, but if he wants to know where I am, tell him you don't know." I squeeze my eyes closed. I hate this.

Silence. "Em. I don't understand what's going on."

"I'll explain it to you. Don't worry, everything will be fine."

I try to chat a bit more with her about school and friends, but she's clearly unhappy. I worry about what she'll say to Vince. She's pretty good at speaking her mind with him. Better than I was.

When I end the call, I call Klara and give her a similar update. I don't know what Vince has told her or not told her, but I have to make sure Cat's going to be cared for. I just tell her I'm staying with a friend until I have a chance to talk to Vince. Then I drop my phone on the coffee table and lower my head into my hands. I feel Owen approach, his weight sinking into the couch next to me, and his hand lands on my back in a gentle, comforting gesture. "I'm sorry," he says in a low voice.

I nod. "This sucks."

18

OWEN

This whole thing is a pig's breakfast. It's the last thing I need. I need to focus on hockey. We need to win. We're heading in the last stretch of the season, when playoff spots and home advantage are nailed down. Pittsburgh is right on our tail in the standings. Nothing is guaranteed.

"How do you get her to school?" I ask Emerie, referring to Cat.

The slump of Emerie's shoulders and her bowed head make my chest hurt.

"We walk," she mumbles into her hands. "I'll just go there in the morning and walk with her."

"And then meet with Mr. D at noon."

"Right."

"I can drive you."

"No, that's okay. It's probably better if you're not with me."

Damn. "Well, you can take my car."

"Eeep. I don't know if I'm comfortable with that. I don't drive much."

I shrug. "It's just a car."

She lifts her head and gives me a crooked smile. "Thank you. You're so good, Owen."

My hand stills on her back. I don't feel "good" right now.

"A good man," she adds quietly, leaning into me. "I'm so lucky we met."

I can't argue with that. I feel lucky to have met her too, even though it's definitely scrambled up my life.

"I don't have much food in the place," I say. "We can order something in for dinner."

She nods.

"I'll take your things into my room." I stand and grab her suitcase then lug it into my room.

I've never had a woman even sleep over at my place, let alone move in.

"I have a lot of clothes appropriate for the beach," she says on a mirthless laugh, following me. "Not much for February in New York."

"I can loan you a sweater or something for tomorrow."

She lays her palm on my cheek. "Thanks. Um, do you think that bed is big enough?"

A smile tugs at my lips. "It works for me."

She throws herself down on it, spreadeagled. "It's massive."

"That's what she said."

She starts laughing, and I laugh too, and miraculously, tension and worries ease out of me. I study her beautiful, smiling face on my bed, and at this moment I feel like this is right. Like everything is going to be fine. Somehow, we'll manage this.

I order food from a nearby place that has a lot of healthy selections, and we eat bowls with brown rice, lots of veggies, coconut, and green curry sauce.

"Do you cook?" Emerie asks me. We're seated on the couch with the TV on, watching coverage of the Olympics that just started. "You must, to eat healthy all the time."

"Yeah. I've learned to make some things. A lot of days I eat at the practice facility. In the off season, I train with a guy who taught me a lot about nutrition, and I try to follow what he says."

"When's your next game?"

"Not until the twenty-fourth."

"What are you going to do with all your free time?"

I shrug. "Work out. Read. Watch the Olympics."

"Yes! I love figure skating."

I say nothing.

Emerie laughs. "Come on, real men watch figure skating."

"Sure. You know what I like best? Other than hockey, of course."

"Of course. What?"

"Those crazy skiers. Pretty much any kind. Slalom, ski jumping, free style."

"Oh yeah! Right? They risk their lives every time."

"It's amazing."

She seems a little less sad now. I'm happy about that. I still haven't figured out what we're going to do about this whole state of affairs. I want to go talk to Moretti and fuck him up. I want to go with her to talk to Mr. D tomorrow, but it's probably better if I don't. Maybe then he'll let her move back in?

Maybe we *should* break up. For real.

That opens the door for Moretti to step right through.

That's not fucking happening.

Shit. My mind's going around in circles. We're damned if we do and damned if we don't.

"Maybe we should fly to Vegas and get married."

Emerie's head whips around, her jaw hanging loose. "What?"

I rub my jaw. "I've been trying to figure out how we fix this. And I can't."

"Well, we can't get married!"

"Yeah, I know." I lean my head back into the couch cushions, my meal finished.

"I'll talk to Vince tomorrow," she says. "I'll convince him to let me move back in for Cat's sake."

"You think that'll work?"

Her lips tilt in a glum smile. "Probably not. I'm so sorry, Owen," she whispers. "I should never have dragged you into this."

"You didn't know." I pull her into my arms, and she snuggles up against my side.

It's too late to break up. I could just do it if I didn't give a shit about her. But I do. I give a lot of shit. Wait, that doesn't sound right. I mean, I care.

A lot.

And she's sure as hell not dating some other guy, even if it's fake dating.

"We'll figure this out," I say.

"Okay, I have another idea." She takes a deep breath and lifts her head. "I'll tell Vince we broke up, and I'll deal with whatever happens after that on my own."

That suggestion doesn't sit well with me either. I mull over why that is while studying her face. "I don't want to break up," I finally say. "And I don't want to lie. And I don't want you to deal with this on your own."

Her eyes get glossy. "I don't want to break up either."

"Well." I swallow. "Let's wait until you talk to Vince tomorrow."

She nods. "Okay."

"Don't worry about it."

"Ha."

"I bet I can distract you." I bend my head and kiss the side of her neck.

She shivers. "That's a good start."

EMERIE

Seeing Cat is gut-wrenching.

She's nearly in tears trying to understand what's going on. I could punch Vince for doing this to her. Maybe I will.

"I asked him why, and he said you need to grow up," she says, her voice high.

I grind my teeth. "Well, it's true that I won't live with you two forever." I try for cheery optimism.

"But…but…"

"You're getting older, too," I say, meeting her eyes. I smooth some hair back from her face. "You're getting more independent. And no matter where I live, I'm always here for you. I'll always love you."

She nods, her lips pouting.

"I don't ever want you to feel alone," I add. "So just know I'm always a phone call or text away. But you'll still see lots of me."

Usually after I drop off Cat at school, I head downtown and get my guitar then move from station to station to play and make music. But I can't do that today. By the time I get somewhere and set up, it'll be time to turn around and come back to meet Vince. I make a quick call to Mr. Cantor. I get voicemail, so I leave a message that I'll be away a few more days. I know he'll worry if I don't show up.

What am I supposed to do for the next few hours?

Anger is growing inside me like a flame getting bigger and hotter. Seeing Cat's unhappiness and confusion is fanning that flame. My jaw is starting to ache from gritting my teeth. Vince is being a dick. This is ridiculous.

But…I'm not his daughter. He owes me nothing. Not even a home. It's kind of hard to argue with that.

I sit in a coffee shop for a while then wander around Nordstrom. I'm not even a little interested in shopping. Finally, I head to the apartment.

But Vince isn't there. All my things have been packed into boxes stored behind the doormen's desk. Anthony helps me load them into Owen's Land Rover. All my possessions consist of a few boxes of clothes. Shit.

Okay, there's more than that. My guitar. Books and music and art I've collected. These are things that are important to me. Not as important as Cat, though.

My heart pinches thinking about the beautiful grand piano left behind there. I love that piano. I love making music on that piano.

I drive back to Owen's apartment. He borrows a trolley thing, and we lug my stuff up to his apartment and pile the boxes in his second bedroom, which he uses as an office-slash-guest room. I identify one with clothes I need and pull some stuff out. I'm wearing the same leggings I wore yesterday and a huge sweatshirt of Owen's, so I change into clean clothes.

"So, he wasn't even there," I tell Owen dejectedly. "I was so pissed, I was ready to lay into him, and I didn't even get the chance."

His lips thin and his jaw tightens.

I tell him about Cat and his eyes flash. But he says nothing.

I know this is a difficult position for him to be in. What's that saying? Between a rock and a hard place. Ha. I feel even worse.

For a moment, I consider just giving up. I'll marry Roman fucking Moretti. How bad could it be? Then he'll be happy, Vince will be happy, Cat will be happy, and Owen won't be putting his career in jeopardy for me.

But then I look at Owen and think about his tenderness and generosity, his strength and resolve, what a huge nerd he is for the sport he loves so much, what a genuinely good man he is…and I don't think I can just walk away from him. Even if it would be the best thing to do. I guess that makes me selfish?

I sigh. "I just need some time," I mumble.

"You're not alone, baby." He pulls me into his arms and presses my face to his shoulder.

His embrace is everything—comfort, safety, home. I've been basically alone since Mom died. I know Cat loves me, and we had each other, but it's not the same as having someone you can lean on. I have Janiya, who's a true and loyal friend, but she's not here. This makes me realize how barren my life has been. I have money. And I've been busy, sure. I have my music, which has probably saved me. But this… this is…love.

I squeeze my eyes shut, indulging in the luxurious feeling of being held and cared for. But self-pity isn't productive. I give in to the moment of feeling sorry for myself then suck in a big breath and lift my head. "Thanks." I smile up at him.

It's almost time to go get Cat from school.

I'm in the elevator descending to the parking garage when it stops on the seventh floor. The doors open, and Lilly steps in.

"Hi!" Her face lights up seeing me. "How are you?"

"Good!" I force a big smile. "You?"

"Still recovering." She pushes the button for the lobby. "That was such a fun trip, though."

"It really was."

She glances at me, as if sensing my lack of real enthusiasm.

"Do you and Easton live together?" I ask.

"No. I live a few blocks away. I just brought Otis home. That's his dog."

"Ah."

I know she runs a doggy daycare, which sounds like just about the best job in the world. I've never had a dog, but I love them. "Are you hiring?" I ask half-jokingly. "I might need a job."

She tilts her head. "I do need help. We've been growing really fast."

I purse my lips. "Hmmm."

She knows I don't work, and I know the others assume I'm some kind of spoiled socialite. Which I guess I am.

We arrive at the ground floor and the doors open. Right in the middle of this. We both look at each other.

"Is everything okay?" she asks with a little groove between her eyebrows.

Emotion clogs my throat and I can't answer. I give a quick nod.

She reaches out and squeeze my arm. "I'm here if you need to talk. And if you seriously need a job."

I nod again. Another good person. "I'm just on my way to pick up my sister at school."

"Come over tonight? Sara's coming to help me plan a charity event we're doing. Paws for a Cause."

A smile trembles on my lips. "I love that. I don't want to interfere."

"Not at all! I'll text you my address."

"Okay. Sounds good." I pause. "Thank you."

Why on earth did I blurt out that impulsive question? I probably make as much money busking as I would working at a doggie daycare if I kept the money. Ugh.

I've spilled my guts to Lilly and Sara. I tell them I asked Owen to be my pretend date to get my ex off my back. And I tell them my stepfather owns the team. That renders them speechless for several minutes.

"Holy shit," Lilly eventually says.

They eye me cautiously.

"I know," I say with a sigh. I tell them about my relationship with Vince, and Cat, then my short relationship with Roman and what's happened.

They're amazed and angry on my behalf.

"Your stepfather can't tell you who to marry!" Sara says. "Who does he think you are? Daphne effing Bridgerton?"

We all burst out laughing.

"I love that show!" Lilly says.

"And the books!" I agree. "And you're absolutely right." I try to explain how forceful both Roman and Vince can be when they want something, but not knowing them, they don't get it.

"We did meet Mr. D'Agostino at the holiday party," Sara says. "But briefly, and we didn't exactly talk a lot."

"Apparently, the guys are afraid of him," Lilly says with a quick apologetic look at me.

I hold up my hands. "You can talk freely about him to me."

"I'm exaggerating," she replies. "But they know who's in charge and he is definitely in charge." She sighs. "Wow, this is...messy."

"I worry about what he might do to Owen," I confess in a thin voice.

"Oh, shit." Lilly looks stricken. "He won't do anything to him. He can't."

"But you just said he's in charge."

"He is, but he can't just trade a player for no good reason. There's a lot of money on the line. They need to make the playoffs—it means more money for the team. And they need Owen."

"That's true," Kate says confidently. "No team owner would mess around with a good team right now. Trades might happen for teams who are out of the playoffs or for teams who need help for a deep playoff run. The Bears do not need to make any changes to the roster. It would be plain stupid."

She knows what she's talking about. I've learned that Kate is super knowledgeable about the sport, which makes sense since she's an agent. I trust what she's saying.

"Not to mention the optics," she continues. "The team owner trading away a good player right before the playoffs start just because he's dating the owner's daughter? That would be a huge public relations disaster."

I nod. "Vince does care about appearances." I'm feeling somewhat better about the situation. "Thanks for explaining that to me."

Kate smiles.

"Anyway," Lilly says. "You can totally have a job at Walk 'n Wag if you want."

"Thank you. I may take you up on that. There's not much I'm qualified to do, but I love dogs. But I haven't given up trying to convince Vince that I should move back in for Cat's sake. I mean, he doesn't want to spend much time with her. He's going to have to take her to swimming and gymnastics. She wants to become a vegetarian! *He* won't make sure she's eating right." My spirits sink at that thought. "I still think this is ridiculously harsh." I bite my lip. "I worry that Roman is holding something over him."

They look back at me blankly.

"He's probably just angry," Sara says. "Because he's not getting what he wants. Maybe he'll get over it."

"Yes." I sigh.

Kate purses her lips. "I don't like to repeat rumors. I usually never do. But I did hear someone...credible...talking about the Bears having unhappy creditors."

My eyes widen. "Oh wow." That's not good. If the Bears owe a lot of money to other businesses and they can't pay it...what does that mean for the team? For Vince? "Well, I'm going to talk to Vince about it all. Maybe if I talk to him on a business level, he'll listen."

"Let's talk about the charity event," Sara says. "We could use help with that, too, if you're interested. It's just a volunteer thing, obviously."

"Of course. I'd love to help. What are you raising money for?"

"The animal shelter where I used to volunteer," Lilly answer. "We're still in the early stages. We haven't even decided exactly what we want to do. We're thinking of a dog walk, or maybe a dog wash."

"There are a lot of dog walks," Sara says. "I think we should do something different."

"If we knew a photographer willing to donate his time, we could do photo shoots," Lilly adds.

"What about Keaton? The photographer for the Bears," she adds for my benefit. "He might do it."

"Great idea!" Lilly taps something into the laptop computer she has on her knees.

"What about a pet fashion show?" I offer. "You could charge a fee to enter, and people could walk their dogs down a runway, wearing their cutest outfit."

"I love that! I bet Layla could help with getting a catwalk for us. We'd need a big space. Maybe we could get a permit for Central Park?"

We continue throwing out ideas. We do some quick research online about permits and costs and estimates of what we think we could make.

This is fun, and for a while I've forgotten my problems. And I realize things like this have been missing from my life—having friends to talk to and having fun.

OWEN

Since Lilly, Sara, and Emerie are together at Lilly's place, Millsy, Hellsy, and I gather in my apartment to watch Olympics. I offer them a beer, but I've returned to my teetotalling ways. My liver needs to recover from that holiday.

"Emerie's over at Lilly's?" Millsy asks, taking his beer from me.

"Yeah." I rub my face.

"What's wrong?"

"Nothing's wrong."

"Ha. You look like your dog just died."

"I don't have a dog."

"Okay, you look like I'd look if Otis died," Millsy says. He loves that dog. "What's going on?"

"Emerie moved in here."

"Holy shit. That was fast."

"Fuck," I mutter. I press the heels of my hands to my eye sockets. "You guys don't know who Emerie is, do you?"

"Uh...your girlfriend?"

My gut clenches. "She's Vince D'Agostino's stepdaughter."

Silence descends heavily around us.

"Whoa," Hellsy says.

"What the hell?" Millsy leans forward, frowning. "Why didn't you tell us that?"

"It's a long story." I sigh.

"Jesus Christ!" Hellsy yells. "You're dating the owner's daughter? And you didn't tell us?"

"Stepdaughter," I correct again. "I didn't know who she was when things started. Their name is different. They're also...not close."

"Why didn't you tell us?" Millsy demands again.

Do I tell him the whole crazy story? Do I tell him about Roman Moretti? That this wasn't supposed to turn into an actual relationship? "Part of it was that I didn't want you all to treat her any differently," I say, knowing it sounds lame.

"Now I'm trying to remember if we talked about Mr. D on the trip," Millsy says. "Shit, Cookie, you could've told us."

"Nobody said anything about him," I assure him.

"So what's the deal?"

"Okay. Fine." I sigh. "Emerie and Mr. D are kind of having a disagreement. He wants her to get back with her ex-boyfriend. Apparently, the ex is the son of a friend of his, and he didn't take the breakup well. Emerie's adamant that they're done." I pause. "She thinks there's money involved."

"That's kind of archaic," Millsy says.

"Right? It's fucked up. He's really pushing this guy onto her."

"He can't force her to date him."

"I wouldn't put it past him," Hellsy puts in.

Millsy makes a face.

"Emerie and I started seeing each other just to get Mr. D to stop trying to fix them up again. And to get Roman Fuckface to leave her alone. That was why I didn't tell you who she was. I didn't think she'd really be around you guys much. But..." I stop.

"You fell for her," Millsy finishes.

I don't want to admit it. "We did have fun together, especially in Aruba."

"Fun," Hellsy says. "I thought we were going to have to drag you out of your room. I bet you were having 'fun.'"

We definitely were.

I go on. "When we got back from Aruba yesterday, he locked her out of their apartment."

They stare at me. "Holy shit. Why?"

"Because she's with me." I gaze glumly at the floor.

"Jesus, he's nuts," Millsy mutters. "I thought he was a decent guy."

"Too much money." Hellsy shakes his head. "It changes people."

"Not us," I object.

"Hey. We get paid well. But I bet we're nowhere near Mr. D'Agostino's level of rich. None of us will be buying a hockey team anytime soon."

"We should totally do that," Millsy says.

We laugh.

"No, really. Why not? A bunch of us could go together."

"And buy the Bears?" I hoist an eyebrow.

"Not necessarily the Bears. I don't mean right this minute. Or even this year. But in the future. We have to do something when we retire."

"I dunno, dude. I think teams cost a lot more than we can afford. They just paid over six hundred million for the expansion team in Quebec."

Millsy chokes. "Holy shit. I didn't realize it was that much."

"We'd need about six hundred guys to chip in," Hellsy jokes.

"Mr. D must have a ton of cash," Millsy says.

"Or a ton of debt," I point out. Then I stop. I frown. What does Mr. D get for marrying off Emerie to Moretti? Emerie said there was money involved. Why? Isn't he already rich as fuck?

"Okay. Backtracking," Hellsy says. "So Emerie's staying here."

"Yeah. I can't let her be homeless." Or let Moretti stalk her.

"Mr. D ain't gonna be happy about that."

He's not wrong.

"What are you going to do?" Millsy asks.

"She wants to talk to him and try to convince him he needs her to look after her little sister."

"Does he?"

I squint. "Well. Her sister's twelve. Not a baby. I kind of have a feeling that Emerie needs to look after Cat more than Cat needs to be looked after."

"Codependent," Hellsy says.

I shoot him a surprised glance. "Yeah."

"Kind of like you and hockey," Millsy adds.

I frown. "What?"

"You're so involved with hockey you have no time for anything else in your life."

"Sure, I do. You guys are sitting here right now."

Hellsy nods slowly. "True. And you came on that trip with us and actually let your hair down."

"Because of Emerie," Millsy points out. "But usually we can't get you to come out with us. You're too busy watching hockey. Reading about hockey. Practicing hockey."

"That's not codependent," Hellsy says. "That's more like addiction."

I bolt upright, my hands curling into fists. "What the fuck?"

They all give me a weird look.

My heart is thudding. I try to calm down. "What are you saying?"

"I'm saying, there's more to life than hockey."

My heart's going to bust out of my chest. Jesus. "I know that."

But do I? I was the same as Emerie when we were sitting on that plane. She was in tears about leaving Cat behind, and I was antsy about taking a week off from training and skating.

Huh.

"So you think Emerie's co-dependent?" Hellsy says.

"I don't know. I don't know if it's at the point where it's unhealthy, but Emerie's really attached to Cat. I can't help but think it might be good for Cat to be more independent. And for Emerie to have more of a life."

"Twelve's not that old," Millsy points out.

"True. What do I know?" I throw my hands up. "I just want to support Emerie. I want to go punch Moretti in the face. And Mr. D too."

"Don't do that."

I blow out a breath. "I know."

"You got any better snacks than flax crackers and kale chips?" Millsy asks.

"Nope."

He sighs heavily.

"Okay, that is insane." Hellsy points at the TV where figure skating is now airing. "She let him throw her up in the air, trusting that he's going to catch her."

"He did catch her." Millsy shrugs.

"But what if he didn't? Holy shit."

We watch more.

"Her face is right in his junk," Millsy comments a few second later on a lift the couple is doing, the girl upside down.

"It is." I say. Then, "Okay, I don't think that's safe." Now they're doing some move where the guy is totally supporting the woman and they're both spinning. "How are they going to get out of that without someone losing an ear?"

They shake their heads.

"Remember when we had a figure skating teacher come work with us when we played for the Warriors?" Hellsey asks Millsy.

He laughs. "We could not keep up with her."

"True." Hellsy nods. "They make it look easy because they train so hard. It's not that easy."

The couple on TV does what the announcers term a "death spiral."

"Appropriate name," I say. "Look at that! Her head is touching the ice!"

"Not many sports are played to music," Hellsy muses.

"I don't understand the judging," I add. "I kind of like games where you score a goal and it's totally objective."

"Well, not always," Millsy points out. "That last goal we had reviewed was not objective.'"

"It was bullshit," Hellsy adds.

"Well, *most* of the time it's objective. I like things logical. Black and white."

"Nothing's black and white, man," Hellsy says, giving me a sympathetic look. "Get used to it."

I swallow my sigh, still pondering his comments about my commitment to hockey. Commitment. *Not* addiction, for Chrissake. I'm not like my brother.

We're watching TV the next might when Emerie's phone rings. She picks it up. "Huh. Klara." She answers the call. "Hi!"

I can hear Klara's voice but not exactly what she's saying.

"She what?" Emerie says, shooting upright. "Oh my God!"

I watch her more closely.

"Is she okay?"

I frown.

"Oh my God. I'll be right over." She ends the call and turns to me, her eyebrows drawn together.

"What's going on?"

"Cat's at Klara's. She ran away from home."

20

OWEN

"She doesn't know where you live," Emerie continues. She closes her eyes. "Shit."

"She's okay?"

"She's safe. Obviously she's not okay, since she ran away from home."

"True. Damn. Okay, let's go."

"You don't have to come with me."

"Of course I'm coming with you." I stand.

"Thank you." She looks like she's going to cry but grabs her purse. We pull on our jackets and ride the elevator down to the parking garage.

"Where are we going?" I ask once we're on 72nd street.

She gives me Klara's address in Harlem. Her hands curl into fists. "I'm getting more and more angry at Vince."

"I see that. It's okay. We'll get Cat. She'll be okay."

She nods and exhales sharply. "But then what?" She pauses. "I should report him to ACS."

I don't think that'll fly at this point, claiming Cat's being abused or neglected, but I feel it's wiser to not say that.

When we get there, Emerie lets me go with her into the apartment building. An older woman with bright orange hair answers the apartment door, her face drawn into lines of concern. "Hi, Emmie."

"Klara. Hi." Emerie hugs her, and I see Cat hanging back in a doorway. I lift my hand at her and wave, and she gives me a tentative smile.

Then Emerie rushes over to Cat and hugs her, too.

"Hi. I'm Klara." The woman extends a hand to me.

I shake it and smile. "Nice to meet you,"

She casts Cat and Emerie a worried glance and bites her lip.

"You shouldn't have run away," Emerie says to Cat. "What were you thinking?"

"I don't want to live with Dad anymore," Cat says tearfully. "Not if you're not there."

Emerie winces. "I'm sorry," she whispers to Cat.

"I wanted to come to you, but I didn't know where Owen lives."

I see the pain flash over Emerie's face. "I'm so sorry, sweetie."

"Can we go there?" Cat asks, glancing at me.

"We should take you home," Emerie says gently.

"No! I don't want to go home!" The agitation in her voice has Emerie instantly trying to soothe her.

"Okay, honey, we won't go there tonight. But you have to go back tomorrow."

"I don't want to!" Her small face reddens as she tries not to cry.

"Is it okay if we spend the night at your place?" Emerie asks me.

"Of course."

Emerie straightens. "Thank you, Klara. I'm sorry about this."

"Don't apologize!" Klara smiles and hugs Emerie. I can see genuine concern and affection on her face, and I feel glad that Emerie and Cat have had someone like this in their lives. "I'm glad she came here, where she's safe."

Cat has a big backpack that appears stuffed full. I lift it and sling it over my shoulder. "Okay, ladies. Let's make like a banana and split."

That earns me a faint smile from Cat.

"If you need me, I'm here," Klara says as we leave.

We make the return drive home mostly in silence. I can feel the energy flowing off Emerie, but I'm not sure if it's anger or relief or something else.

In my apartment, we take Cat's things to my office, which has a bed for guests. Luckily the room's a good size and even with all Emerie's boxes, there's room for Cat. I leave them there, saying, "I'll let you two talk."

Emerie shoots me a grateful glance, and I gently close the door.

Rubbing my face, I trudge to the living room and turn on the TV. I can hear voices from the bedroom but not what they're saying. What would I say, in Emerie's place? I know nothing about kids. You assume when someone has money that their needs are being met. Obviously not.

I remember watching that movie on the plane and talking to Emerie about the hierarchy. Cat obviously didn't feel safe or secure at home despite the luxurious surroundings. I rub my aching jaw and try to relax it.

Not only is Vince pissed that I'm dating his stepdaughter, but I'm now harboring his daughter. I am so fucked.

Emerie emerges a while later, closing the door behind her. She walks over and sits next to me. "She's getting ready for bed."

"What did she tell Vince?"

"She snuck out and left him a note. She said if I wasn't living there, she didn't want to either."

I bite back a smile. "Good for her."

"No! It's not good!" Then she sighs. "Okay, I'm glad she wants to be with me, but...he's her dad. She has to go back."

"She doesn't want to."

"What time do we need to get Cat to school?"

We figure out a plan.

"I'll sleep with her tonight," she says softly, meeting my eyes.

"Yeah. Sure." Not ideal, but I get why. "Did you call your stepfather?"

"Yeah. He hadn't even found the note yet. I would have liked for him to worry a bit. It might have been good for him." She purses her lips. "I told him where we are."

"Oh."

She meets my eyes. "I'm sorry."

"At this point, it is what it is."

"What does that mean?"

"Let's talk about it in the morning."

She studies my face, nods, then kisses me, which as always turns longer and hotter and...I wrap my arms around her and devour her taste, trying to fill myself with it, since I won't have her in my bed. We both pull apart breathing heavily, her eyes glazed. She smiles and touches my cheek. "I'm sorry about this. Good night."

"Night, beautiful."

I watch TV a while longer, then head to bed. Alone. For the first time in weeks. And goddammit, I miss Emerie.

Fucking bizarre. I never wanted to get involved with anyone during the season because it would be distracting. And this is exactly why. I've seen Millsy and Hellsy and Morrie go through this. Relationships aren't a straight line to happiness. They're a fucking roller coaster. Up. Down. Spin around. I don't have time for that.

We need to get this shit figured out and back to normal before we start playing again. Which is only two days away.

What that looks like...I have no clue.

I lay awake for a long time, thinking about that.

Cat shows up first in my little kitchen. "Good morning."

I can't be annoyed about her being here. She's a kid. Her eyes are heavy and pink, and her lips sag. My heart clenches with sympathy. "Morning. How did you sleep?"

"Eh." She makes a face. "The bed is nice. And I'm glad I'm with Emerie. But it was hard to sleep."

"Same here. Want some breakfast?"

"I guess so."

"I have bread for toast. Granola and Greek yogurt. Or I can make you one of these." I hold up my smoothie.

"No FrootyOs?"

I laugh. "No. Those will kill you, kid."

She eyes me. "That's what Em says. I'll have some yogurt, please."

I open the fridge and find it. "I have berries." I hold up a container. "Or granola. Or both."

"I'll take both."

We get her set up with a delicious and nutritious bowl.

"Want coffee?" I ask.

"Okay."

"I was kidding. You don't really drink coffee, do you?"

"No."

I laugh. "What's your first class of the day?"

"Math. I love math."

"Huh. Good for you. If you love math, you can do anything."

She gives me a skeptical look. "Even play hockey?"

I grin. "Do you want to play hockey?"

"No. I suck at sports."

"Well, at least you didn't say you can't play hockey because you're a girl. Because girls can totally play hockey."

"I like watching it." She scoops up some yogurt.

Emerie strolls out then, dressed in jeans and a black sweater that hugs her curves. Her hair's on top of her head in a messy bun and she's wearing her glasses, which I discovered are real on the trip, although she has several pairs. I like these ones—big, roundish clear plastic frames.

"Oh, you're eating," she says on seeing Cat's bowl. She looks at me. "Thank you."

I nod. "Coffee?"

"Yes, please."

I know she doesn't eat breakfast but has to have her coffee with lots of sugar and real cream. Things I don't usually have, but which I now keep on hand. She gratefully accepts the big mug from me and takes a mouthful.

"Do you like math, Owen?" Cat asks me.

"Yeah, actually I do."

"Cool." She finishes her yogurt and jumps off the stool at the counter. Without asking, she locates the dishwasher and places her bowl and spoon inside. Good kid.

"Are you ready?" Emerie asks her.

"I don't want to go to school today."

Yikes. I remember Emerie telling me about when Cat was little and refused to go to school because of her anxiety. Jesus, I hope this isn't triggering more problems for her. I meet Emerie's eyes and see the hint of worry there.

But she smiles sympathetically. "I know. But there's no reason not to. Owen's going to drive us this morning."

Cat pouts, then shrugs. "Okay."

Whew. "Let's scat, alley cat." I say.

Emerie directs me over to the west side, and we make the drop off.

"Now what?" I ask.

"We're going over to Vince's. I mean, I'm going over to Vince's. I've had enough of this. Cat's unhappy. I have to do something." Her chin sets with determination.

I put the SUV in gear and say nothing. She's not going alone, but we'll argue about that when we get there.

I navigate the old, narrow streets full of delivery vehicles and other traffic and park near the apartment building. When I get out, she pauses. "You can wait here."

"Nope." I shut my door and round the vehicle to hold hers. She slides out, her gaze fastened on my face. I squeeze her hand. "I'm coming with you."

"No." Her eyes widen. "You can't."

"I can. I am." I brush my mouth over hers. "I'm doing this. Don't argue."

"Owen…" Her eyebrows slant downward, her look pleading. "I'll be fine."

"I know you will. You have totally got this."

One corner of her mouth kicks up.

"I'm only here for backup. Let's go."

We enter the building, and she breezes right past the doormen.

"Uh, Ms. Ross…wait. You can't—"

"Change of plans, Anthony!" She waves at him and steps into the elevator.

I follow. The doors slide closed. "How are you going to get in?"

She holds up a key, a nefarious look on her face. "This."

I realize what she's done. "That's Cat's."

"Yep."

I grin.

We enter the big apartment. It's quiet, and Emerie pauses in the foyer then lifts her chin. She walks down the hall and pauses at an open door. "Hi, Vince."

I'm standing behind her so he can't see me.

"What the hell…how did you get in?"

"Never mind. We need to talk."

"Fine."

He didn't even ask about Cat. Motherfucker. Heat runs through my veins and my jaw clenches.

Emerie is amazingly calm. She walks farther into the room, which I guess is Vince's home office. For now, I stay out of sight.

"Cat was so unhappy she ran away," Emerie says, her tone gentle and compassionate. "Don't you care about that?"

"Of course I do."

"You need to let me move back in," she continues quietly but firmly. "I'm the one who looks after her. What is your plan for school and homework and activities? I know Klara helps, but she can't do all that."

"It's handled."

Emerie says nothing for a moment and my heart squeezes. He's telling her they don't need her. That must hurt.

"Why are you doing this?" Her voice contains genuine curiosity. "This seems excessive. I know you want me and Roman to get back together, but I've told you…it's not happening."

For long seconds, he's silent. "You'll feel differently about that when Owen Cooke is gone."

I freeze. *When* I'm gone. Not *if* I'm gone. Jesus Christ. I press my hand to my forehead.

Another pause. I wish I could see them.

"You won't do that," Emerie says, but I pick up the faint tremor in her voice.

"Why not? Hockey players are expendable. There are all kinds of players waiting to get their break in the NHL."

He's not wrong. Still, that burns. Sweat breaks out under my arms.

"He's a good player, Vince. And a good man. He's an important part of this team. Would you really mess that up and hurt the team because of this? Why?" She pauses. "Is it because of money?"

He doesn't answer that question, saying, "You have an inflated sense of his worth. Did that come from him?"

I narrow my eyes, hands curled into fists.

"It's reality," Emerie says. She sounds so confident, I'm impressed. "And I'm sure Brad Julian would tell you that, too."

"Sure." Vince's tone is dismissive. "But *I'm* in charge."

"What would convince you? Not making the playoffs?"

"We will make the playoffs."

"Maybe? Maybe not. By then it's too late to fix it. You're out until next year. The playoffs are a big source of revenue for the team and the league. You can't take a chance on that."

Wow. She's done some homework.

"You can't do it, Vince. If this gets out…it's really bad PR. The league wouldn't be impressed at all. Remember all those times we went to the commissioner's place for dinner?"

She fucking knows the commissioner of the league?

I swipe sweat off my brow.

"You're not going to tell him," Vince says. "Don't be ridiculous."

"I will." Her voice is clear. "You already know I don't care what people say about me. I'll tell this whole vile story. The league has enough issues right now with inconsistent reffing, and a player accused of revenge porn."

Yikes. She knows about that? Not our team, but still a big embarrassment for the league. Has she been studying? I can't help the little smile that tugs my lips. My little hockey nerd in training.

"The last thing they need is a scandal about a player being benched or traded because the owner's pissed that the player is dating his stepdaughter."

Silence vibrates in the apartment.

She's got him. I sense he's paying attention.

I'm here for backup, but she doesn't need me. She really does have this. I'm so proud of her I could burst. Some of the tension eases out of me, my smile broadening.

"I want Cat happy. I want her cared for. And I want you to leave Owen alone. You can lock me out. Fine. I'll survive. Just don't hurt them."

Holy shit. Pride swells up huge inside me. She's fucking amazing.

She appears in the doorway, jerks her head to the front door, and leads the way out. She pauses in front of the French doors to the living room, staring in.

I follow her gaze.

"My piano," she whispers.

She loves that piano.

She pulls in a quick breath, lifts her chin, and walks to the door.

21

EMERIE

Vince isn't backing down.

I'm homeless. And family-less.

Cat's the only family I have now, and I've lost her.

Okay, I know that's over the top. She's not lost. But that's how I feel right now.

Owen takes me home. I mean, to his place. I'm trying not to cry, but he keeps shooting me concerned glances as he drives.

Up in the apartment, I drop my purse and sink down onto the sectional. I stare across the room.

He sits next to me, curls his arm around my shoulders, and hugs me.

"I don't know what else to do," I whisper. "She ran away from home to be with me. What do I tell her?"

"Are you really asking my advice?"

One corner of my mouth lifts as I look at him. "I appreciate you asking that and not jumping in to try to fix everything."

"I want to."

"Thank you." I touch his cheek. "But I need to deal with it."

"You were amazing back there."

"I didn't get what I want."

"You stood up for yourself. And for Cat. And for me." He presses his lips to my temple. "You're strong. You can handle this. You can handle anything."

I'm not so sure of that. But him telling me that helps.

"And I'm here for you," he adds.

My heart expands and I turn into his embrace. "Thank you."

I can't think straight. I can't put a coherent thought together to make a plan. I'm trembling, and Owen's big hands stroking my back feel so good.

"How about a bath?" he asks.

I lift my head. "A sex bath?"

He grins. "No. Not this time. A bath by yourself. With those bath salts I got you."

"I love those bath salts. Okay."

"I'll go run the water for you."

What a sweetheart. Him being so nice to me is making me even more emotional. A nice soak in the tub should help. I do some of my best thinking there.

The bathroom smells amazing when I walk in, scented steam filling the air. He's lit the big candles I set on the shelf and laid out fresh, fluffy towels. I look at him, and so much feeling fills me, over-flowing, and the words almost slip from my lips. *I love you.* But I don't say them.

"Thank you," I whisper.

He smooches my lips and leaves me alone in the bathroom. I undress and slip into the hot water. My body softens at the volup-tuous pleasure. I close my eyes. I can't do anything right this minute, so I may as well just give in to this.

In the silence, my mind eventually quiets, too.

I'll talk to Cat after school. I'll have to be honest with her. I dread how that could go. Last night she was so upset, and I don't want to see her like that again. It fucking killed me.

I can't ask her to move in here. This is Owen's home. I don't have a home of my own to take her into. But I guess that has to be my next step. Finding a home of my own.

Oh God. How hard is *that* going to be in Manhattan? Especially with no steady source of income.

I take a few deep breaths to push back the panic brewing. I can do it. I can do anything. Owen says so.

Cat should stay with Vince. She has a beautiful home there. Vince has the money to give her whatever she needs, including people to look after her. And legally? Well, I doubt I have any legal rights to Cat. I need to shut down that idea right now. I can't fight Vince on that.

What *can* I do? I can make sure Cat knows she's loved and valued. I'll do that any way I can.

I settle deeper into the water with a new sense of resolve. I'm not giving up. I'm accepting the reality of this situation and determined to make the best of it.

I sit in Owen's empty apartment and look around. He's off skating with the guys. I'm alone. I don't usually busk on weekends, but I guess I could now.

I sigh.

I miss Cat.

A heaviness has settled inside me. What am I feeling? I'm a little sad, yes, but it's more than that. I feel…lost.

I don't know who I am anymore.

I'm trying to take care of Owen and not be in his way, but it doesn't quite give me the same sense of purpose that looking after Cat did.

I've been trying to get hold of Vince, but he's not taking my calls and I haven't been able to see him. I attempted to go up to the apartment with Cat after school one day and got stopped by the doormen, who have their orders. They looked embarrassed but still wouldn't let me up.

I've helped Cat with homework over video chat and talked to her on the phone for an hour one day "about a boy." I'm trying to stay upbeat, but right now…I'm lost.

I wander over to the window and gaze out. The sky is overcast, a low mist hanging in the air. That doesn't help my mood.

I have to do something.

Music. Music always saves me.

I get my guitar and sit down to start playing. Music comes to me. I think about Owen and how happy he makes me. I think about feeling lost. I think about finding a new me. Another me. No, another *part* of me.

Who do I want to be?

I write a whole song and sprawl back into the chair, happy, energized, satisfied.

Then I get out my computer and fire it up. Nash keeps telling me I should start a Soundcloud account. He says I could make more money. I've never been motivated by the money, but maybe now I should think about it.

I type and click and scroll, going to the "For Creators" page, taking in information about it. Okay, I can set up a profile. That's easy.

I watch a tutorial video. Do I really want to put my music out there in the world for anyone to listen to? It's scary.

I read about monetizing. My fingers still, and I gaze at the screen, my stomach tightening. I don't know anything about this.

But I can learn.

OWEN

Over the next couple of weeks, Emerie and I evolve into a new routine. Except it's not the same as my usual routine. For one thing, I'm still on a break from hockey. And for another thing, Emerie's here, and that's distracting.

On the other hand, being distracted by her is pretty damn fun. Especially in bed. And in the shower. And hell, in the living room on the couch.

I help her go through some of her things and pull out her music. She has another guitar, a bigger one than the one she carries around busking. I watch her lovingly stroke the sleek curves of it. I want her to play for me.

She wants some of her other things out—candles, books. I hold up a a stone sculpture and study it. My eyes widen. "Whoa. What is this?"

The couple appear to be having doggy style sex.

Emerie laughs. "Oh! Janiya sent me that from India. It's an erotic sculpture from a temple there."

I study it. "Okay."

"The carvings are supposedly good luck and she thought it would bring me good sexual luck. And hey—it worked!"

I laugh.

"I'll put it next to your bed." She takes it from me.

"If I get any luckier sexually, I'll probably have a heart attack."

"Ha. But I'm glad you feel lucky. I do, too." She gives me a cheeky grin.

I still go skate with the guys and work out. I convince Emerie to eat my quinoa with roasted carrots and grilled chicken and to try my super protein smoothies. She convinces me to order pizza. Once.

When I get home, she has dinner ready for me. She even made one of my favorite recipes—spicy chicken skewers with black bean salsa. She picks up food and does my laundry, even though I tell her she doesn't have to do that. So I drive her when she has to take Cat to gymnastics or talk to one of the teachers at her school, and knowing she loves baths, I run her baths in the big tub and fill it with these tension-reducing, relaxing bath salts I picked up for her one day that smell fantastic.

One night we go out for dinner to a new restaurant with Morrie and Kate, and another night we go play Skee-Ball with Millsy and Lilly, Hellsy and Sara.

And we watch our countries' hockey teams compete against each other in the Olympics. Luckily, this doesn't make us hate each other.

And she busks. I worry about her, but I know that music is important to her. I feel the same about hockey. So, I support her

One night, she plays her guitar and sings for me. She played this song in the subway once when I was listening. I remember the line: *And suddenly...all my love songs are about you.*

I watch her face while she sings and our eyes meet, and I fucking love that she's singing to me. Just me. Maybe even about me.

"I still can't believe you write these songs," I say. "You blow me away, Em."

"Thank you." She pauses. "Lilly offered me a job."

I blink. "Doing what?"

"Dog walking. Or helping in the day care."

"Huh. Do you want to do that?"

"It would be fun. But honestly, on a good day busking, I can probably make more money. I do love dogs, though."

"I like dogs, too. Just never had time for one."

"Yeah. It would be hard when you travel so much."

I grin. "That's what Lilly's for."

"I went to the animal shelter she used to work at. The one we're planning the dog fashion show for?"

I nod.

"So many cute dogs waiting to be adopted! I wanted to bring them all home."

"I guess Mr. D wouldn't go for a dog."

"God, no." She makes a face.

I want to get her a dog.

What the fuck am I thinking? If *this* has disrupted my schedule, a dog sure as hell would. I can't get a dog.

Tomorrow we get back to regular practices, and our first game is the day after that. I don't know how this is going to work with my regular schedule. Things have been going okay. In fact, I'm kind of happy she's here. Maybe we can make this work without interfering with my game.

22

OWEN

Back to the usual routine. The break is over.

I've gotten used to waking up with Emerie in my bed. The day of my first practice, we get up at the same time, which means some shuffling in the bathroom to get ready. I got used to having her around, but I'm not used to sharing my bathroom when I'm getting ready to go to practice, and she has a lot of shit spread out along the vanity. It flusters me, being bumped out of my groove.

She guzzles her morning coffee while I whip up a smoothie in the blender. Again, having someone else in the small kitchen at the same time is a bit of a pain.

"Do you want my Land Rover to take Cat to school?" I ask. "Hellsy is driving us to practice today."

She purses her lips. "That's okay. I'm still afraid I'm going to smash it up. And some days you'll need it when it's your turn to drive."

"Okay."

She leaves first to go take Cat to school, and I spend a few minutes scrolling through social media and catching up on the hockey blogs and sportscasters I follow for news, reminding myself of what the standings were before the break. Then I'm off with the guys to practice.

The coaches work us hard. I'm feeling it after some time off, even though I've been skating and working out. That week in Aruba distracted me from staying in game shape. Damn.

We start with some O zone drills, which immediately makes me think of Emerie and her dirty little mind. I smile. And miss a pass. Shit!

"Focus, Cooke!" Coach yells.

Right. Focus.

"Go to the net!" Coach shouts at Murph.

I skate hard, shoot the puck, Murph at the net waiting to tip it in. We miss. Circle back. Try again. And again.

I'm soaked with sweat and breathing hard by the time we're done, but I stay on the ice after everyone else has left, practicing one-timers with assistant coach Meknikov.

When I was a kid, I was a good skater, but I couldn't shoot. My dad used to take me to special shooting practices to learn the proper technique. And I practiced. Practiced. Practiced.

I practiced a lot with Eric.

I miss a shot from Coach Meknikov.

Jesus. What is wrong with me?

When my technique got better, I worked on one-timers, and I still do. Goalies are so good these days, you need a fast, hard shot so you don't give them an extra second to prepare by stopping the puck on your stick.

I want the puck on the middle of my blade and lots of torque on my stick. Coach shoots the puck to me but not always *right* to me, making me move fast to get in the right place. My arms and shoulders are aching, but I keep going until I'm satisfied.

"Good work," Coach says as we skate off.

"Thanks. It's hard having that long of a break."

I hit the shower and then meet up with the guys in the player lounge for lunch. We get caught up on what we all did, hearing from Gunner, JBo, and Bergie about the All Star Game and some of the parties they went to.

"The days of Playboy bunnies at the All Star parties are over," JBo says in response to a question about that from Jammer.

"Yeah. Times are changing," Bergie agrees.

"You're saying you didn't go out somewhere after with lots of hot chicks?" Murph says.

"Hell yeah, we did." JBo grins.

I have a phone call scheduled with my agent that afternoon to talk about some endorsements he's working on. I sit in my office, trying to ignore the boxes full of Emerie's belongings stacked along one wall.

"I have a couple of interested companies," he tells me, naming a big sporting goods manufacturer, a men's grooming products company, and a luxury car brand.

"Do I get a car?" I ask, joking.

"We can negotiate that."

I was kidding. But hell, I'd take a car. He goes over the details and says he'll get back to me.

When I end the call, the apartment is silent. Wow. It's been a while since things were this quiet here. I have some bills to pay, so I go online and do that, then I pick up a book I'm reading called "The Mind of a Champion."

I've just settled in when Emerie arrives home. I take one look at her face. "What's wrong?"

Her bottom lip quivers. "Cat doesn't want me to take her to school, or pick her up after, anymore."

I set down my book. So much for reading. "Oh. She *is* twelve."

"I know, but geez! Terrible things can happen! It's a big city! With crime!" She flops down on the sectional beside me.

I smile. "She's growing up."

"I know." She sighs. "She has friends who live nearby, and they walk to school together. She wants to walk with them."

"So what are you going to do?"

"I told her I had to talk to Vince first, but if he was okay with it, I was too. And he is."

"Good."

"But I'll worry about her."

"Of course you will." I caress her cheek with my knuckles. "But she's a smart girl. She'll be fine."

She *will* worry about Cat. And I'm a little worried about Emerie. Not having this duty of taking Cat to and from school is going to be hard on her. First, she's not even living there with Cat anymore, and now Cat doesn't need her for this.

She settles into a brief sulk, then straightens her shoulders. "What are we doing for dinner tonight?"

"I was going to make that squash recipe."

She wrinkles her nose. "Oh."

"Why? What did you want to do?"

"I thought we could go out."

"We have to dial back on that, sweetheart. I'm back to my normal schedule now."

"Right, right. That's okay. I'll help you cook."

"Okay." She's not the best cook, but she's learning.

As I stir the pearl barley into boiling chicken broth, and Emerie cuts up the butternut squash, she says, "I wish a had my piano here."

"Yeah? You miss it?"

"I do. I'm doing more song writing and..." She stops.

"What about your guitar?"

"Yeah. I have that." She focuses on her knife for a moment. "I feel like I have a lot of things to say. Music has always been how I deal with my emotions."

"I can tell you put a lot of emotion into your songs."

I get her grating Parmesan cheese while I slice up a bunch of different kinds of mushrooms.

"Would it be okay if Cat comes over here on Sunday?" she asks.

"Of course."

There goes more of my routine. This Sunday's a day off. I planned to watch a bunch of video. But that's okay.

We slide the baking sheet of cubed squash into the oven to roast, and I heat a pan with olive oil to sauté the garlic, shallots, and then the mushrooms. Emerie stirs the barley, then chops the herbs. Soon we're sitting down to our dinner of grilled chicken with the barley and squash side dish.

"This is really good!" she says.

"It is. And super healthy. Mushrooms are one of the few nonfortified foods to contain vitamin D, which is important for improving muscle efficiency and function."

She nods. "That's what you need." She tilts her head. "Maybe I should start working out."

I grin. "Sure."

"Kate belongs to a gym that she really likes. Maybe I could tag along with her some time. Yeah. I should do that."

"That's a great idea." That would be a good use of her newfound time. Not that I want her out of my way. I just...I have goals. I have to focus on them.

23

EMERIE

I go out with Sara, Lilly and Kate one night. They surprise me by taking me to a little pizza joint for pizza and beers. For some reason, I thought these gorgeous, smart, talented women whose boyfriends are rich, famous athletes would want to go somewhere trendy and upscale, but here we are at a little hole in the wall place with plastic chairs and a wobbly table.

We squeeze around the tiny table, the giant pizza we ordered taking up all the space. It's really good pizza.

I talk to Kate about her gym, and she's enthusiastic about taking me there and introducing me to people. She's very fit—she used to play hockey and clearly stays in great shape.

Then we talk about the fundraiser we're working on—even Kate has been roped into helping. She's good though. While Sara and I have some great ideas, she's very practical and businesslike about making the ideas happen. Or nixing them when they're too out there.

"I can't wait for this," I say. "Seeing dogs on the runway! I wish I had a dog to enter!"

"Well, Otis will definitely be participating." Lilly smiles. "I need to find a great outfit for him to model."

"He is the cutest thing." I've gone for walks with Lilly and Otis a couple of times in the park near us, and I love him.

"So…you're still staying with Owen?" Sara asks.

I lift a piece of pie with delicious melty cheese hanging off it and set it on my plate. "Yes." I sigh.

"What's the sigh for?" Lilly asks.

Oops. "Did I sigh? I didn't know I sighed. Nothing."

They all eye me skeptically.

"Do you miss your sister?" Sara asks sympathetically.

"So much." I make a face. I tell them about her not wanting to be walked to and from school anymore. "I feel like I'm losing her bit by bit. I feel a little—" I stop. Invisible. I feel invisible. Like I did as a teenager.

My stomach clenches hard and I swallow, staring at my pizza. This is always what I've been afraid of. And it's happening.

"All parents must feel like that," Sara says. "As their kids grow up and become more independent. But I'm sorry you miss her."

"I do still see her. She comes over on Sundays and we hang out."

"Owen's okay with that?"

"He's very sweet to her. He bought her mint chocolate chip ice cream, which he would *never* have in his freezer."

They all nod.

"And he bought her a Bears jersey. It's adorable." Then I sigh. "But then he disappears into his office to watch hockey video."

"Are things okay with Owen?" Kate asks.

"I guess." I pick at a string of cheese and lift it to my mouth. "I just feel a little…superfluous." Invisible.

Oh God. It's not just the situation with Cat making me feel this way. It's Owen, too. A cold lump forms in my chest.

"What does that mean?" Sara asks.

"He's really busy." I try to keep my voice steady. "He spends a lot of time watching hockey videos. I mean, a *lot*."

"Apparently he's is quite the hockey nerd," Lilly says. "He knows everything about the game."

"Yes. He does. He also watches a lot of hockey games. And reads about hockey. And sports psychology. He works out a lot." I make a face. "I know hockey's important to him. But we don't do anything else."

Sara's thick eyebrows fly up. "Nothing? Not even the devil's dance?"

For a beat, there's silence and then the other women all collapse into laughter. My tension eases and I have to smile.

"Sara!" Lilly wheezes. "The devil's dance?"

Sara grins. "You know what it is."

"Yes," Kate chokes out. "But come on...that makes it sound evil! Sex is *good*."

"Yes, yes, it is," Sara agrees. "Though I'm still a newbie at it." She shrugs and looks at me. "I was a virgin until I met Josh."

"Oh. Well." I blink at that sharing.

"I don't think you can call yourself a newbie anymore," Lilly says. "It's been a year of nonstop boinking for you two.'"

This has taken the attention off me and Owen. "Sounds like a good year."

"It has been," Sara agrees with a contented smile. "But back to you and Owen. You're not telling us you aren't sleeping together?"

"Uh, no. We're doing that. Definitely. Most of the time he's focused on hockey, but in bed I have to concede he is *very* focused on me." I pause. "I've never been so sexually satisfied in my life."

"Ohhhh." They all make the same happy noise together.

"Nice," Sara says. "Owen's very...big."

"So is Josh," Lilly points out.

"I mean, all our guys are big," Kate says. "They're hockey players."

"True. But Owen's *really* big." Sara eyes me expectantly.

"Yes. He's big," I agree with a demure smile.

"Ah ha." Sara grins.

"The man can melt my panties off me with just a look," I say. "But he doesn't talk to me much. And we don't do anything besides eat the occasional dinner together if it's not game day or he's not on a road trip." That lump in my chest materializes again.

Sara tilts her head. Kate purses her lips. "Is he not happy?"

I consider that. "That's a good question." I suck on my lower lip. "I don't think being that focused on one thing is good for him. It's not that I'm whining because we never go out. It probably sounded like that." I make a face. "I asked him once why he's so dedicated. He told me..." I pause and look at the women. "He had a brother who died. He said he doesn't want to waste the gift he's been given. Like he feels his brother did. But..." I stop again, my mind whirring. "I think it's more than that."

"I didn't know he had a brother," Lilly says quietly. Her forehead creases. "Easton's brother died, too. But I don't think Owen talks about his brother."

"I know. He's never mentioned him again. And he doesn't talk to his parents much either." A thought takes hold. I'll think more on it later. "Anyway, it's not that he seems *un*happy. Just focused on other stuff. Except, in bed, like I said. So I feel conflicted about whether he wants me there or not."

"Oh, trust me, if things are hot in the sack, he wants you there," Lilly says.

"Agree," Sara says.

"I try to stay out of his way," I tell them. "I know hockey's important to him. I know how driven he is to be the best. I don't want to interfere with that. I've caused him enough problems." I roll my eyes.

"You mean with your stepdad," Kate says.

"Yeah."

"He's still with the team," she points out.

"He is. But...he didn't make the All Star team. I can't help but wonder if Vince had something to do with that."

"Oh my God!" Kate stares at me.

Sara and Lilly blink. "Seriously?"

I shrug. "I know Vince doesn't have a say. The fans vote for some players, and the league decides the rest. But he could have influenced them." I bite my lip, then tell them about the showdown at Vince's place and my threats to go to the commissioner of the league if Vince does anything more to Owen.

"Holy shit! You are badass!" Kate picks up her beer mug and holds it up to me in a toast.

I smile wryly. "Thanks."

"You know the commissioner?" Lilly squeaks, eyes huge.

"Oh yeah. I've met him a few times."

"Eeeek. Could you have a word with him about some other things?" she asks.

I laugh, recognizing that she's joking. Sort of. "I need to find a place of my own."

"Um...you could move in with me," Lilly says. "Actually, Easton and I are talking about moving in together. I didn't want to do it too fast, because I...had reasons. Long story. Sometime I'll tell you. Anyway, my apartment is available as my roommate right now. For a couple of months. Then you could have it to yourself or find another roommate."

I nod slowly. "Wow. Thanks. Your apartment is great. I'm not sure if I can afford it."

"I already offered you a job," she says kindly.

"I've been thinking about that. I do have some money, so I'm okay for now. But..." I scrunch up my face briefly. "I like living with Owen. I like *him*."

They study me.

"Are you in love with him?" Lilly asks softly.

"I don't know?" I drop my gaze.

I can't love a hockey player. That doesn't fit with my life.

Of course, my life looks nothing like it did a few months ago.

It's probably not a good idea for me to love anyone. Because they're not going to love me back. Like Vince. Or they'll leave me. Like my dad. My mom. Cat. Well, she didn't leave me, but...same thing.

Even Owen...I feel like he's drifting away. And fuck, that hurts.

He has more important things to focus on than me. I totally understand that. But it still hurts.

I can't fall in love with him.

OWEN

"Cooke. I need a word."

I've just come off the ice. Sitting in the visitors' locker room in St Louis, I look down at my sweaty self, then back up at Mr. Julian.

"After you've showered and changed," he adds.

I look around and meet the eyes of the other guys. I shrug.

"Any trade rumors?" Brando asks, looking around.

"It's still a few weeks to the trade deadline," Jammer replies.

I meet Hellsy's eyes. He knows what I'm thinking.

"There hasn't been a lot of talk about this team," Gunner says. "We've got all the pieces in place for a playoff run already."

Everybody nods.

The worry that I've pushed to the back of my mind leaps to the forefront. My gut tightens, but I strip off my gear and head naked to the showers. Scenarios run through my head as I shampoo and scrub, but I talk myself out of being seriously concerned.

I dress in my jeans and Bears hoodie and find Mr. Julian. We go into an unused media room to talk. He grabs a chair and gestures for me to sit, too.

I wait.

"You're dating Mr. D'Agostino's daughter," he finally says.

Fucking fuck.

His tone is neutral so I'm not sure where we're going with this. "She's his stepdaughter, but yes."

He nods slowly. "Did you think that was a good idea?"

"I didn't know who she was when our relationship started." That is true. "Also, she's a grown woman and has a right to date who she wants to."

"And she didn't know who *you* were?" One eyebrow arches.

"No, she didn't. She hates hockey."

He's silent again. "Is it serious?"

Fuck. What the hell do I say to that? I'm fucking nuts about her. I think she's falling for me too. But serious? "I don't know."

"If it's not serious, you might want to think about how deep into things you get with her."

Ha. My gut tightens. Too damn late for that. "Why is that?" I ask calmly.

He rubs his forehead. "Fuck," he mutters. Then he looks up at me. "Look, I have a good relationship with Vince. I've told him we're not going to make changes to the team that aren't based on building the best team to win the cup."

Our eyes meet, and I understand. Mr. D has asked him to get rid of me.

I know he knows that I know.

"But I can only push so hard," he continues.

I get it. Ice water runs through my veins. "I understand. And I appreciate your support. I certainly don't want to cause problems for you or for anyone else on the team."

"I know you don't." His mouth lifts into a wry smile. "You're a good guy, Owen. We have no right to tell you who you can date. And I don't want to come between a couple in love. Hockey will end. Family and love are all we really have."

I'm surprised at his sentimental take. I've never really thought about that. I've never thought about hockey ending. I've been totally focused on just being the best.

I walk out of the room feeling heavy, my gut churning.

Shit. Fuck. This sucks.

I don't want to cause problems for Mr. Julian. He's been nothing but good to me. He cares about the guys. When we had problems a couple of seasons ago with a bully coach, he listened to us when we approached him. And he made changes. I don't want to play anywhere else. And I feel I owe him better than having the owner of the team putting pressure on him to do something.

I was really hoping this wasn't going to happen.

EMERIE

Owen's been away a whole week on a trip to Dallas, Winnipeg, St. Louis, and Minneapolis. Tonight's the last game of their trip, and I'm so excited that he'll be home tomorrow. Or rather, late tonight. I've missed him so much.

There are only a few games left in the regular season. The Bears are still fighting with Pittsburgh for a playoff spot. That team is hot and talented, and lots of the sports dudes online are saying they'll be in for sure.

The Bears won in overtime in Dallas and lost in Winnipeg and St. Louis, and their chances of a playoff spot seem to be slipping away. Owen's been a little off his game. Not that I can tell, but the TV commentators talk when I watch the games saying he's a step behind, playing sloppy, making mistakes. When I talked to him after the St. Louis game, he was down on himself about a turnover (not the delicious kind) that cost them a goal.

I'm watching the game again tonight, of course. Who would have thought I'd be so invested in a hockey game? I can't believe it myself, but I've become hooked on the excitement, the speed, the skill...I wouldn't say I love it, but...okay, I kind of do.

I'm also invested in them winning. It's such a meaningless thing, really. It's a game. But now I'm a fan, and I want them to win.

I can see the Bears are getting frustrated. They're down three-two with only a couple of minutes left in the game. They've pulled Colton from the net. This always seems so risky to me, but Owen told me that they're losing anyway so why not try it? I guess I understand.

I watch as Minneapolis shoots the puck down the ice. One of the Caribou gets it and goes to our net. The empty net.

"Oh my God," I groan, but then Owen comes flying down the ice, trying to stop the guy from scoring.

It all happens so fast, I'm not even sure what I just saw—Schneider pops the puck into the empty net just as Owen hits him. Schneider goes down and slides into the boards. And he doesn't get up.

Instantly, a mob of players surrounds Owen. I'm staring at the TV, my heart thudding, but I can't see him. I can't see what's happening. The announcers are talking about Schneider still lying on the ice. I cover my mouth with my hands. I hope he's okay.

"What a vicious hit!" an announcer says.

"What!" I shout at the TV. "Owen is not vicious!"

The refs are blowing whistles and trying to get things under control, but everyone's still pushing and shoving. Finally, they separate the players and I can see Owen, his mouthguard hanging out as he yells back at some of the other players. He looks...

I want to throw up. He looks wrecked. He shoves another guy away from him. A linesman is taking him off the ice.

"He'll be gone with a major," the announcer says.

A trainer comes out to help Schneider, still on the ice.

The Bears players follow Owen as the linesman pushes him towards the bench, but he ends up going down the tunnel. The camera moves back to the ice, to one of the Minneapolis Caribou players who's yelling, his face red with anger. Another ref is trying to calm him down.

This is ugly. So ugly. I hate it.

They end up having to take Schneider off the ice on a stretcher. I feel sick watching it. I know hockey can be dangerous, but this is the first time I've seen something like this. It's horrible.

Then the game resumes. I don't know how the players can focus after that. I rub my mouth as I watch. It doesn't matter. The Caribou scored, they're up by two goals, and it's pretty much impossible for the Bears to come back with two goals in the time that's left.

It's like a train wreck I can't look away from. I have to watch the post-game interviews because of course they're talking about the hit. Some of the things the Caribou players are saying are alarming. Frightening, even.

They're talking about how the next time they play the Bears they're going to make Owen pay. They're talking about him person-ally, using words like disgusting and dirty. They're saying he hit Schneider intentionally. That he was *trying* to hurt him.

That's not Owen. Not at all! Oh my God!

25

EMERIE

I listen to the TV guys analyze what happened, and I'm actually yelling at the TV. It's not that I don't care that someone was hurt—I do! I don't want that guy to be injured. But to think that Owen did it on purpose—that's crazy!

I watched it happen, and yeah, it was fast, but he was just trying to stop Schneider from scoring. They're saying he skated all the way from the other end of the rink to hit him, but that's not what happened.

Finally, I have to stop watching. I can't take it anymore. The other players are threatening Owen, the TV guys are saying it was dirty, it was intentional, and he should be suspended. And I just keep seeing that look on Owen's face. I keep thinking about how he must be feeling. And I'm hurting for him.

I pace around the apartment. Owen won't be home until about three in the morning, likely, maybe later. I can't sit still, though, and I sure as hell can't fall asleep. I'm a mess. I'm angry. I'm worried. I'm frustrated. Agitated.

I do get into bed and try to read. I think I doze off for a while. Then I hear Owen come in the door. I clamber out of bed, tangled in the covers, and rush to him, my stomach in more knots than a macrame wall hanging.

He looks destroyed. His face is stiff, his skin flushed. His tie hangs loose around his neck.

I start toward him to hug him.

He shakes his head and holds a hand up. "Just…leave me alone. I'm not in the best mood right now."

"I know. I watched the game. I just want to hug you and make you feel better."

"You can't make me feel better." He tosses his coat over a chair and plods toward the bedroom.

I watch, my fingers twisted together, my eyes hot, my chest aching. I've never in my life hurt so much for another person. It startles me.

I feel so helpless. I can't change things. I can't make things better. I also can't just leave him alone. I pad to the bedroom after him.

Ignoring what he told me, I walk up to him and wrap my arms around him. He's taken off his suit jacket. His body is rigid, vibrating with tension. Heat pours off him, the fabric of his dress shirt damp. I press my face to his chest. He's smells freshly showered but his unique scent as always fills me up.

Slowly, he lifts his arms to hug me back. The vibrating increases, turning to trembling. A raw, tortured sound rises from his chest. I squeeze him tighter. "It's okay," I whisper. "It's okay."

His arms band around me, and we stand like that for a long time. I feel the hard shudders that work through him, the rough noises of repressed sobs. He cups my head and clasps me to him, pressing his face against my hair. I just hold him, tears stinging my own eyes at his pain.

The world narrows to us, in this room, in the darkness. I would do anything to take this pain away. It's unbearable to me that he's suffering like this. A fist squeezes my throat, cutting off my breath, making my lungs burn.

I hold him. It's all I can do.

"I could have killed him." His voice is ragged and raw.

"You didn't."

"I could have. I hurt him. What if I ended his career? What if—"

"He's okay," I interrupt gently. "He wasn't admitted to the hospital. They checked him and released him."

"How do you know that?"

"I was watching all the coverage. That's what they said."

His body is tense, and then he lets out a long exhalation and relaxes slightly. "Oh." He falls silent again. "I didn't do it on purpose."

"I know. I *know*. I knew right away."

"Thank you." He rubs his face against my hair. *"Thank you."*

Owen doesn't go anywhere the next day, just broods and wanders around the apartment. He's been scheduled for an in person hearing tomorrow with the Department of Player Safety. Apparently, this means it could be really bad. Meanwhile, he's suspended

I torment myself by reading the coverage of the incident online.

Schneider has a concussion and won't be playing for a while. Concussions are bad, but I'm relieved that he's not hurt worse, after seeing him taken off on a stretcher. Just thinking that makes me nauseous. I know Owen was torturing himself thinking about how bad it could be.

I even search the rules to find out what a charging penalty is, exactly. I just want to understand. I read the rules and, yes, I guess Owen did deserve a charging penalty. He did travel a fair distance, but I still believe he didn't do that with the intent of hitting the other player. He was trying to stop a goal.

The media gets quotes from other players on the Caribou, who of course say that it was dirty and unnecessary, that Owen didn't even try to play the puck. They talk to Easton, who stands up for Owen, saying, "I've known Cookie for a long time and he is not a dirty player. The last thing he'd ever want to do is hurt someone. There's no way that was intentional. I'm sure he hates that Brent is hurt." Owen's coach even says that he thought the hit was clean and unfortunately Schneider had his head down trying to score the goal.

But it's when I'm reading some of the comments on different fan accounts that I freak out. Not only are the Caribou players calling Owen names, the fans are, and it's way worse.

My mouth drops open in horror as I see people saying they hope the Caribou intentionally injure Owen and lay him out on a stretcher; saying there should be a target on Owen; and then I gasp when I read that "his parents should pay for this, too."

What?

I swallow. I have to tell Owen about this. But I don't want him to read this shit.

It turns out I don't have to tell him, because his dad calls him. He goes into the bedroom to talk to him, and comes out looking even worse. Totally defeated, with a slump to his big shoulders I've never seen.

"What's wrong?" I ask, my stomach tossing. I rub the hem of my sweater back and forth between my fingers.

His jaw looks tight enough to break his teeth. "Someone spray painted my parents' house."

"What? Oh my God."

"They wrote 'Cooke must pay.'"

My eyes spring wide. "Oh no!" I press my hands to my mouth. "Dear God."

"And someone came up to my mom in the grocery store and told her he hopes I get my neck broken." He shakes his head, his mouth a thin line. "What the fuck."

"What is wrong with people? That's nuts!"

"Mom was crying." His voice breaks. "I fucking made her cry."

I frown. "*You* didn't make her cry. Some asshole did."

"It was because of me." He shoves a hand through his hair. "They've been through enough, for Chrissake. They don't deserve this. And it's because of me. Fuck." He sits on the couch, his shoulders slumped.

Oh my God. A dark swirl of pain rips through me.

"I've tried so hard," he continues, head down. "I've worked so hard."

"I know. I know you have." Everything inside me hurts, my chest squeezing painfully. Is this what's driving his need to work so hard at hockey? His brother? He never talks about his brother, other than that night he told me about him. And now he feels like he's let his parents down?

"Tell me about it," I say softly. "About your brother."

He shakes his head.

I rub his back. I don't know what else to say.

He dresses in a suit and tie for his hearing with the Department of Player Safety. He looks so handsome and professional and yet raw and broken. I see how hard he's working to keep his emotions in check.

"Do you want me to come with you?" I ask.

He shakes his head, his jaw tight. "No. It's fine. Mr. Julian will be there." I see the faint wince. Is he worried about letting down Brad Julian, too? "Also a couple of guys from the union and Harlan." His agent.

"Will Vince be there?"

"No."

"Okay, good." I still don't totally trust Vince. What is *he* thinking about what's happened? This sure isn't going to endear Owen to him.

Owen takes the subway to the league headquarters on Sixth Avenue, and I wait at home. I sit with my guitar trying to calm my nerves, but nothing helps. I feel like he's on trial, and I guess he is. He'll get to tell his side of the story, but there are a bunch of other things they'll take into consideration—the injury, what kind of behavior caused the incident, and Owen's past record. Which is spotless. He's never been suspended before, or even fined. He barely gets penalties! This was the first time he ever got a misconduct.

That night we find out they're suspending him for eight games.

"Fuck." He blows out a breath, standing in the living room. "That's fucking bullshit."

"Yeah." I sigh, too.

It could have been worse. His history probably helped. But it feels bad because other players have been involved in incidents that seem worse but had lesser penalties. Owen could appeal it, but he won't.

"I deserve it," he says quietly.

I admire him so much for taking responsibility for what happened. He's never tried to blame someone else or criticized the league. He feels like shit about it, but he owns it.

"Eight games…wow."

"There are only five games left in the regular season," he adds heavily. "So I'll miss the first three game of the playoffs."

"Shit."

That's a huge disadvantage for the Bears. He's just behind team captain Daniel Bergen in goals and assists. Look at me, with all my new hockey knowledge. I'd laugh except nothing seems funny right now.

"Emerie."

I look up at him. "Yeah?"

"You need to leave."

I frown. "What?"

He rubs the back of his neck. "I can't do this."

I still don't get it. "You can't quit hockey."

"I mean, I can't do this." He gestures back and forth between us. "You and me."

My stomach cramps up so sharply I nearly double over. I stare at him. "What are you saying?" I croak.

"We need to end things."

2 6

OWEN

My life is so fucked up right now, I might as well fuck it the rest of the way up.

"*Why?*" Emerie stares at me, her blue eyes wide and hurt.

"Hockey has to come first."

She flinches. Her face tightens, color draining from it.

I look away. I can't look at her. I can't stand what I know I'll see in her face. More disappointment.

She walks over to the window and stares out at the sparkling city lights across the river. The air in the room is thick and heavy. "I know," she finally says quietly. "I know I have to go."

That's not what I expected from her. In a way I'm relieved, but mostly just...hurting. Inside, I'm hollow and frozen.

She disappears into the bedroom. I sink down onto the sectional and bury my face in my hands. Fuck!

This is ripping a hole in my gut. I clench my fists and try to breathe.

I know I have to do this. I'm so messed up. I've tried so hard. I've tried so hard to be the best. And now I've let everyone down. *Everyone.* In the worst way.

I've let down the fans, who are trying to defend me to other fans who now hate my guts. I've let down the team. Mr. Julian had my back today, but fuck, I never wanted to put him in a position like this. I've let down my teammates. Now I can't help them win.

I've let down my parents.

I've tried so hard.

And I've failed. More than just failed. I've imploded spectacularly.

Everything seems impossible right now.

I can't let someone else into my life. I knew I shouldn't get involved in a relationship. I said what I said—hockey has to come first. Always.

My eyes burn, and I rub the heels of my palms into them.

A while later, Emerie emerges from the bedroom with her suitcase and guitar case. Fuck. She's leaving.

"You don't have to leave right his minute," I choke out. "Where are you going?"

"I found a roommate." Her smile is bogus, but she's trying so hard. "Lilly's letting me move in with her. We already talked about it. I knew I had to get my own place."

"Do you need a ride?" Lilly's place is just around the corner, but I feel I have to offer something.

"No." She shakes her head emphatically. "I'm good. I can't take everything right now, but I'll get the rest of my things at some point."

"Any time. I can help."

Her smile is killing me. I want to stab myself in the chest for making her look like that—wounded but brave. "Thanks. Do you want this back?" She holds up the key to my apartment.

I blink. "Uh." I'm stumped by this.

She sets it on the coffee table.

I watch her walk to the door. It's like having one of those bad dreams where I'm so terrified, I'm frozen in place, unable to move. I just want to wake up.

"Thanks for letting me stay here." She opens the door. "And for being so supportive about Cat. And Vince. I know I caused problems for you, and I regret that so, so much."

I want to protest. But yeah, there were problems. I manage to stand, my muscles stiff, shoulders bunched.

And then she destroys me.

Facing me, she says, "I love you, Owen. I believe in you. No matter what. I love you for everything you are."

I stare. My heart literally stops beating. I can't breathe.

She loves me.

Then my heart explodes into hypersonic rhythm. I can barely hear over the rush of blood in my ears.

"I only want the best for you. Please...you never talk about your brother. I think you should do that. And talk to your parents." She holds my gaze for an excruciating eternity that has my guts twisting, then turns and walks out, the door closing behind her.

There are two things I have to do. I'd rather take a slapshot in the nuts, but I man up.

I call Brent Schneider. This is probably the toughest phone call I've ever made in my life. But I genuinely want to make sure he's okay and to apologize to him.

"How are you doing?" I ask him.

"I'm doing okay." His tone is guarded. "Still some post-concussion symptoms but getting better."

"I'm glad to hear that. Really. I called to apologize for what I did. I...I'm not making excuses, just trying to explain. I lost my focus. Things have been a bit messed up for me lately, and...that doesn't excuse it. At all. I just want to say I'm sorry I hurt you."

"Thanks, man. Appreciate that."

"I want you to know it wasn't deliberate. I would never do that."

He sighs. "I don't know you. But you don't have a rep as a dirty player. That said, I'm still kind of pissed."

"I don't blame you. I just hope you're feeling better and back on the ice soon."

"Thanks. And…thanks for reaching out."

We end the call. I sit for a few minutes with the discomfort of that. I deserve it.

The other thing I have to do is face the media.

I make myself go to practice the next day and then afterward, sitting in front of cameras, microphones, and cell phones, I begin. "First of all, I just want to say I'm glad that Brent is going to be okay. Concussions are no fun, but I'm relieved that he was okay after, and that's the most important thing." I rub my face. "I reached out to him yesterday and apologized on the phone. And I'm apologizing again now. I'm sorry my play injured him." I pause for a steadying breath. "I know that my intent doesn't change the result, but I want to say that it was never my intention to injure him. I would *never* do that. I was trying to prevent a goal, which is why I was skating so fast. It wasn't until the last second when I got to the net that I decided to make the hit, and I thought it was a clean hit."

I'm trying to keep my chin up, my shoulders square, and my voice steady. I've been super emotional about all this, and I don't want to break down in tears on TV.

"I also want to apologize to the team. And to management. And to the fans. I know I'm letting everyone down by not being able to play during this important stretch. The suspension decision is made, and I'll live with it. Regardless of my personal feelings about the length and severity of the punishment, I accept it. I won't be appealing it. What I *don't* think is fair…" I pause, swallowing. This is the hardest part. "…is my family being attacked because of what I did. That is not right. They've been attacked online and bullied in person. I get that fans love their team, but that is not acceptable."

That's been the most horrendous part of all this—that people, complete strangers, have attacked my family. They've said disgusting things about me, but I can live with that. That's part of the deal. But not going after my family.

As someone with a bit of fame, I'm fair game. I get that. And the internet gives people a sense of protection or safety when they say horrible things about people. People who are real, live, eating, breathing people. People with feelings. It fucking sucks.

It goes too far when fans think they own us. When they think they can say someone—another human being—should be hurt or killed. That's just not right.

It makes me furious, but mostly because what the hell can I do about it? Nothing.

I get some attention from Robby, our head athletic therapist. In the hit on Schneider, I also hurt my shoulder. It's not bad, but I've been ignoring it, and he does some ultrasound therapy then works on stretching and mobilizing my shoulder joint.

I skip lunch with the guys. Just not feeling it. I drove myself here today, so I drive home.

Was Emerie watching the press conference?

It doesn't matter.

I miss her.

Too bad. Toughen up, fluffy.

Some hot, rough, sex would be nice right now.

No.

That's not what it was about with Emerie.

I hope she's okay.

Never mind her. Stop thinking about her.

Yeah. That'll work.

At home, I meander aimlessly for a while. I walk into my office and stare at Emerie's stuff. I gaze out the window. I grab a bottle of water, drink some of it, then wipe off the kitchen counter. Things were always messier when Emerie was here.

Fuck, I miss that, too.

I heave a sigh and pick up the book I'm reading. Stretching out on the couch, I try to read. My mind won't stop, though.

I love you.

She might as well have reached inside and ripped a hole in my gut.

She can't love me. Not when I've screwed up this bad.

Despair swamps me.

How did this happen? How did I manage to destroy everything? How could I have fucked up so badly when I've worked so hard?

I'm so fucking pissed at myself. At that moment, I hate myself. My jaw locked, I let out a hoarse, strangled noise of pain.

Talk about your brother.

What for? He's gone. And talk about him to whom? Like my parents would want to talk about that. Or anyone would. Millsy lost his brother, too, and I doubt he wants to hear my sad story.

27

OWEN

I wake up to banging on my apartment door.

Groggy, I open my eyes. It's the middle of the afternoon, and I'm on my couch. I've been sleeping here a lot lately.

More knocks reverberate through the apartment.

"What the hell?" I yell, swinging my legs to the floor. My book thuds to the rug, and I lurch over to the door like I'm hammered.

I yank it open and see my teammates standing there—Millsy and Hellsy. And Millsy's dog.

"Hey."

They squint at me. "What were you doing?"

"I think I fell asleep."

They push past me to enter my pad, not waiting for an invitation. Otis is jumping around, excited to see me. I bend down to rub the guy's head. He had a rough start in life, but he's got a good home now with Millsy. I kind of love the little dude.

"Were you drinking?" Millsy asks.

"No. But in hindsight, that might have been a good idea."

"You don't drink," Hellsy points out.

"Sure, I do. Sometimes."

"Where's Emerie?" Millsy asks.

I swallow. "She moved out."

He nods.

Somehow, I get the feeling he already knew that. I narrow my eyes at him. "What?"

"Why'd you do that?" he asks, taking a seat on the sectional.

Hellsy sits too, in one of my chairs. Otis sniffs around the apartment.

"Is he going to piss on my floor?" I ask Millsy, pointing at the black and white Frenchie.

"Nah. I just took him out."

They look all casual and laid back. Like my life isn't a huge goddamn goat rodeo and they're sitting in front row seats.

"Do what?"

"Dump her." Millsy crosses one ankle over his knee. "You seemed really happy with her."

"After what just happened, you can ask that?" I shake my head. "She doesn't need to be part of my shit show of a life."

"Ah. So you were doing it for her."

I give him the dirtiest look I can. "What are you saying, Mills?"

"Okay, fine. If I have to explain it in one-syllable words, I will. You can't break up with someone for their own good. That is totally patronizing and arrogant."

I blink.

"You don't know what's best for her," Hellsy adds. "Only she knows that."

"I do know what's best for her!" I shove a hand in my hair. "And it's not me."

They both give me long, level looks.

"Seriously, dude?" Hellsy asks.

I drop my ass onto the couch. Otis leaps up beside me and sits, too, giving me big brown puppy dog eyes. "Guys. I fucked up. Big. Huge. That hit…" I shake my head.

They both nod. "Yeah."

My look is probably baleful.

"You did," Hellsy says. "Everyone does at some point."

"Nobody's perfect," Millsy adds. "No matter how hard you try." His gaze lasers onto me.

"So." Hellsy shrugs. "Let me pour you a tall glass of get the fuck over it. And here's a straw so you can suck it up."

"That's it? After what happened, I'm just supposed to suck it up?" Anger heats my blood.

"What else are you going to do about it?" Millsy asks.

"Sometimes good people make bad decisions," Hellsy adds. "It doesn't mean you're a bad person. It means you're human."

I sigh with frustration, my jaw tense. "I know I'm not a bad person. But I'm sure as hell not good enough for Emerie."

"Ah. A pity party." Millsy nods. "Cancel it."

"Jesus," I mutter.

"We're hockey players," Hellsy says. "We fall. We get up. We learn. We grow. We move on."

"Why do you think you're not good enough for Emerie?" Millsy asks.

"Doesn't that seem obvious?" I sweep out a hand.

"No. It really doesn't."

"Fuck. I'm not talking about this shit."

"Oh hell no." Hellsy leans forward. "You saw what we went through. Me, Millsy, Morrie. He's on his way over, by the way."

I throw up my hands. "What is this? An intervention?" Christ, just saying the word makes me shudder. How many times did we try that with Eric? It never worked.

"If we didn't talk about what we were feeling, we wouldn't have made it," Hellsy says. "But we know it's hard."

"*Fucking* hard," Millsy agrees. "But we're not going to let you get away with macho bullshit like denying your feelings. Trying to stay tough on the outside."

"I'm not denying my feelings. I'm pissed."

"At who?" Hellsy asks.

"Myself!"

He nods. "Okay. Good start. Why?"

"Because I fucked up! Jesus, you're asking obvious questions."

"Everyone fucks up," he says again. "Why is that so terrible for you?"

Slowly I move my head from side to side. They're not giving up. I don't want to do this. Finally, I say, "My brother died."

They watch me. They know that.

"I…" I rub my forehead. "He fucked up. So bad, he gave up. I know how hopeless he felt."

Millsy straightens. "Is that how *you* feel?"

"If you're asking me if I'm suicidal, the answer is no."

"Okay." He settles down.

"He threw away everything. His talent. His family. His life. I vowed I would never do that."

"Okay." A notch pinches between Hellsy's eyebrows.

"I was determined to play in the NHL like Eric should have. I've worked so hard to get here. To stay here."

"Yeah. You work hard." Millsy exchanges a look with Hellsy.

"My mom was crying the other day because someone came up to her and told her I should be carried off the ice on a stretcher."

"Fuck." Millsy scrubs a hand over his face. "That's sick."

"Jesus." Hellsy looks skyward. "Some people."

"As for Emerie…" I stop. "First of all, I don't want her going through bullshit like that. Also, I don't have time for relationships. Maybe if I hadn't been so distracted by beach vacations and having fun and…and all her family shit, that hit wouldn't have happened that way."

"You're blaming her?" Millsy's mouth drops open incredulously.

"No!" I gape at him. "No, no! It's not her fault. It's mine." I rub the back of my neck, which feels as hard as a frozen puck. "The morning of the game, Mr. Julian talked to me."

They give me identical questioning looks.

"He didn't come right out and say it, but apparently Mr. D'Agostino does want to get rid of me."

Hellsy's jaw drops.

"Shut the fuck up." Millsy gapes at me.

"I got what he was implying. He stood up for me, but he can't forever, if Mr. D wants me gone."

"Jesus Christ." Hellsy mutters.

"So he wants you to break up with Emerie." Millsy frowns.

"Again, he didn't specifically say that. But… I got the message. And shit, Mr. Julian's a straight shooter, right?"

"Right," they both agree slowly.

"I don't want to cause problems for him. Or for the team. We've got a good group here. We've got a chance of going all the way this year."

"Oh Christ." Millsy looks sick.

"So, I was a little off my game." I hold up my hands. "I told Brent Schneider this, too. It's no excuse. And it proves my point. I need to focus on hockey."

They both regard me solemnly, their mouths in identical flat lines.

My phone buzzes. It's the doorman.

"Probably Morrie," Hellsy says.

I tell the doorman to send him up, and a moment later, he knocks. Otis goes nuts barking and bouncing around as I head to the door to open it.

"Hey, man." Morrie grabs me in a bro hug. "How're you doing?"

"Shitty. Come on in. I'm being tag teamed."

He laughs softly and follows me into the living room. "Are you ganging up on the poor guy?"

Millsy and Hellsy smirk. "Yep. And we're making progress."

"Excellent." Morrie takes a seat and Otis leaps onto his lap. He absently pets the dog's head. "As someone who's been through months of therapy, I'm glad to hear that."

I don't know much about Morrie's background. He just signed with the team this past summer, and we've only been playing together a few months. But he, Hellsy, and Millsy know each other. They all played junior hockey together and were involved in a tragic bus crash that killed a bunch of people. They survived, but that doesn't mean they were fine after. They've been through a lot.

They've started a campaign focusing on mental health issues for men because of what they experienced, and I really admire that. I'm not one of the guys who needs it, though.

"He broke up with Emerie because he's not good enough for her," Millsy tells Morrie.

Morrie nods, focused on me. "Too bad you have nothing going for you."

The other guys snort. On some level, I recognize the humor in this, but nothing's funny right now.

"You know everything there is to know about hockey," Morrie says. "You must study it twenty-four-seven."

I say nothing. It's a slight exaggeration, but yeah.

"He watches every game," Millsy says. "And tons of video of our team."

"That's how I learn," I say. "How I get better."

"Oh yeah, for sure." Millsy nods. "You're the hardest working guy on the team, hands down. Staying after practices, putting in extra ice time. Working out."

"Is it possible…" Hellsy purses his lips. "…hear me out here…that hockey has become an addiction for you?"

"That's ridiculous."

"Hockey's not a drug," Morrie points out.

"No. But people who are workaholics often use work as a way to distract themselves from what's really going on in their lives." Hellsy watches me as he says that.

"Oh, that's bullshit," I say. "I'm not a workaholic."

They all say nothing while eyeing me with doubtful expressions.

My insides shift uncomfortably. "What?"

"I'm starving," Morrie says. "Let's order pizza."

Jesus. I just want them to leave. I'm annoyed and tired and salty. I want to be alone. But they plow ahead and order pizza.

"You got any beer?" Morrie says when that's done.

"I might have one. You can share it."

That's not enough to get rid of them. Hellsy goes out for a jog to the superette over on Broadway and returns with a six pack of some kind of ale.

As they crack them open, I offer glasses, which they decline.

"You don't talk about your brother much," Millsy says. "I lost my brother, too."

"I know." Millsy's brother and father were also killed in the bus crash.

"It's hard," he says. "I still miss him. I talk to him, sometimes. Not as much as I used to, but I still do."

I didn't know that. Talking to your dead brother is pretty…sad.

"You ever talk to Eric?" he asks.

"No." I look down at my bottle of water. I think about that. Hell. I know why I don't talk to him. I just don't want to admit it. I swallow a sigh and say, "Probably because I was so pissed at him for years before he died."

Millsy's chin goes up. "You were pissed at him?"

"Yeah. I know it's dumb. He was an addict. It's a disease. He couldn't help that. But I was mad at him. For a long time, I thought he should just quit using drugs. Just get his shit together. Quit causing problems for Mom and Dad." I pause. "It was hard to accept that he couldn't. Even when he tried. It was just too powerful for him."

"Addiction's a bitch, man," Morrie says quietly.

I nod. Now I'm thinking about Eric. About what he was like before he started taking narcotics. How much fun we had. How he looked out for me. How competitive we were at the local community center rink, playing even when it was dark and freezing cold, trying to outscore each other.

I do miss him. I miss that Eric.

"We didn't play together very often because of the age difference, but one time we were just playing pick up at the rink. I kind of bumped this other guy, like, not even a check. He turned around and punched me in the head. Eric came shooting over and shoved him. He was way bigger than either of us. The guy fell on his ass, but then he got up and bolted off the ice and never came back."

The guys all smile.

I feel like there's a hard lump in my chest. I rub at it absently.

"Is he why you don't drink much?" Millsy asks.

Is it? "I guess so," I say slowly. "Another way I was determined to not be like him. To not be a drunk." I snort out a mirthless laugh. "Life goals."

Jesus. That's pathetic. These guys are probably cringing. But when I look at them, they're not. They're nodding. Like they understand.

They hang out until the pizza comes. Pizza's not on my healthy eating plan, but fuck it, I've barely eaten anything the last few days. I have to fuel my body somehow. So I scarf down the meat-lovers with extra cheese.

Otis is sitting in front of me, polite but watchful in case a piece of pepperoni falls to the floor.

"You already knew Emerie and I broke up, didn't you?" I say to Millsy.

"Well, no. I just knew she moved into Lilly's apartment."

I nod.

"Lilly's going to move in with me," he adds.

"Congrats," I say automatically.

"Yeah, that's good news, dude," Morrie says. "Cheers." He lifts his beer bottle.

"Thanks." Millsy grins. "Otis is happy, too."

Otis is in fact smiling. I have to smile back at him.

When they eventually get around to leaving, Millsy says, "So, you're coming to skate tomorrow, yeah?"

I roll my eyes. "Yeah."

Tomorrow's a game day, so I can go skate and hang out with the guys then go back to watch the game. I hate watching games when I could be playing. But it is what it is.

28

EMERIE

I e-transfer Lilly the money for my half of the rent for the next month. I have enough in my savings to cover this, but when she moves out, paying the full amount every month is going to be a challenge. I'll figure it out.

I wander around the apartment. It's in an old building, and I like the shiny, honey-toned hardwood floors, pale walls, and original dark woodwork. The living room is long and narrow with two windows overlooking the street and one long wall of exposed brick holding a fireplace. The kitchen is tiny but functional.

Lilly's probably going to take a lot of things with her like dishes, glassware, cutlery. Furniture? Easton likely has all they need, but who knows? I'm going to have to go shopping. Normally, shopping would excite me. Not now. Bleh.

I lean against the counter in the tiny kitchen.

Being with Owen opened up my world. Opened it up to possibilities. To bigger things and deeper emotions. I met new people and went on a trip and had fun. I got up the nerve to start my SoundCloud. Now I don't have Cat. And I don't have Owen. I don't even have myself anymore.

For some reason, I think of that movie Owen and I watched on the plane. The guy who was trying to find his identity and his struggles, the questions about his art—what it meant to him, what it meant to the public, what was he trying to say?

I've never asked myself those questions. Why not?

I grab a bottle of water from the fridge and guzzle some down. Suddenly, I feel hot and sweaty. Uncomfortable.

Craig in the movie thought that the reason he wasn't successful was because people didn't understand his work. He thought being successful was being famous. And he learned that wasn't it. Because he never tried to do the work of becoming his best self.

I don't want to be famous. I just want to be my best self. And music is a big part of that.

I think of Owen and all the work he does to become his best self. But...is he doing it for the right reasons?

God! I press my fingers to my eyes. So many questions.

I pull out the paper from my purse. It's a flyer being passed around to buskers in the subways—the same one Nash showed me a while back—about the American Busker competition.

I set it on the kitchen counter and smooth the creases.

If I'm going to try to figure out who I really am, maybe I need to do this. It's crazy. I don't care about adulation or recognition. At least...I don't think I do. But maybe just doing something that scares me is enough to learn who I really am.

With courage flowing through my veins, I grab my laptop and go to the website to sign up. My fingers hesitate. What am I doing?

Just do it.

I type in my info.

There. I'm signed up. The auditions start in a couple of weeks.

I'll tell Nash tomorrow. Maybe he'll do it too.

"Don't take this the wrong way," Lilly says the next day when she gets home from work and we have a chance to talk more. "Because I'm glad you're moving in. But why are you here?"

I huff out a laugh. "Well, I knew I couldn't stay with Owen forever. And…" I swallow. Cough. "We broke up."

"Oh no." She drops her hands and gazes at me in dismay. "What happened? Or…you can tell me it's none of my business. But if you want to talk about it, I'm here."

I gave her a wan smile. "Thanks. I'm kind of still processing it."

"Understandable. From the expression on your face, I gather it wasn't your decision?"

"No." I rub my mouth.

"Men are such dumbasses."

"Yeah. They can be."

They can be pretty great, too, though. I sigh inwardly.

"Did you see Owen's press conference yesterday?"

"No. I don't want to see it."

She pushes out her bottom lip sympathetically. "I understand."

"He blames himself for what's happening to his parents," I say sadly.

"Social media can be brutal."

"Yes. And just because he's a hockey player—a public figure— doesn't mean he doesn't have feelings. Why do people think it's okay to talk about them like that? It's been a shocking eye-opener to me about what public life is like."

"It's definitely an adjustment," she agrees. "When I started dating Easton, I accidentally stumbled into a fan forum and saw all the horrible things fans were saying about me. Female fans." She rolls her eyes.

"Oh no!"

She grimaces. "Oh yeah. Those ladies want the hockey dudes for themselves."

"Oooof." Since I'm talking about Owen, I let it all out and tell her what happened after he learned about his suspension. "He said he can't do it," I finish, my voice thin. "Us. He said hockey has to come first."

"Oh no." Her forehead creases with distress. "Fuck him."

It's so nice that my female friends are all on my side. Except Owen was her friend before I was.

"It wasn't a surprise. I was already clueing in that I don't come first with him." *I don't come first with anyone.*

"Right. You were talking about it that night we went out for pizza."

"Yeah."

"I really thought Owen cared about you."

"I did, too. We got so close on our trip. I guess it was getting back to reality that made him realize I was interfering with his hockey life. I felt this was coming, even before this whole mess. He was always so busy doing other stuff." My heart is splintering, sharp and painful. And yet, even though my heart is bruised and throbbing at Owen's rejection of me, I meant what I said to him. I *do* want only the best for him.

"I'm sorry." Her eyes are warm with sympathy.

"It's okay." I flick my hair back over my shoulder, trying to ignore the ache in my chest. "I know I should come first."

I'm just not sure when that will ever happen.

"How is Cat doing?" Lilly asks.

"Actually...good. Kids are resilient. She's adjusting to our new schedule. She doesn't even want me to take her to and from school anymore. She's growing up."

"She needs you less."

"Yes." I try not to pout.

"I totally admire you for how you've looked after her. Losing her mom so young is tragic. For both of you."

"Thank you." I regard her for a long moment. "I started a Sound-Cloud account," I blurt out.

Her eyes widen. "No way!"

"Yep."

"That's great!"

I shrug and drop my gaze. "I don't know how it'll go."

"I think it'll be amazing," she says confidently. "It's worth a try, right?"

Is it the trying that counts?

"Better an 'oops' than a 'what if,'" she adds cheerfully. "Right?"

I consider that. "I guess so. Yes."

"I'd love to hear you sing more. We were all saying that after our trip."

I can't exactly invite them to the subway to listen to me. I think of the open mic nights Elijah has tried to convince me to do. I could tell my new friends to come…oh God. I can't do that. Can I?

29

OWEN

What the hell am I going to do for the next few weeks?

I'm filled with apathy. I don't care about anything right now.

Without hockey, who am I?

My life is all hockey, all the time. I can't play. The terms of my suspension allow me to work out at club facilities and practice with the team, and I can go to the arena and watch the games from the press box. I strangely have no desire to watch hockey, study hockey video, or read about hockey.

I don't want to leave this apartment. I don't want to see fans. I don't want to see anyone.

But after a few days, I'm coming out of my skin. I have to do something.

But what?

I've been involved with a program through the Bears' Foundation called Play Well. It teaches kids about health and fitness. When we players drop in, it gets the kids excited and motivated.

I call Shelley at the Bears Foundation to ask about doing that while I'm off.

She's not enthusiastic.

"Given what's just happened, this might not be the best time," she says carefully.

Shit. All the air leaves my lungs, leaving me deflated. So much for that idea.

"Okay. I get it."

"Definitely in the future, though!" she says brightly.

"Yeah. For sure."

I end the call and fall back onto my couch. I stare at the ceiling.

Maybe I could do some kind of volunteer work outside of the Bears' Foundation?

I don't know how to go about that, but hey, I can google. I start researching and pause when I come across a place in Brooklyn that offers support for teenagers with substance abuse problems.

I don't know if I can help anyone. I haven't had substance abuse issues myself. But I know how it feels when someone you love has.

I don't know if this place even has volunteer opportunities. Maybe you have to be a social worker or a doctor. I guess I can find out.

I make the call and introduce myself. "I guess I'm looking for a way to share my experience and perspective," I tell the man, whose name is Mike. "To try to help."

We talk for a while. He has a gentle manner that makes it easy to open up to him.

"Why don't you come in tomorrow," he says. "We have a group session at ten. You being a professional athlete will give you a platform that might have some influence on the young people."

"Okay." A seed of hope germinates inside me, animating me. "That sounds great."

I don't know what I'm going to say. All I can do is tell my truth and be myself, I guess.

"We're a peer-driven drug and alcohol addiction recovery support center," Mike tells me the next day when I arrive at Light House. "We work in collaboration with state and local community-based organizations. All our services are free of charge. Our goal is to inspire and empower our members with the recovery skills necessary to become healthy, purposeful and successful members of the community."

I nod and look around as he leads me through the building, which is actually an old home. We walk into a room that was probably a dining room at one time. Chairs are arranged in a circle, some of them occupied by teenagers. A couple of boys stand to one side talking. Mike introduces me to Donna. "She'll be facilitating his meeting," he says.

"Hi, Donna. Nice to meet you."

We shake hands.

"Have a seat," she says with a smile.

I take a chair, and soon everyone is sitting in a circle. I imagine this is what an AA meeting is like. I rub my palms on my khaki pants.

Donna introduces me. I catch the spark of interest at the fact that I play for the New York Bears. Then we go around the circle for the kids to introduce themselves. There are six boys and two girls.

"I'll let you tell your story," Donna says to me.

"Okay." I look around. "I've never done this before. So bear with me." I don't get much reaction. Tough crowd.

I tell them my story. I talk about Eric. I tell them I don't know what it's like to be an addict...except...maybe I do. A little?

I tell them about my feelings when Eric was dealing with his substance abuse issues. I get a lot of nods of recognition.

I hate that these kids have probably put their families through something similar. How the hell am I going to reach them when their own families can't? What the fuck am I even doing here?

I push aside the doubts and forge on. I talk about my anger and resentment. "And I think…" I pause, because this only just came to me. "Sometimes we use other things to cope with the pain." I think about Eric. "I don't know what kind of pain Eric was in. I don't know what kind of pain you're in." I make some eye contact. "I didn't want to admit that *I* was in pain. So I played hockey. That was all I did. It kept me from thinking about things. It kept me from feeling things." I swallow.

"Hockey's not a bad coping mechanism," one kid says dryly. "You make millions of dollars."

I half-smile. "Yeah. But it's never a good thing having only one thing in your life. It holds you back from a lot of other things. Important things." Like Emerie. Like...love.

The kids have questions for me, and I try to answer them as best I can. They make me think. Then I listen as Donna asks the group a few questions based on the things I've said, that maybe make them think, too.

At the end of our time, I'm exhausted but in a totally different way than after a game or a hard practice. I feel good, though. Maybe I had some small impact on one of these kids. Maybe I helped myself more than I helped them.

Being a professional hockey player probably got them to listen to me. But here, it doesn't matter if I'm the best hockey player. In fact, it doesn't matter anywhere—except to me. And as I walk out of Light House, it strikes me that being the best I can doesn't necessarily mean being the best hockey player.

And I have a lot of work to do on that.

30

EMERIE

Cat wants to go to a hockey game.

I don't think I can do it.

It's Saturday night, so there's no reason not to. And I want to spend time with Cat. Owen's not playing, which is the main reason I wanted to watch hockey. I wanted to watch him.

Okay, maybe I like the game a bit. But it reminds me of Owen, and that makes me sad.

We're going to sit in Vince's box since that's free.

Really looking forward to seeing him. *Not.*

So much for my tough talk and certainty that Owen and I would be together. I feel like a fool, now. Vince is probably enjoying it. He better not think that means I'm open to dating Roman.

I told Cat Owen and I broke up and that I was sad about it, but I didn't want to make a big deal of it. I was surprised how upset she was.

"You mean I won't see him anymore?" she asked, eyes filling with tears.

"No. I'm sorry."

"I like Owen!"

"Me, too, Kit Cat. Me too." I gave her a hug.

She's been over to my new place to see it. She met Lilly and Otis, who she adores.

I pull on a pair of loose jeans with a frayed hem, the black lug-soled boots I often wear when busking, and a black turtleneck sweater. I leave my hair loose and don't bother with contacts, putting on my big, black-framed glasses. Black seems to suit my mood.

I taxi over to the west side to get Cat, then to the arena. Cat's wearing the jersey Owen gave her, which chokes me up for a minute.

"So, what's new?" I ask her on the way.

"Mmm. Well, Dad took me to swimming this week. And he stayed and watched."

Whoa. I try to mute my shock. "That's nice."

"And I asked him for help with my homework, and he helped me with a geometry problem."

Again, whoa. "You can call me if you need help."

"I know." She shrugs. "He was right there, so I asked."

"Is he home more?"

"Yeah. He is."

Mind. Blown. "I'm glad."

We near the arena and hop out of the cab. I love how the area buzzes with energy on a game day. The air is mild with the promise of spring in the soft breeze.

We ride the elevator up to the press box level and head down the hall to Vince's box.

"Hello, Emerie," he says neutrally.

"Hi, Vince. How's it going?" I take a seat.

"It's going fine."

"Thanks for letting us watch up here."

He nods. We make painful small talk for a few minutes. Then he says, "Cat tells me you have a new place."

"Yes."

"You and Cooke aren't seeing each other anymore."

"Yes." I press my lips together. "But does *not* mean I'm interested in getting back together with Roman."

"I know."

I give my head a little shake. What?

"Hey, don't worry about me." My breezy tone covers my sarcasm. "My heart's broken, but I'll survive. I always do. He was just another person who didn't see me." My throat squeezes but I smile, though it feels like a grimace. "I know I never mattered to you. So I'm used to it."

His face tightens.

"I'm sorry I acted out. When I was a teenager. It was hard losing Mom, and all I wanted was to know I was loved and that I belonged somewhere. I thought I could get your attention that way. It worked but in the wrong way." I laugh lightly. "I just pissed you off even more. But I got my shit together and figured out what was important. I had to make sure Cat didn't feel the same way I did."

He stares at me. "I wasn't angry at you."

"Oh, come on." My smile wobbles. "Sure, you were."

"I was heartbroken, too," he says quietly.

I go motionless and shut up.

His jaw tightens.

"What?" I stare at him.

"Losing Kim," he says in a low voice. "I loved her. Of course I was heartbroken."

I blink slowly, once, twice. Now I'm confused. He was heartbroken? He might as well have told me he's flying to the moon tomorrow.

He has a heart?

"I'm sorry," I whisper. "Of course."

"Did you break up with Cooke because of what he did to Brent Schneider?"

My forehead puckers. "No! Of course not."

"That was ugly."

I stare at him. "He didn't intend to hurt that man. He would never do that. In a split second, going eleventy billion miles per hour, he made a wrong decision."

He listens, eyes sharp.

"He feels terrible about it," I add, although that's an understatement. "He feels terrible that people would *think* he would do that. I can't believe you do."

"I never said I think that."

"His whole life is hockey. Everything he does is to make him a better player. You should be grateful to have him on your team."

Vince sighs. "I know."

31

OWEN

I return to the press box just in time for the national anthems.

I don't hear the music. I just hear Emerie say in her fake cheery voice, *Just another person who didn't see me.*

I shouldn't have stopped to listen outside the door of Mr. D's box. But I heard her voice, and...I eavesdropped. And had my heart fucking sliced up.

I saw her.

I *saw* her.

I saw *her.*

I saw a beautiful, big-hearted woman who cares about her sister and gave up so much so she wouldn't feel the same sense of invisibility. So she would feel seen. I saw a talented musician who sacrificed a music career for her sister. I saw a woman who loved me. Whose heart I broke.

I know I never mattered to you. So I'm used to it.

She's used to not mattering.

She should never be fucking used to that. She *does* matter. She matters so goddamn much. And I'm an asshole for not telling her that.

I've been a miserable prick since she left. And not just because of what happened on the ice that night. Or the fucking abuse I've taken and that my parents have taken.

It's because I miss her.

She didn't stay at my place that long. I kept telling myself she was a distraction. I kept telling myself I needed to ignore her so I could focus on hockey. That was the worst thing I could have done to someone who feels invisible. Who feels like she doesn't matter.

I did it to protect myself. And I fucking hurt her.

Christ.

That's what asshole Vince D'Agostino did to her, and now I've done the same.

I sit only because everyone else is. I'm staring at the ice but don't even see the players or the faceoff.

I'm a shithead.

Beave shoots me a glance. "You okay?"

"Yeah. Why?"

"You made a noise...I thought maybe you have diarrhea or something."

I choke. "Um. No."

"Okay," he says doubtfully, returning his gaze to the ice.

"I'm gonna get a coffee." I stand.

"You don't drink coffee."

"I do now."

I hate coffee. I stumble over to the buffet area where the team puts out food for the press and staff. I fill a cardboard cup from the coffee urn and slurp some down. Ugh.

Everyone's focused on the game, the crowd cheering for something. I should be focused on the game. Right now, I don't give a shit. I have to get my head on straight.

He feels terrible that people would think he would do that. I can't believe you do.

I hear her words to Vince again.

You should be grateful to have him on your team.

She defended me to Vince.

Even though I broke her heart, she defended me. Christ.

I love her.

But I don't deserve her.

Do you ever choose which will be the last bite you eat, so your mouth will remember it?

I smile twists up my mouth.

There should be a rule that if they shoot the puck over the glass, they have to go get it.

I huff out a laugh and rub my mouth.

I remember how hard we laughed when she thought the end of the belt of her life jacket was a snake in the water. She laughed at herself. I love that.

I remember her standing up to Vince. I remember her playing her guitar and singing to me.

I love her. Even though I think she should do more with her musical talent. Even though I think she was consumed with her need to take care of Cat at her own expense. Even though she got me involved in that crazy scheme that may have cost me the All Star Game. That could still cost me my job here. After this suspension, nobody would question why Mr. D would trade me away.

For some reason, that doesn't strike fear into my heart like it once did. Because after the last week, losing my job here doesn't seem nearly as bad as losing Emerie.

I'm surviving without hockey. I've found something that gives me a purpose other than hockey. And I lost something that gives me a purpose other than hockey. Mr. Julian's words have replayed over and over in my head: *Hockey will end. Family and love are all we really have.*

He is so fucking right.

I look down at the empty cup in my hand. I drank the whole cup of gross brown water. I crumple it and drop it in a waste bin, then return to my seat.

Is it possible...that hockey has become an addiction for you?

I hear Hellsy's voice in my head, asking that question.

Ridiculous.

I think about more of the shit they said. About people who are workaholics using work as a way to distract themselves from what's really going on in their lives. About how Millsy talked to his dead brother. But I never talked to Eric. Because I was pissed at him.

Pissed at him for giving up. For hurting Mom and Dad. For hurting…me.

Jesus. The pressure behind my eyes grows, my throat constricting. "I need more coffee," I choke out to Beave, before rushing out of the press box.

I arrive in Sarnia around four in the afternoon.

The team's on a road trip to Detroit and Pittsburgh, and I'm not with them. So I made a quick trip, flying to Toronto then renting a car and driving here.

It might be too late for Emerie and me, but I want to be a better person. I don't deserve her in my life, but I want to try. Because being the best person I can be is more than being the best hockey player. *Hockey will end. Family and love are all we really have.*

Mom and Dad are both still at work, so I cruise around town, visiting old haunts like the arena where I watched junior hockey as a kid, dreaming of playing with a team like that. I drive by the community rink I played at as a kid, the school I went to until I was drafted by Kitchener, the burger place I used to hang out at with my friends.

Memories of Eric are all tied up here, too. When I moved to Kitchener at age sixteen, Eric was already deep into the addition cycle. His hopes of a hockey career had been shattered. I felt guilty that I'd been drafted by the OHL but determined to make the best of it like he hadn't been able to. If I could do anything to give Mom and Dad a spark of happiness in their lives, I'd do it.

I park out front of the house just as Mom pulls into the driveway. I let them know I was coming, so it's not a surprise. She waves at me as

I climb out of the car and start toward her. It's a wet spring day, the pavement shiny, the grass just starting to green up, the trees still bare.

"Hi, Mom."

"Owen." She hugs me, though I tower a foot over her. I get my height from my dad, but I'm taller than him, too. "It's so good to see you."

"Yeah." I squeeze her then step back. "You, too."

"Come on in."

I have a small bag, but I leave it in the trunk of the car until later.

The smell of the house has memories rushing back—the cookies Dad bakes, the cinnamon candles Mom loves. She fishes mail out of the mailbox and glances through it before setting it on the kitchen counter.

"I'm going to change," she says. "Help yourself to a drink or a snack."

I nod, and she whisks down the hall in her suit and heels. She's a manager at a local bank. I open the fridge and pull out the milk. I've spotted the cookies on the counter, and I definitely need milk with them.

I've already downed two cookies when Mom comes back, now wearing yoga pants and a fitted long-sleeved hoodie.

"Great cookies, Mom."

She laughs. "Thanks. Do you like the almonds in them?"

"Love it."

"Dad should be home in a bit. You want to tell me why you're here? Or should we wait for him?"

"We can wait for him."

We chat about random stuff. My cousin Mika is getting married this summer. The next-door-neighbors had to put down their dog, Barry. "Geez. He was old when I lived here."

She laughs. "He would have been five."

"I remember when I hit a baseball into their yard and I went to get it, he wouldn't give it back."

Dad arrives home and greets me with a big hug. He offers a beer, but I decline. Then I wonder why. Why do I make such an effort to be perfect—no drinking, no drugs, no junk food—when it all ends up being for nothing?

Dad cooks most of the meals, and he gets things out of the fridge and gets to work. "How are you doing?" he asks as he browns ground beef for tacos.

I don't need to ask what he means with his serious question.

"Crappy."

He shakes his head, focused on the frying pan. "I knew you'd take this hard."

"Wouldn't anyone?"

He gives me a look. "No. I'm sure most guys don't like it when they hurt someone, but it is part of the game. You've been injured yourself."

"Yeah.

"But I don't think most guys are as hard on themselves as you are."

My lips twist up. What can I say? He's right. I beat myself up over a missed shot on a shootout. Over a dumb turnover at the blue line.

"He's right," Mom says, cutting up tomatoes.

"I know," I say in a low voice. "I didn't do it on purpose."

"We know that," Mom says. "Of course we know that."

I remember Emerie saying that, too. Fuck me. I'm a fucking lucky bastard to have people who believe in me no matter what, and I didn't even know it. And what did I do? I sent her away.

A burn hits my chest.

"I'm sorry you're being put through what you are," I add. "I feel sick about what's happened."

"That is not your fault," Dad says. "People are assholes."

I smile. "Yeah. They are."

"So why are you here?" Mom asks. "We don't see much of you anymore." She's looking at the tomatoes, not at me, but I can feel her hurt pulsing in the air around us.

"I know that, too." I clear my voice. "I need to talk about Eric."

Mom's head snaps up. She blinks, then glances at Dad. "Okay."

"I'm not sure where to start." I curl my hands around my empty glass. "I'm...angry at him."

Dad squints. Mom's eyes widen.

"Oh," she says.

"I don't think I even realized it," I go on. "But...I think I need to talk about it. I need to...deal with it."

"You haven't dealt with it by now?" Dad asks gruffly.

Mom sets her hand on his arm. "It takes time," she says softly. "Everyone's different. Everyone deals with loss in their own way."

I nod. "So here's the thing." I swallow. "When Eric was having problems—"

"He was a drug addict," Mom cuts in. "We can say that."

My throat squeezes. "Right. Okay. He was doing drugs and getting in trouble and...I didn't want to be like that. I saw him wasting his talent. He was a great hockey player."

"He was," Dad says quietly. He turns off the stove and moves the pan.

"When I went to Kitchener, I worked as hard as I could. I didn't want to waste what I had. I didn't want to be like him." My voice catches. "It was the same when I got drafted into the NHL. When I started playing with the Bears."

Mom presses her fingers to her mouth.

I meet her eyes. I force the ugly words out. "I was mad at him."

"Oh Owen. Your feelings are what they are. I understand you feeling angry at him. I was angry, too. So many times." She sighs. "I was also brokenhearted, frustrated, sad...well, my emotions pretty much ran the gamut."

"I know it wasn't his fault," I say. "But I can't help it. I was mad. I didn't want to feel that way. So I tried to stop feeling anything. I tried to stop thinking about him."

"How'd that work out for you?" Mom asks.

"It was going great. Until..."

They both eye me curiously. "The hit on Schneider?" Dad asks.

"Actually...no." I feel like I'm being strangled. "I, uh, met a girl."

Mom lowers her chin, her eyes sparking. Dad frowns.

"Tell us more," Mom says.

"I care about her. A lot. But I think I f— er, I think I messed up."

"How so?" Mom asks gently, and her non-judgmental words and tone settle me.

"I've been so focused on hockey. It's been my whole life. I didn't think I had room in my life for a girlfriend. But...she's in my life. Or she was." I drag a hand down my face. "I thought she was interfering with hockey, and then this whole shitstorm happened, and I thought it proved me right. So I broke up with her."

Mom inhales sharply but says nothing.

"What's she like?" Dad asks.

"She's amazing. She's a musician. She plays guitar. And piano. And sings. She's raised her little sister. She lost both her parents. Her stepdad is...ah, shit." I swipe my tongue over my top teeth. "He owns the Bears. She's Mr. D'Agostino's stepdaughter."

Dad stares. "Jesus Christ."

"I know. And he's been an asshole to her. But she's so strong and caring, and fun to be with."

Mom smiles even though her eyes look glossy like she's going to cry. "She sounds wonderful."

"And she's beautiful," I add. I stare across the room, unfocused. "Her name is Emerie."

"And you chose hockey over her," Mom says.

I close my eyes. *When you put it that way...* "I'm an idiot. But...that's why I'm here. I need to figure this out. I think I've been trying to avoid thinking about Eric by thinking about nothing but hockey."

Mom makes a soft sound of agreement.

"I still love him. And..." I choke up again. "I miss him. So much."

"I know." She reaches over and squeezes my hand. "Us too."

"I feel crappy that I was angry at him."

Dad's been quiet. But now he says, "Is that why you've pulled away from us?"

"I didn't realize it. But yeah. I think so. I felt guilty. I shouldn't be angry at my dead brother. I didn't want to talk about him. Or think about him. I didn't want you to hate me for being such a selfish, shitty person."

Mom's eyes grow wet. Dad is stoic, but his Adam's apple is moving like the bobble head players the team gives out.

"We love you and we always will." Mom sniffles. "We always loved your brother, even after everything he put us through. He couldn't help it."

"I *know*. And that makes me feel even worse." I pause. "Can we talk about him now? The good stuff. And the bad, I guess."

"Of course."

We spend the rest of the evening reminiscing about Eric, good, bad, and ugly. It's all part of him and who he was. And it's part of us, too.

When I go upstairs to go to bed in my old room, I walk into what used to be Eric's room. It doesn't look the same. I sit on the bed in the quiet darkness and let the memories run through my head like a movie...playing with Legos in here, jumping on the bed to see if we could touch the ceiling, breaking the lamp when we played mini sticks with an actual puck. I can see his face, his big grin, his wild cowlick. I never knew. When we were kids, I never knew it would end that soon.

My eyes burn and a hot knife stabs into my heart. And yeah, I shed a few tears.

32

EMERIE

I'm still confused about what happened at the hockey game.

Okay, I knew Vince cared about Mom. I saw them together. He clearly doesn't like kids, but he loved her. I guess he was going through his own shit after she died, but I still don't totally forgive him for how he treated me. He was the grown up. He needed to be a better parent figure.

I know it messed me up, and I've worked on doing better. I didn't deal well with it as a teenager—the loss, the grief, the feeling of abandonment—but I picked myself up and got back on track.

Or did I?

Here I am, alone. No boyfriend. No family.

I look around my little apartment. Lilly's at work. I'm settling in here, but it's still new.

I feel like my skin's too tight. And hot. My heart is galloping.

It's like I'm terrified. But of what? Everything is fine. Fine.

I stand and walk to the window. Spring flowers are blooming in the parks and the trees are becoming green. It feels fresh and hopeful.

I need some of that hope. What am I so scared of?

Maybe it's time for *me*. Never mind that I haven't been a priority in anyone else's life since Mom died. I need to make *myself* a priority.

I go into my little bedroom and get my laptop. I go onto the internet and find the site for open mic bookings. I see the one at the Mystic Nomad in Hell's Kitchen that Elijah mentioned. Saturday from four to seven. I can sing two songs. I can't sign up in advance, I just have to go there.

I see Lilly's head pass by the window and then hear her coming into the hall of the building. I close my computer and paste on a smile as I turn to greet her.

"Hi!" The auburn highlights in her wavy dark hair glow under the lights. "How was your day?" She sets a couple of full shopping bags on the floor as she takes off her jacket.

"Good. You're home tonight?"

"Yeah. I invited Sara and Kate over to watch the game. I hope that's okay."

The Bears play in Pittsburgh tonight.

"Of course!"

"You can watch with us," she says.

"Sure. That'll be fun."

"I got some snacks." She lifts the bags. "And wine."

"Need any help?"

"Yeah, that'd be great."

I follow her to the tiny kitchen and help her arrange a charcuterie platter, cutting up cheeses and breads. We have a glass of wine and nibble cheese and cashews while we work. She tells me doggie stories and updates me on arrangements for the Paws for a Cause fashion show. We got a permit to hold it in Central Park at the end of June, and we have lots of entries, so it looks like we're going to make good money for the shelter.

All this distracts me but doesn't quite quell the uneasiness in my gut.

Kate and Sara arrive with more wine, dressed in Bears jerseys with their guys' numbers on them. I don't even have a Bears T-shirt. I guess it doesn't matter now. I'm just another fan, not a WAG. I push down the sadness I get when I think about Owen.

We settle in to watch the opening faceoff. I've watched enough games now that I know some of the players and I generally don't embarrass myself with stupid questions. Although, I do still have questions. "Why do they put tape on their sticks?"

"I think it helps grip the puck," Lilly answers. "Because the wood—"

"Carbon fiber," Kate corrects.

"Oh, right." Lilly nods. "The stick is smoother, so they rough it up with the tape."

"Okay."

Is Owen with them? Is he watching the game from the press box again? I keep these questions to myself.

We cheer when Brandon scores for the Bears, and groan when Pittsburgh ties it up before the end of the first period.

During the intermission we take bathroom breaks and refill wine glasses.

"Can I tell you guys something?" I ask.

"Sure."

I look around at them. "I've sort of kept this secret because I didn't want my stepfather to know what I was doing, but it doesn't matter anymore, and I want to tell you all."

"Are you pregnant?" Lilly gasps, her hand flying to her throat.

"No!" I shake my head vigorously. "Oh my God, no, that's not it. It's about what I do during the day...for a living...sort of."

Kate's eyes widen. "Are you a sex worker?"

"No!"

"If you are, it's fine," she says. "Sex work is work."

"No, no!" I have to laugh. "Let me finish!"

"Okay. Sorry." She sits back.

"I'm a busker."

They all blink.

"I sing and play guitar in subway stations."

"Whoa." Lilly's mouth falls open. Then she closes it.

"That's...well, you're a great singer," Kate says, looking a bit like I just told her I sing opera.

"Thanks." I bite my lip. "I know it's weird, but I like it. I make good money, but up till now I gave most of it away, since I didn't need it."

They're all gazing at me like they don't know what to say.

"I've never seen you there," Kate says.

"Well, you might not recognize me. I wear a wig and dress differently."

"I interviewed a busker for my podcast," Sara says. "Elijah Thomas. Really cool guy."

"I know him." I smile. "He's a great guy."

"I was surprised to learn that a lot of buskers do it because they like it," she goes on. "Not always because they can't find other work."

"That's true. It's been great for me. Other than the time I got robbed. And once I got punched in the head."

They all gasp.

"It's all good." I wave a hand.

"Do you want a different job?" Lilly asks. "I mean a different music career."

"I've been thinking about that a lot lately. Busking worked for me because I could still spend a lot of time with Cat. But now...I have more time. I'm not sure what I want."

"You could be a famous rock star!" Lilly says.

"I'm not a rock star." I shake my head.

"A Broadway star!" Kate says.

"No. I don't have a Broadway voice. I'm not sure I want to be a star of any kind." I bite my lip. That anxiety in my belly intensifies again. "I just want to sing."

"You have an amazing voice," Sara says. "You should definitely sing. However you want."

"Thank you." I take a deep breath. My stomach is hard as a rock now, and I'm sweating again. "I appreciate that. I felt like my family was taken away from me when Vince locked me out. He wasn't the best stepfather, but at least he was there. And Cat." I swallow painfully.

"You still have her," Sara says softly.

"Yes. She's just growing up. The thing is, I never really felt like I belonged in Vince's home, even though I tried. I acted out when I was a teenager, desperate for attention. But then I realized I needed to focus on Cat. I guess that made me feel like I had purpose in my life. Vince locking me out, and then Owen shutting me out at his place triggered all those feelings again. And him ending things made that even worse." So how do I do that? How do I belong somewhere? "I'm afraid," I whisper to the other women.

Lilly's eyebrows slope down. "Of what, hon?"

"I don't know." I press a hand to my stomach which has been hurting all day. "I guess a lot of things."

"Oh man. We all have fears," Sara says.

"Some people are afraid of mascots," Kate says.

"I'm afraid of spiders," Lilly puts in.

"I mean *big* fears," Sara says.

"I'm afraid of being alone," I choke out. "I've always been afraid of being alone. Afraid that no one will love me. Losing Cat…well, not losing her, but leaving her…was so hard." I swallow. "And then… Owen." I stop because I'm going to cry, and I don't want to cry in front of these amazing ladies. I take a sip of wine, then another.

"I guess that's why I was so focused on Cat," I finally continue.

They purse their lips, nod, murmur understanding.

"But maybe this is exactly what I need," I say, lifting my chin. "To be alone. To be responsible for just myself, looking after *me*. And being happy with me."

"That could be," Sara says slowly.

"I've been afraid of success. Or I guess it's actually a fear of failing. I've been happy busking and singing the songs I want to sing, and if I'm lucky, a few people will like it enough to throw some money in my guitar case. I've been afraid to go any further than that with my music. Because…" I choke out the words. "What if I can't?"

They all make sympathetic sounds, gazing at me.

"I think we're all afraid of that," Kate says. "I sure was when I started out as an agent. Could I really do it? A woman in a man's world. And at first, I got told a lot that I couldn't." She shrugs. "I proved them wrong."

"That's very true," Sara agrees. "But Em, you don't have to go any further if you don't want to. You need to do what makes *you* happy."

I let that sink in. "Right. You're right." Then I blurt out, "I'm going to do an open mic night."

They all grin.

"That's awesome!" Kate says.

"You convinced me." I exhale sharply.

"We'll come and cheer you on!"

"No!"

Their faces fall.

"I mean... oh boy. Really?"

"Of course! It'll be amazing!"

"I'm so grateful to have you as friends."

They all make noises of agreement. "We're here for you, Em."

The game has started again, and we haven't been paying attention. The blare of the goal horn alerts us to this, and we realize that Pittsburgh just scored to take the lead.

"Damn," I say. I smile at the others. "Thank you for being so supportive."

"Just know...you belong with us." Lilly meets my eyes. "Whatever happens with Owen...we're your friends now."

Whatever happens? It already happened. It's over. But I smile at her with sincere gratitude and affection. "Thank you."

33

OWEN

I get back from Sarnia feeling a lot different than I did when I left. I'm on a mission. But it's a different mission than before.

Emerie was right. Talking to my parents was what I needed to do. And I've had a lot of time to think.

I text Millsy. *You home?*

While I wait for his reply, I text Hellsy and Morrie as well.

Millsy and Hellsy are both home, so I tell them to get up to my place. *I have beer.*

I'm not above a bribe.

Morrie's shopping for new sneakers but says he can come by in about half an hour.

Millsy arrives first, with Otis of course. The little dude bounces in and makes himself at home on my couch.

"What's up?" Millsy heads to my fridge.

"I went home to Sarnia for a couple of days."

"Oh yeah?" He grabs a beer and pops the top off. "How are your folks?"

"They're doing okay. There haven't been any more threats." I roll my eyes.

"That's good. That is so shitty."

"Right?"

Hellsy walks in. "Hello, gentlemen. What's going down?"

I tell him about my visit, too, offering him a beer. "How was the road trip?"

"We kicked ass," Hellsy says, stretching out in a chair. "Two wins."

"Yeah. I watched. Gunner was fanfuckingtastic."

"No shit."

"You guys don't even need me," I say.

"Fuck yeah, we do."

I laugh. I'm sort of joking, sort of not. It's been great to see the team come together and pull off wins even though I'm not playing. It did give me a sharp reminder that I'm replaceable. But that's okay. Because now I know that even without hockey, I'm worth something. Helping those kids has made me feel more worthy and effective than I think I ever have.

We yammer about the games until Morrie shows up. He's carrying a glossy shopping bag and pulls out a box to show us his purchase.

"Versace?" I stare at the shoes. "Seriously? Versace sneakers?"

"Aren't they sick?" He admires them.

"Don't tell me how much." Hellsy holds up a hand.

"Eleven hundred bucks."

"Shit!"

"Come on, admit it. You want them."

When the bullshit settles down, Morrie says, "So, who called this meeting?"

"I did." I take a deep breath. "I need to talk to you guys."

To their credit, they don't give me shit about this.

"I went to see my parents so I could talk to them about my brother."

They don't even look a little surprised about this. Assholes.

"You were right. Talking about this stuff is hard." I rub my forehead.

"It is," Hellsy quietly agrees.

"I've tried not to think about Eric since he died," I tell them. "When

I did think about him, I was mostly resentful. Or bitter. I thought of ways for me to not be like him. To take care of myself. Eat healthy, work out, play the best I can. To not let anything interfere with hockey."

They all nod. Morrie takes a pull of his beer.

"Which means I've never really gotten over losing him. Maybe I never will." I stop as my throat chokes up. After a long, slow breath, I go on. "I never let myself feel sad. I never let myself feel the pain of his loss. I never let myself accept what happened and move on. Because I was stuck in anger."

"It's hard, man," Millsy says in a low voice.

I nod. "And I was stuck in fear. Fear of being like him. So I worked even harder."

"You're not like him," Hellsy says firmly.

My smile is twisted. "I am in some ways. But I got fixated on that." I drag in another deep breath. "Emerie told me she loves me."

With sober expressions, they watch me.

"You don't love her?" Morrie asks.

I close my eyes. "I do. Fuck. I want her more than anything I've ever wanted. But I fucked it up. I didn't think she could love me because I wasn't perfect. And I thought I didn't have room in my life for her. So I broke up with her."

"We told you before...nobody's perfect."

"Yeah. I'm not. And I'm not any better than Eric just because I've succeeded. He had a disease that he couldn't fight any longer. I need to accept that. I need to get over that."

"So tell her that."

"Jesus." I swipe a hand over my brow. "And I thought *this* was hard."

Morrie grins. "Right? Laying your beating heart in front of a woman for her to stomp on it is pretty fucking scary."

"We've all been there," Millsy says fervently. "But you know what? It is so worth it. My mom told me—and this is from a woman who lost her husband and her son in one night and couldn't cope—that loving someone is worth the risk. For her to say that made me believe. And she was right."

I know how happy he is with Lilly. And the other two guys are happy in love too.

"Thank you." I lift my chin. "Thanks for the straight talk that day you came over. And thanks for this."

"Group hug?" Morrie asks.

"Nah, man, I'm good," Hellsy says.

"Okay," Morrie says. "What are you going to do? To get Emerie back."

"I don't know."

"An apology is always good. Some good grovel."

"Dress up as the Bears' mascot," Millsy says with a smirk in Morrie's direction.

I've heard that story, and it's epic. "I'm not going to do that. But yeah, I need to apologize for how I screwed up. I need to show her how much I love her."

"Okay." Morrie leans forward. "We're here for you, bro. Let's brainstorm."

EMERIE

Cat wants to go to another hockey game. I consider calling Vince and trying to convince him to take her to the game with him, but he's always busy doing deals and networking while he's there, so I don't bother. I try to tell Cat I don't feel like going, but she's really insistent that she wants to see this game.

It's the second game of the playoffs. The team really pulled together without Owen and locked up a playoff spot. This is the last game of Owen's suspension. They'll be so glad to have him back. He'll be glad to play again.

We go up to Vince's box. He's not there yet, so I get Cat popcorn and a drink and a Coke for myself. I'm not sure what to expect from Vince after the last time.

The intensity of a playoff game is hiked way up. The atmosphere in the building is electric. Even I feel the increased pressure, the buzz of excitement. Vince arrives after puck drop, nods to us, and takes a seat. He brings a couple of other men with him—Roman's dad, who is one of Vince's business partners, and another man I've never met. Vince introduces him as an "investor."

The first period ends with the score tied one-all. I sit back in my seat and laugh. "I'm exhausted. I can't imagine how the players feel."

The other two guys leave to go mingle or something and Vince pulls out his phone.

I look at Cat. "Want another drink?"

"Sure."

We stand just as Owen walks in.

All the breath leaves my lungs. As usual, just seeing him makes my knees weak and wobbly. My heart thuds hard against my breastbone.

"Hi," he says, fixing his gaze on my face.

"Hi."

There's an intensity in his eyes I haven't seen since...maybe in Aruba? Or maybe on the ice. But also...vulnerability.

He's focused on me. Then he glances at Cat. "Hey, Kitty. Want to meet Kevin Beaven?"

Cat's eyes widen. "Yes!"

Kevin's right behind him. "Hi!"

"Hi, Kevin!" Cat bounces.

"Come get an ice cream," Kevin says. "You can meet Nate Karmeinski. He's here too."

"Oh no, is he hurt, too?" She follows him out.

I expect Owen to go with them, but he doesn't. He walks farther into the room and looks at Vince. "Mr. D'Agostino. I'm glad you're here. I need to say some things to Emerie and also to you."

What? I blink rapidly, pressing a hand to my chest where my heart jumps wildly. I hold onto the back of a seat to steady myself.

Owen turns his intent gaze back to me. I feel like I'm in a tractor beam—mesmerized. Frozen in place.

I adore this man.

His gaze on me is burning hot but also tender and needy with a hint of uncertainty. I can see the tension his big shoulders hold.

"Hi. How are you?"

"I'm okay." *Say it again, Em.*

"I went to visit my parents."

"Oh! Really? That's…great. I think?" I know I told him he should do that. But what if I was wrong?

"It was great. You were right." He holds my gaze steadily. "I've been sort of an idiot."

I frown.

"We had a good talk. We talked a lot about Eric."

"Ohhhh," I breathe. "That's…good." I bob my head slowly up and down. I glance at Vince, not sure if he knows about Owen's brother.

"I've been angry at him."

"At…Eric?" I cock my head, my insides quivering.

"Yeah. Angry at him for dying. Angry at him for giving up. Angry at him for not trying harder. For leaving me." He bows his head and looks at his hands holding the water bottle.

My heartbeat sticks in my throat.

He looks up, focusing on me again. "I never really dealt with losing him. Never accepted it. It's kind of…driven me."

I press my hands together and lift them to my mouth. I understand what he's saying. I comprehend it right to the marrow of my bones. His entire purpose in life has been about Eric. I gaze at him. "I know."

Our eyes meet. And hold. "Yeah. You do. And I'm sorry."

"Sorry for…?"

"For not putting you first."

My heart tries to burst out of my chest. "Oh, Owen."

"I'm so sorry." He lays his hand over his heart. "I was so lucky to have you in my life. And I hurt you. And I fucking hate that."

I nod, my eyes stinging.

"You believed in me," he continues. "When a lot of other people didn't. I can't tell you how much that means to me."

I swallow. "Did your parents believe in you too?"

"Yeah." His lips curve into a slight smile. "You were right. They're one hundred per cent behind me, too."

"Oh, good." I exhale.

"I was trying to not be Eric. To be better than him. I thought I had to be perfect to do that."

You don't. You don't have to be better than him. You don't have to be perfect.

But he says it before me and I'm so, so glad he knows this. "I know now that was wrong."

I nod, my throat so strangled I can't speak.

"It might be too late for us," he says.

I feel a sharp pinching sensation behind my breastbone.

"But I want to be a better person. For you. I don't deserve you in my life, but I want to try. If you'll let me."

I cover my mouth with trembling hands. I have some things to say, too, but I don't know if I can get them out. I swallow painfully. "I've learned some things about myself, too."

"Yeah?" His eyes soften, still warm.

"Yeah. I may have gotten too invested in looking after Cat. And maybe lost a bit of myself in the process." I curl my fingers tightly together. My heart is still racing, my skin icy. "I did it out of love."

"I know." His smile heats my skin.

"And maybe out of fear."

His eyes shadow now. He takes a step closer, tension working between his eyebrows.

"I was afraid of being alone. Of not belonging. Of not being loved."

He closes his eyes for a few long seconds, looking like someone just speared him with a butt end. "I'm so sorry, Em." He opens his eyes and they're shining with emotion and…maybe…tears? "I am so sorry. I was afraid, too. I was terrified that I could care more about something other than hockey, and I just couldn't let myself."

"I know. I understand." I blink back my own tears.

"I'll regret that for the rest of my life," he says quietly. "That I made you feel unwanted. Unloved. When the truth is, I do love you."

Oh God. Oh my God. I press my fingers to my lips, my eyes wide.

"And I'm sorry I didn't tell you that earlier. You're the most important thing." He holds my gaze steadfastly. "I want to show you that."

"You hurt me," I say, my voice thin. I guess I'm still afraid. Afraid to trust that he means that. "How do I believe you now?"

"I'll show you. I'll show you every day, if you'll let me. And I'll start showing you right now." He turns to Vince.

My heart jounces in my chest.

"Mr. D'Agostino, I know you had other ideas about who Emerie should be with. And I'm sorry you were disappointed. I know I made a huge mistake and caused a lot of problems for the team, and if you were to trade me now, no one would question it. I'm prepared to live with that, if that's what your decision is. But I love Emerie. And if she'll have me, I want to spend the rest of time showing her how much she's loved. How much she's needed. And how much she matters."

Vince stares back at Owen.

Owen just put his career on the line. For me. Emotion unfurls inside me, hot and soft and brilliant, nearly dropping me to my knees.

Vince's face is tight and inscrutable. Then he huffs out a laugh and shakes his head. I swear the look in his eyes is respectful. "You're okay, Cooke."

What does that mean? Does it mean what I think it means?

I stare at Vince. "You're okay with this?"

He glances at the door as if making sure nobody can hear us. "I owe you an apology too, Emerie."

My chin nearly hits the floor.

"For a lot of things," he mutters. "I know I haven't been a great parent. If anything good came of all this, I've realized I need to do better for Cat. And for you, if it's not too late."

I stare, my mind like a blender on high speed.

"You've done so much for her. I appreciate it."

I swallow. "Th-thank you."

"Yeah, I wanted you and Roman back together." He sighs. "For financial reasons. I won't bore you with the details but…after that day you came and chewed me out, I kept thinking about it. Roman's been…aggressive. I though it was the solution to my problems. But you were right. I can't solve my financial issues in a way that will hurt the team. And my family."

"Financial issues?" I whisper.

He waves a hand. "Don't worry about it."

Oh sure. Now I *am* worried. And curious. Vince has always had money. I pull in a shaky breath. "Is everything okay, Vince? Are you okay?"

"Oh, yeah. Fine." He pauses. "You can move home if you want."

Oh. My. God. My head becomes an empty space. Then I shake it and say, "I appreciate that. But no. I need to look after myself. I still want to look after Cat. But she's becoming a young woman, and it's time for her to grow, too. And…time for you to be more of a presence."

"You're okay?" he asks gruffly.

I nod and smile. "I'm great." I look at Owen.

His eyes glow with love and pride. He holds out his hands to me.

I love him.

I go to him.

He wraps me up in his arms, and the feel of him soothes me. I breathe in the scent of him, the heat of his skin. His heart thuds against me, as hard and fast as my own, and when his mouth finds mine, I melt into him. I slide my arms around his neck and hold on while the world fades away around us. All I can hear is static, all I can taste is him.

His mouth slides over my cheek and he whispers in my ear, "I love you, Emerie."

"I love you, too."

We draw back to peer at each other, both of us shaking, both of us near tears.

"I'm so sorry," he says again.

I touch his cheek. "Thank you."

Vince clears his throat. "The second period's starting," he says gruffly.

Owen and I look at each other "Wow," I say.

"Yeah. Wow."

Cat and Kevin return. Kevin sees me in Owen's arms, grins, and flashes a thumbs up.

"Wait. This was planned?" I ask Owen.

"Yes. Thanks for getting her here, Cat."

She beams. "You're welcome. Did you two make up?"

"We did."

"Yay!"

"You may as well watch the game here," Vince says to Owen.

Their eyes meet.

Owen lifts his chin and says, "Thank you, sir."

34

OWEN

We walk into my place later that night. Vince shocked the hell out of both of us by offering to take Cat home.

I left the foyer light on, but the rest of the place is dark except for the city lights glittering through the windows. Once the door is shut and my keys are dropped on the console table, we turn to each other.

"I have something to show you," I say.

She bites her lip on a smile. "And I can't wait to see it."

A laugh cracks out of me. I pull her close and hug her tight. "You have a dirty mind, babe."

"What? What did you mean?"

I hear the laughter in her voice and give her ass a little tap. "Come on. In here."

I lead her into the living room and snap on a lamp.

She stops. "What the...?"

She's staring at the glossy black baby grand piano now sitting in the corner. Open-mouthed, she turns to me.

"It's for you." I gesture to it.

Her head slips side to side in disbelief, her eyes huge. "I don't understand."

"You were so sad that you had to leave your piano. So I got you this one. I know it won't fit in your apartment, but it can stay here, and you can play it any time." I walk to the piano and pick up the apartment key I left sitting on it. "You can have this back."

I feel like I've taken off all my hockey gear and I'm standing in front of her naked, while she's holding a stick. I'm defenseless. Exposed.

"Are you serious?" She takes a few hesitant steps closer. "Oh my God, Owen."

"It's just a *baby* grand," I say.

"Just a baby grand? It's a Steinway!" She runs a hand over the sleek surface. "This is crazy!"

"Possibly," I agree. "I didn't know what was going to happen tonight. You could have told me to fuck off and die."

Her lips twitch. She takes a seat on the stool.

"I had it tuned. They said you have to do that after you move it. But I don't know the difference."

"Yes." She plays a quick scale. "Oh my. It's...beautiful." She holds both hands over the keys, then starts playing something I don't recognize. Her slender fingers move gracefully on the keys, creating melodic magic. She pauses and looks up at me. "It's like it has its own voice. It *sings*."

I watch her, my chest full of emotion as she plays part of another song. "Do you like it?"

"I love it. I can't believe you did this." She slides off the stool and stands. Then she runs at me and jumps me.

I have a split second to prepare, and I catch her. She wraps her arms and legs around me and kisses me. Hard.

"I want to do you so bad right now," she mumbles, peppering kisses over my cheeks, my eyes, my forehead. "Oh my God. I can't even..."

"I won't put up a fight," I say, and I carry her into the bedroom.

I carry her to the bed where I lay her down gently, reverently, as if she's fragile and precious. She is precious. I'm still in my suit, and I strip out of my clothes and join her on the bed to remove hers, tugging her jeans down her smooth legs along with her panties. I pause when they're off, tracing the tattoo on her delicate ankle—a fine line swirled into the shape of a treble clef and music notes. "Love this," I murmur.

I help her sit up to lift the sweater over her head. She reaches behind her to undo her bra, and I toss it aside, my gaze wandering over her lush body.

"My gorgeous girl," I whisper.

She reaches up to push my hair back off my forehead, letting her fingers trail over my cheek and jaw. The tenderness of her gesture makes me feel like a fist is squeezing my heart.

"I love you, Owen."

"I love you too."

I hold myself above her on my arms and kiss her, my tongue sliding into her mouth. Her taste hits my veins like a drug—she tastes like sweet longing and dirty sex and Emerie. She tastes like her music sounds—soulful, smooth, and rich.

Fire lights up every nerve ending in my body, and I lift my mouth from hers and kiss her bare shoulder, sliding my open mouth over her skin. Her soft moan inflames my senses even more.

I kiss her throat and lick my way down between those gorgeous breasts. Her back arches and I close my mouth over one nipple, loving the sweetness, the feel of it on my tongue, the soft resilient flesh pressed to my lips.

Heat pours over my body, liquid pleasure running through my veins.

We roll and twist together, mouths fused in long, deep kisses. I worship her with my tongue, my hands, everywhere I can reach. I slip my hand between her legs, find her velvety wet center, and circle my thumb over her clit until she vibrates.

Her body ripples under my hands, and I'm swept away in sensation, in the almost unbearable sweetness and erotic pleasure, but also in the emotion of it, something powerful and huge swelling inside me.

I lifted my head. "Do we need a condom?"

She gazes back at me, trust glowing in her eyes. "No."

I lift her thigh and push into her body, watching her face. Her lips part, her eyes gaze up at me, her hands on my chest. Our gazes hold while heat builds and shimmers around us. The love and devotion in her eyes is my own reflected back at me, and my heart thuds in a slow, heavy rhythm against my ribs. "I feel so lucky right now," I whisper.

She gives me a trembling smile back. "Me too."

I slide slowly in and out of her slick heat as she squeezes around me, her hands pressed to my chest. Sensation coils inside me, heavy and hot.

"Owen."

I gaze down at her, riveted by the sight of her beautiful face as I thrust deeper, harder. She lifts into me, and I watch her eyelids lower and her mouth open. Hot little whimpers and soft sighs escape her lips, building as she gets closer, and closer. Her fingernails dig into my pecs. Then her body tightens, her pussy rippling around me, her cries exquisitely beautiful in my ears.

"I love watching you come. It's the most beautiful thing I've ever seen." I fall over her, burying my face in the side of her neck and breathing in the familiar scent of her, flowers and spice and Emerie. My chest clenches at the perfection of it, the overwhelming intensity of it, the rush of emotion inside me so strong.

I've never had intimacy like this. Sex, yeah. But this is more. It's life. And love.

My thighs quake and my balls tighten, the tension at the small of my back sizzling painfully. Electricity tingles up my spine, scorching every nerve ending in my body and I come, my cock jerking inside her in almost painful, wrenching spasms.

She wraps her arms around my back and holds on tight. My face buried in her hair, I draw in long, ragged breaths.

"Oh, Emerie." I move on her, lifting my head so I can kiss her. A long, tender kiss of devotion and promise. "Emerie. I love you."

We curl up together under the covers, wrapped in a delicious warm afterglow. I run my hand down her sleek back to cup her ass and gently squeeze. "Christ, I've missed you," I breathe into her mouth. "So fucking much."

"I missed you, too."

I hold onto her. I'm never letting her go.

We're lying in the middle of my huge bed, face to face. We can't stop touching each other—faces, shoulders, arms, hair. "What you said about being afraid of being alone just about killed me. I…have a confession."

Emerie purses her lips. "What?"

"I overheard you talking to Vince. At the game the other night. When you said you were used to feeling invisible…Christ." I swallow. "It was like taking a butt end in the gut. I realized what an asshole I'd been. I was trying to protect myself by focusing on hockey and not you. I should have talked to you about it. But…"

"It's hard. I know." Her fingertips drift over my beard stubble.

"Yeah." I sigh. "Another thing Morrie, Hellsy, and Millsy were right about. They're on this mission to get guys to talk about their feelings."

"Oh yeah. The world would be a better place if that happened."

"Fuck. I have to admit they're right."

"That's another thing we can help each other with. Okay?" Her eyes search mine. "Whatever you're feeling…tell me. You already know I love you no matter what."

"Yeah." My heart clenches. "Same." I rub my thumb over her soft lower lip.

"I think you impressed Vince tonight."

One corner of my mouth lifts. "Well, at least he didn't seem pissed off."

"Maybe he's finally accepting that Roman and I are done forever."

"Ugh. You had to say that name."

"Sorry. Never again. I *hope* he's accepting it. And I hope he's given up on trading you, or whatever."

"We'll deal with it if he does. But if I end up in Winnipeg, I don't know how much money you can make busking."

She laughs, then sobers. "You'd be okay if I kept busking?"

"Of course. It's part of you. It's what first stopped me in my tracks and gave me goosebumps."

Her mouth softens. "Thank you," she whispers.

"I think I fell in love with you, watching you sing in the subway."

"Ah." She pulls in a sniffly breath. "Thank you. I saw you watching me, you know."

"I tried to hide so you wouldn't think I was stalking you."

"News flash. You're too tall to hide."

I grin. "Yeah, I guess so."

"Tell me more about your brother."

I search her face, and she gives a tiny, encouraging nod. So I talk. I tell her about the memories Mom, Dad, and I shared, all the good stuff, some of the bad. And the bitterness I've been feeling for so long about his death finally slides away, leaving sadness, yes, but also acceptance. Peace. "I miss him."

"You always will." She cups my face. "That's okay."

"Thank you for telling me to talk to my parents. It was what I needed."

"I'm glad."

"I was afraid to see them all these years. Because I was so guilty about how I felt about Eric. I thought they'd hate me for being angry with him." Regret is a dull heaviness in my chest.

"Oh no." Her forehead creases.

"They don't hate me. They understand. And...there's something else I want to tell you about."

"Okay." Her eyes are luminous with acceptance. Of whatever I'm about to say. I'm so fucking lucky.

I tell her about going to Light House. How I needed to do something when I was suspended and hockey wasn't it.

"That's amazing," she says softly, touching my cheek. "I'm so proud of you."

"Thanks. I'm kind of proud of myself, too. I'm going to go back."

"Good."

I pull her hand to my mouth and kiss her palm. "I guess I have to thank my buddies for that, too."

Her eyes widen.

"Morrie. Hellsy. Millsy. They staged an intervention." I snort.

"Oh." She blinks.

"They tried to get me to see that my obsession with work and hockey was like an addiction. And I was using it to hide from stuff in my life I hadn't dealt with."

"Ohhhh. Wow. Yeah."

"Will you help me? If I start obsessing about it? I know now, and I want to do better. I want to be there for you more. But if I slip…"

"I'm there for you. Always."

I close my eyes, emotion flooding my chest, hot and soft. "Thank you."

"Because you'll help me, too…right?"

I focus on her. "Of course."

"I…uh…started a SoundCloud account. I'm putting my music on there."

"Really? Wow! That's great, Em."

She smiles. "I'm terrified."

"You got this."

"I'm excited, too. It's going okay. And there's something else."

"Yeah?"

"I'm going to do an open mic night. Saturday."

"Whoa! Really?"

"Yes." She gives a nervous smile. "The girls convinced me. I want to do this. For me."

"You'll kill it."

"I don't know about that. I want to have fun."

"Perfect. Have fun. I'll be there for you."

"Gah!"

"I like it when you sing to me."

She grins. "Also…I entered a contest. For buskers."

"I didn't know there was such a thing."

"It's new. This is the first time they've done it here in New York. We have to audition, and only twelve people will make it to the final. It'll be a public event in Central Park. I don't know if I'll make it to that, but…I'm going to try."

"That's amazing!" Excitement pulses in my veins for her. "You'll do great!"

"We'll see. But thank you. It's something for myself. To push myself. Just for me."

"Yeah. I'm proud of you, beautiful."

"Thanks. I'm proud of me too. I thought about what you said. When you told me I'm an artist."

Right. On the plane to Aruba.

"I didn't consider myself an artist. All I did was busk."

I shake my head, ready to correct her, but she goes on. "But if I believe that being a successful artist means reaching people with your art, maybe…maybe I do that. In a small way."

"You definitely do," I say. "I didn't give you enough credit for that. Busking seems…like not enough for your talent, but you *do* reach people. You *do* touch their lives. I've seen it." I press a hand to my chest. "I've *felt* it. Your music got inside me and made me feel things."

"Thank you." Her eyes glow. "That's the best compliment. And I know now that's what I want. I don't want to be famous or make a lot of money. I know I can't change the world, but maybe I can have some small impact with my music."

I get that. "If you only ever want to busk, I'm one hundred percent behind you on that. If you want to do more…I'm there for that, too."

She leans in for another smooch. "I love you."

"Love you, too, beautiful."

35

EMERIE

Here I am at the Mystic Nomad.

What the hell am I doing?

A swarm of bees buzzes in my belly. I haven't felt like this since I started busking. I take a few deep breaths, trying to relax, remembering how my nerves eased back then. This is no different.

Except people are here to actually listen to music.

Aaaaaah!

I've warmed up my vocal cords and tuned my guitar. I've practiced the two songs I'm going to sing. Over. And over. I even have a couple of extra songs ready just in case, as Elijah advised me. He had lots of good advice. I've gone to a few open mic nights at other places to check them out. That made me more comfortable. I know the Mystic Nomad is a good venue for my music because it's quieter. It's cute—an old building with wooden floors, brick walls, the stage in front of an empty fireplace. The wall behind the low stage is draped with strings of little white lights.

Every small, round table is occupied, including two with my friends. And Owen. Although it's dark, with small candles glowing on the tables, I can see them all from where I stand off to the side of the stage.

Owen. The candle on the table highlights the planes and curves of his beautiful face. I love him so much. I love him so much it scares me. I can't lose him. But I have to be brave in love as well as my music. Because the happiness he makes me feel is worth it.

The host of the evening, Sebastian Meyer, a well-known local musician, approaches me with a smile. "You all set?" he asks. "You're up next."

I nod mutely.

"Stage fright?" he asks.

"Just a little."

"No worries. We all have it. It gets your adrenaline going. Gets oxygen pumping to your brain. It actually helps you perform better."

I stare at him. "I never thought of it that way."

His smile is reassuring. "There you go."

"Thanks."

The performer on stage finishes her cover of an Adele song to a round of applause, and Sebastian jumps onto the stage, clapping, thanking her. Then he introduces me.

My friends all hoot and holler, which is embarrassing but also gratifying. I step onto the worn, patterned carpet, lifting the strap of my beloved Martin D-28 over my head. It's bigger than my Little Martin, which I use for busking. It's my prized possession, the guitar I always wanted to own after I started learning to play. I love it for its rich, warm tones that complement my voice. I pat it. It will bring me luck.

I step in front of the microphone. Holy shit. Am I really doing this?

I smile.

"These two songs are originals of mine," I say into the mic. "I hope you enjoy them." Another small cheer rises from the tables on my left. "The first one is called 'Without Love.'"

I lift my eyes, and with my signature fingerpicking style, I pick out the opening melody of my song. I wrote "Without Love" after Owen broke up with me, but it wasn't quite finished. Now I've finished it. It's sad, yes, a song of heartbreak and loss, but it's also hopeful and ultimately triumphant.

This may be a different venue. The audience may be different. But *this*…playing, singing… is familiar to me. I sing from my heart, letting my voice soar, telling my story.

The applause when I finish is satisfying. My heart gallops, and I find Owen in the audience. He's clapping and grinning. Our eyes meet, and warmth spreads through me, settling me.

I play my next song, "Dreams of You." It's different than the first. Elijah told me since I can only play two songs to choose ones that are completely different. This one is slower and more romantic. Dreamy.

My eyes are closed when I finish, lost in my music, and I'm startled out of it by cheers and whistles. My friends are on their feet, shouting their approval. I look around the room. Everyone else is clapping enthusiastically, too, smiles on their faces.

I don't know if I'm any good at reading the room, but…I feel good.

"Thank you. Thank you."

I've been told to leave the stage quickly to make room for the next performer, so I do that. My face is hot, my hands trembling as I set my guitar into its case. I stand to rejoin Owen and the others, and he's right there, lifting my case for me.

"You were amazing." He bends down to press his lips to my forehead. "Fucking amazing, Em."

"Thank you." I lean into him, into his warmth and strength, breathing in his beloved scent. *I'm okay. I did it. I'm okay.*

He wraps an arm around me and squeezes then leads me back to the table. I take the seat next to him. A man on stage is playing a violin, and I don't want to disrupt his performance, so I exchange smiles with my friends. Lilly grips my hand briefly. They all seem just as excited as I am.

Wow.

My mind is racing. I try to listen to the music, but I feel like I'm floating outside my body. Owen clasps his fingers around my hand, and it grounds me.

I clap for the performer when he's done, and for the next one. I've learned that it's polite to stay and listen to the other artists, and I'm calming down and listening and enjoying the music. The waitress comes around for drink refills, and I ask for a bottle of water, which I proceed to guzzle down.

I'm doing it. I'm living on my own. I'm making music that moves people. And I put aside my fears and opened myself to love—which is the scariest thing of all.

But also—the *best* thing.

EPILOGUE

OWEN

I watch Emerie up in the wings of the temporary stage in Central Park, holding her guitar. I'm in the crowd gathered on the grass. It's a warm June day, the sky overcast, but it doesn't feel like rain.

It's her turn. The emcee, a local radio deejay, announces her name and she strides out onto the stage, waving at the crowd. I clap loudly, hands in the air, as do my teammates around me and their wives and girlfriends.

Today is also the dog fashion show, in a different location in the park. How they ended up the same day was some really shitty timing, but we had to deal. There was no way we weren't going to be here to support her. We managed to find enough volunteers to take over for a few minutes so we could race over here to hear Emerie perform.

Cat is beside me, jumping up and down. She thinks Emerie's busking is super cool. And on the other side of her is Vince. Also clapping. Here for Emerie.

Vince is still kind of an asshole, but he's stepped up for Cat, and he's even invited Emerie and me over for dinner a few times. I've also seen him at Cat's gymnastics open house and her birthday party. He's picked up Cat from Emerie's apartment a few times.

Emerie takes her place in front of the mic. The judges—pop singer Abrianna, country singer Jeb Irwin, and Broadway star Khalil Brown —sit at a long table on the right side of the stage. Emerie's image is projected onto a big screen on the left. She's so beautiful. She's wearing a pink flowered dress and her long hair flows in waves over her shoulders. I see the nerves in her eyes, the slight tightness of her smile. But her open mic nights have helped prepare her for this—the biggest audience she's ever played to.

I can't help but think of the first times I saw her play in the subway. How her music touched me. How she sang about soul mates, and I didn't know if there really was such a thing.

Now I know there is. And she's mine. She's my best friend. I feel alive when I'm around her yet calm. She makes me feel things, things I tried not to feel for so long, but balances all different emotions. And I think I balance her. We've both had a lot of growing to do, learning about ourselves and about each other and who we want to be. We have fun together. Yeah, we've both learned the importance of friends and fun. And like she said to me that day she walked out my life, which turned out not to be forever, thank God, I want the best for her. I'll do whatever it takes to give her that.

She sings, "Without You," which has been getting tons of attention on her SoundCloud. Her voice is getting better and stronger. As the last note fades, the crowd goes wild. She finds me in the crowd and meets my eyes. She presses her hand to her heart and mouths, "I love you."

I nod, letting her know I feel the same, my smile so big my face hurts.

"Thank you!" she calls to the audience. "Thank you so much!" She bows, waves to the crowd and heads offstage.

The judges will have some time to confer on the top three, which they'll announce in reverse order—third, second, first place.

I leave the others and make my way to the stage to find Emerie. She spots me and moves toward me through a bunch of people, holding her guitar. I wrap my arms around her and spin her around.

"You totally killed it," I tell her.

"Oh God. I did it."

"I'm sure you'll win."

"It doesn't matter." She leans back in my arms and smiles up at me. "I did it. What happens in the contest doesn't matter."

"Emerie. Hi."

We both turn to look at the man stopped near us. Roman.

My gut clenches. Christ, I haven't seen him in months. What the fuck is he doing here?

Then I notice a woman with him, petite, with long, shiny black hair...and holding his hand. Huh.

"Roman. Hi." Emerie turns in my arms and I release her. Not totally. I keep a hand on her waist.

"Congratulations. That was an amazing performance. I had no idea..." He stops. "You're very talented."

"Thank you."

"I'm blown away," he says. "Uh, this is Sophia Delos Reyes. My girlfriend. Sophia, Emerie Ross and Owen Cooke."

"Nice to meet you," Emerie murmurs.

Sophia smiles warmly. "I loved your performance. Just beautiful. I hope you win!"

"Thank you so much."

"Just wanted to say hi," Roman says. "Congrats again."

They move away, and Emerie turns to me, eyes wide. "He has a girlfriend!"

"Thank fuck. If he was stalking you here, I'd have to punch him."

She laughs softly. "You can't do that off the ice, honey."

I laugh, too. I don't even do that *on* the ice.

After learning that it had been Roman pressuring Vince to break us up using money as enticement, or threat, however you want to look at it, I was ready to go after him. Luckily, he seemed to finally get the message that his bullshit wasn't going to work. Vince finally stood up to him and told him he could shove his money up his ass if he thought Vince would sabotage the team. Or Emerie. Which made me respect Vince a little more. And despise Roman.

Our season ended a while back. It was a long, hard season, but we all felt proud of how we played.

The truth is, hockey's not my top priority anymore. I still want to do the best I can. But my top priority now is Emerie. Making her happy. Supporting her. *Seeing* her.

ANOTHER EPILOGUE

THE HOCKEY TIMES
New York, New York

Citing losses of $42 million over the last two seasons and an inability to negotiate a more favorable lease at the Apex Center, owner of the New York Bears Vince D'Agostino has filed for reorganization under Chapter 11 of the Federal Bankruptcy Code.

"This will have absolutely no effect on Bears games, on our payroll, on the club's playing schedule, or any of our hockey operations," D'Agostino said in a statement. "The team, our season-ticket holders and our corporate sponsors will be protected during this reorganization."

"This is no doubt disappointing," NHL commissioner Thomas Yang said. "But the team ownership has committed to work to resolve their financial issues and we are optimistic that the franchise will be financially and competitively successful in New York."

There are rumors that former team star Johnny Risley is planning to sue the team over deferred payments still owed to him, but this has not been confirmed at this time.

Thank you so much for reading The O Zone!

Bears Hockey continues with

GOOD HANDS

Two people who only want sexy hookups have their lives turned upside down by a positive pregnancy test...

One-click Good Hands now!

And read on for an excerpt!

Do you want to read the sex scene from The O Zone my editor told me to cut? Sign up for my newsletter for exclusive access to it!

Brandon

"You must be the guy who's going to buy me a drink."

I turn to see a pretty blonde smiling at me. I smile lazily back at her. Hell yeah, I'll buy her a drink. I'll buy her a drink all day long. "Cute line."

"Thanks." Her smile broadens. "I have lots."

I laugh. "You go around getting guys to buy you drinks a lot?"

"Only the ones who remind me of a magnet."

I tilt my head and lift an eyebrow.

"You remind me of a magnet because you're attracting me to you."

I laugh again. "Nice. What would you like to drink?"

"I'd love another Ariba." She holds up an empty glass, which I take from her.

"When in Aruba," I say. "I'll be right back, beautiful."

I head to the bar. My friends and I are hanging at this spot on the beach in Oranjested, having just finished dinner. We're here in Aruba for a week of sun, sand, and sex. At least, I'm *hoping* for the sex. As one of only two single guys with the group, that wasn't a given. On the other hand, women usually find me attractive…and tonight is now looking promising.

I've had women approach me before so this isn't unusual, but her cheeky lines and saucy attitude, not to mention her flirty smile, are super appealing. I mentally rub my hands together as I order the cocktail and another beer for myself. Then I cross the wooden deck and step back onto the sand where she's waiting for me.

I hand her the drink.

"Thank you. I'm Lola."

"Hi, Lola. Nice to meet you. I'm Brandon."

She sips her fruit-garnished drink through the straw. Her shoulder length pale hair stirs in the breeze off the ocean. The lights strung above us illuminate her face, and yeah, she's beautiful, with amazing, clear turquoise eyes. Her loose, button-down white shirt has the cuffs folded back, and is partially tucked into cut-off denim shorts that leave a sweet length of tanned leg visible. The combination of pale hair, light eyes, and tanned skin is incredibly sexy.

She's checking me out, too. Fair. *Check away, Lola.*

"So you're here on vacation," she says.

"Yep. With some friends." I wave a hand in the general direction of the group, who gathered around a picnic table on the sand. Lola's part of another group we met up with, discovering some of them are also from New York, and also discovering they're hockey fans.

"You're a hockey player, too?" she asks.

"Yes, I am."

"Cool. I like hockey."

I didn't catch where she's from. "Are you from New York, too?"

"Yep."

"Do you come to our games?"

"Sometimes, yeah."

"Awesome. How long are you here for?"

"Tonight's our last night," she says with a regretful sigh.

"Damn."

"I know, right? I love it here."

"She says that now." A woman passing by pauses to interject. "We had to drag her by her hair to get her here."

Lola shakes her head and huffs. "Sure, Kaylee."

The woman grins and continues on her path toward the bar.

I smile. "Your friend?"

"Cousin. And best friend." Lola rolls her eyes.

"Why didn't you want to come to Aruba?"

"I did...but I'm super busy at work and taking a vacation is hard." She looks briefly troubled, then shrugs. "But I did it and it's been super fun."

"Is it your first time in Aruba?"

"Yeah. How about you?"

"Same. Tell me some things I should make sure to do while I'm here."

We start chatting about the things Lola and her friends have done —snorkeling, sailing, horseback riding. "And we did the cave jump thing," she says. "That was fun!"

"What is that?"

She describes driving ATVs along the coast, seeing the rock formations and caves, and jumping into a natural pool.

"I'll have to check with our cruise director to see if that's part of our itinerary," I say.

She blinks. "You're on a cruise?"

"I'm kidding. We call my friend Nadia the cruise director because she likes to plan everything." I grin. "Tomorrow we're doing a sunset catamaran cruise."

"Oh, that sounds amazing. One night we did a bar hopping tour on a party bus. That was fun, too."

Our conversation turns more personal. "What do you do for a living, Lola?"

Sipping our drinks, we drift away from the group

"I'm a change manager manager." She makes a face. "I know it doesn't sound exciting, but I love it."

"Well, that's what's important. But you have to tell me what a change manager manager does. I assume you manage change."

She laughs. "You got it! I work for Synoptic Global Services."

I'm sure I look blank, but I nod.

"We're an international insurance consultancy. We provide independent insurance due diligence, insurance program review, and financial solutions to the mergers and acquisitions business."

"Ah. That explains it." I'm still totally lost.

"Insurance for M&A businesses helps buyers and sellers mitigate risk and helps close a deal. Like, buyers and sellers are usually concerned about how taxes or ongoing litigation or contractual obligations a business has might impact a merger or acquisition."

"I assume you're talking about really big businesses."

"Yeah." She nods. "Right now, my job is working on a project for one of our clients to ensure their insurance programs are optimized to deliver better protection, improved broker service, and additional premium savings. My job is to create a plan to implement the changes—milestones, time frames, resources. Then I help implement the changes, making sure everyone's engaged and on board. I deal with resistance to change, handle communications. I also do training for management and supervisors so they can do the same with their teams." She shrugs. "There's more, but that's basically it."

"Holy shit. That sounds impressive."

"Thank you." She tilts her head, eyes shining. "I love my job. I just wish…"

"What?"

"Well, this particular job is a term. One year contract. I've been doing contract work with Synoptic for eight years." She sighs. "It would be nice if they'd actually hire me."

"Ah."

"One of their VPs is retiring later this year. I'm really hoping if I do well with this project they'll consider me for his position." She holds up two crossed fingers and a big toothy smile.

"Vice president. That would be also impressive."

She gives her shoulders a little shimmy. "I've been working toward that my whole career."

"Well, you seem very intelligent and capable. I'm sure you've got this in the bag."

"You don't even know me." She grins and purses her lips around her straw briefly. "Or the business. But thanks for the vote of confidence."

I watch her pretty lips close on the straw and feel a stirring in my southern regions. Her lips are sexy, but her intelligence and confidence are even hotter.

"I just play a game for a living," I say.

She bursts out laughing. "It's a little more than that."

"It's a big business game," I acknowledge. "Lots of money on the line."

"Fame."

"Eh. I guess. I'm not a superstar. But yeah, lots of people know who I am. It's easier to hide in a big city like New York."

"Compared to…?"

"I played a couple of years in Montreal. You can't hide from anyone in that city. They're hockey crazy." I smile, though. "It's cool."

"Hockey's pretty popular in New York."

"Yeah, it is. And this year we're doing well. Gearing up for a playoff run after this break."

"You'll be all rested up and raring to go."

I'm raring to go all right. The way she looks at me, the way she listens to everything I say, attentive and curious, is a huge fucking turn on.

We talk about New York. She's lived there since college. She's cautiously vague about where she lives, saying only Hudson Yard, which isn't that far from me in Lincoln Square. I don't mind that she's careful; women have to be.

"It's a tiny condo," she says. "A studio. But I had a bad experience living with a crazy roommate and I wanted to live alone."

"Yeah, me too. I did the roommate thing for a few years when I started playing, and when I moved here. I'm too old for that now."

"Ha. How old are you?"

"Almost thirty."

"Hey, me too. My birthday's in September."

I grin. "So is mine. What day?"

"September twelfth."

"I'm the eleventh!" I laugh. "I'm a whole day older than you."

"I've always liked older men," she says in a flirty tone.

Our eyes keep meeting and heat pulses between us. The sound of the ocean waves on the nearby sand are a rhythmic push-pull that mirrors the pulsations around us and my quickening heartbeat. The sultry tropical breeze brushes over us and I feel like it's her fingers on my skin. I want her fingers on my skin. Or *my* fingers on *her* skin. That would work, too.

The breeze teases the opening of her shirt, giving me a glimpse of pink lace. Jesus.

"Yeah?" I reach out to push a strand of hair off her face. "You're fucking gorgeous."

Her gaze hangs on mine, her lips curved. "Thank you. Did I mention that I find you attractive, too?"

"Like a magnet," I say, studying her face, the small, slightly pointy chin, narrow nose, high cheekbones.

She laughs softly, shifting closer to me in the shadows, the lights of the bar now behind us. "Yeah. A really strong magnet."

Her scent reaches my nose—a combination of coconut and tropical flowers and sunshine. And warm woman. Heady.

"Magnets can also be repulsive," I murmur, my nose nearing her hair.

"You are definitely not repulsive."

"Good to know." I pause, our noses almost touching, our eyes heavy lidded. Our breath mingles.

"Just so you know, my lips won't kiss themselves," she whispers.

AUTHOR NOTE

I have to be honest here and tell you this book was an utter disaster to write. I started off with a story in mind and somehow it totally changed by about halfway through and then it became a big mess. Thankfully Kristi Yanta saw what it could be and gave me so much great input. Revising was a little intimidating, but in the end, I absolutely love this story and these characters!

I didn't set out to be a crusader for men's mental health, but somehow that happened, too. More men need to read romance novels!

I'm so grateful for the team I have around me—Stacey Price, my goddess assistant, Heather Roberts, another goddess, Kristi Yanta, yes, a goddess. It's a goddess team of amazing talented women! And this time Katie Kenyhercz is part of the editing team—thank you, Katie! Also big thanks to my daughter who does the spreadsheet stuff. I literally break into a sweat every time I open an Excel spreadsheet—she says she gets excited. What? But yay! And thank you (again!) to my friend PG Forte for the brainstorming help with busking and the American Busker competition. She knew exactly who Emerie was as soon as I described her.

And as always thanks to *you*! You are my "why". I love to write and tell stories, but it's way more fun when I share them, and even more fun when people like them. Thank you for reading!

OTHER BOOKS BY KELLY JAMIESON

Brew Crew

Limited Time Offer

No Obligation Required

Aces Hockey

Major Misconduct

Off Limits

Icing

Top Shelf

Back Check

Slap Shot

Playing Hurt

Big Stick

Game On

Last Shot

Body Shot

Hot Shot

Long Shot

Bayard Hockey

Shut Out

Cross Check

Wynn Hockey

Play to Win

In It To Win It

Win Big

For the Win

Game Changer

How Sweet It Is

Screwed

Firecracker

ABOUT THE AUTHOR

Kelly Jamieson is a best-selling author of over forty romance novels and novellas. Her writing has been described as "emotionally complex", "sweet and satisfying" and "blisteringly sexy." She likes coffee (black), wine (mostly white), shoes (high heels) and hockey!

Subscribe to her newsletter for updates about her new books and what's coming up.

Find out what's new...
www.kellyjamieson.com

Contact Kelly
info@kellyjamieson.com

Made in the USA
Monee, IL
14 April 2022

94763056R00166